Praise For THE BOOK OF THE MOST PRECIOUS SUBSTANCE

"I f****** loved it."
—Lauren Beukes, auth‹

"There's two types of magic at ‹
characters are trying to do, mixi‹   ...‹ sex and spells,
and then there's the magic Sara Gran is doing to us, as we
compulsively read this literary thriller. And there's a third
magic we only wish we could do: pay in blood to go back,
read this book again for the first time."
—Stephen Graham Jones, author of *The Only Good Indian*

"Sara Gran's *The Book Of The Most Precious Substance* is
a mix of book buying mystery, erotica, and a pinch of
Clive Barkerian obsessive existential horror, but it's all Gran.
And it's all brilliant."
—Paul Tremblay, author of *The Cabin in the Woods*

"Gran perfectly captures the eccentric world of antiquarian
bookselling while portraying a profound and magical
reckoning with loss and the possibility of going on. She has
outdone herself." —*Publisher's Weekly* (starred review)

Praise For Sara Gran's Previous Books

"For those who haven't read Sara Gran,
trust me, you are in for a singular mystery experience."
—Maureen Corrigan, *The Washington Post*

"Terrific." —Sue Grafton, *A Is for Alibi*

THE BOOK
OF THE MOST
PRECIOUS
SUBSTANCE

Also by Sara Gran:

Marigold

The Infinite Blacktop

Claire DeWitt & the Bohemian Highway

Claire DeWitt & the City of the Dead

Dope

Come Closer

Saturn's Return to New York

The Book
of the
Most Precious
Substance

a novel

Sara Gran

DREAMLAND BOOKS
LOS ANGELES

DREAMLAND BOOKS
LOS ANGELES

Library of Congress Control Number: 2021922661

February 8, 2022

Trade paperback 978-0-578-94709-9 | Ebook 978-0-578-95779-1

First edition paperback original 2/22

www.dreamland-books.com

Interior and exterior design by Zoe Norvell | www.zoenorvell.com

1.

I first heard about the book from Shyman.

We were at the big annual book sale in the community college gymnasium on Lexington near Grammercy Park. Most book dealers specialized in an area of study: military history, revolutionary literature, modern first editions. I didn't. I specialized in books that interested me and were profitable. I liked books that were beautiful, with unusual bindings or remarkable illustrations. I liked obscure topics, like lesser-known religions or forgotten corners of history. I liked books about art. I liked counterculture. On my table at the moment were a dozen books from the 1800s with forgettable words and good bindings priced at fifty bucks each; a few bird and butterfly guides from the same era with original lithographs priced at two hundred each; a travelogue written by a Russian visitor to Tibet in 1901 (the only copy I'd ever seen or heard of) for five hundred; a little stack of British pulp fiction from the forties and fifties;

another stack of perverted and wonderful Olympia Press editions in green paper wrappers (no Nabokov or Miller, sadly, the gems of the run); a handful of gossipy out-of-print paperbacks about groupies and musicians I'd found in a thrift shop a few weeks before; a book on Haitian voodoo from the 1930s with remarkable photographs; and a series of letterpressed pamphlets on Southern cooking published by the Charleston Junior League from the 1930s through the 1960s. My most expensive book was fifteen hundred bucks, a rare and beautiful survey of a little-known Swedish artist named Hannah Kline. My cheapest, the British paperbacks, were twenty bucks each.

Business was brisk. It was a week after Valentine's Day. The fair itself was in the exact dead center of the business, in the middle between thrift-store dollar paperbacks and seven-figure rarities. It had slowed the week before, and we were all worried the slushy mess outside would slow down sales, but our worries weren't justified. Now we worried about all the moisture ruining our books. Book people aren't exactly silver-lining types.

And then Shyman showed up at my table.

"Hey, Lily," he said. "I was looking for you."

"Hey," I said. "How's your day going? Selling anything?"

Shyman himself looked like the exact dead center of most book dealers: a fifty-something man with an irregular hairline and patchy, unbecoming facial hair, clothes that were somehow too big and too small at the same time, and a look on his face like he could very easily be persuaded to sit down and never get up again. Like most book people, there was a shadow in his face, a hollow echo in his laugh, that let you know he'd rather be around books than people. Who could blame him? It was why so many of us were in this business. People had let us down. People had broken our hearts. We liked books and animals and messy rooms full of things that weren't people.

But you could also see, in better moments, the man Shyman used to be: handsome, erudite, a scholar with a beautiful wife and a promising career ahead of him. The promise of which, obviously, had not come true. Shyman was very good at what he did, which was sell books about military history. As far as I knew, he wasn't really interested in anything else. He had come to the book world through a handful of failed PhD attempts. He ended up with no degree and no job but with a library of military books that had increased in value threefold since he began graduate school. He lived on Long Island somewhere. Not the fancy part.

"Eh," he said. "It's OK. But listen. You know something called the *Pretiosus Materia*? Something like that?"

I thought it was Italian and I thought he was mispronouncing it.

"*La Pretiosus Materia?*" I said. Not that I spoke Italian. But I spoke a little French and a little Spanish, and figured it was something like *The Precious Materials*.

"Latin," he said. "Not Italian. *The Precious Substance*. You know about weird stuff. I thought you might've heard of it."

"I don't think so," I said.

"Well, if you can find it," he said, "I got someone offering six figures for it."

"Six figures?" I asked.

"High six figures," he said, "and I strongly suspect he would go to seven if he had to. He wants this book. Of course, if you can find it—"

"If I find it," I said, "we share."

"If you find it," Shyman went on, as if I hadn't spoken, "you or whoever finds it, I'm willing to give twenty percent. That's fair."

"Fifty percent," I said.

"Twenty."

"Fifty."

"Twenty-five."

"Fifty."

"Twenty-five."

"OK," I said. "Thirty-five."

"Let's make it interesting," said Shyman. "Thirty-three percent. If you find the book for me, I buy it for my client, I give you thirty-three percent of what I make from it. If I make anything."

"OK," I said. "Deal."

We shook on it.

I needed money.

I started that night.

2.

Before I could start looking for *The Precious Substance,* I had books to sell. I sold all my Olympia Press books to a man around my age, early forties, with an armful of thousand-dollar books I would have liked to spend the day with. I sold the butterfly books to a woman with a small tattoo of a heart on her cheek. We talked about butterfly guides for a while; she was an entomologist and a book collector.

Then Lucas Markson approached my table. Lucas was a regular customer who had become an acquaintance, or maybe a friend. I still wasn't quite sure which. Lucas was the head of the rare books department at a big university library uptown with a big acquisitions budget. I'd known him for more than five years but Lucas was still, in many ways, a mystery to me: He always seemed to have money and always looked decent—both rarities in the book world. He was close to six feet tall with an appealing face and a kind of charm that was unusual in book people. He was handsome, with a pleasantly prominent nose that added some character. He dressed well: tailored shirts, slim jackets, blue jeans worn just right. The only stain to mark him as a book person was a strange little nervousness that sometimes led him to make eye contact, or fail to, at unexpected moments. Other than that he was suspiciously normal.

Lucas's father had been some kind of wealthy finance person; he'd mentioned once that his father had never loved him or his mother, and that he was sure this lack of love was what had led both his parents to an early grave. Like many, he claimed to be native New Yorker, but was really from a wealthy part of Westchester. He'd moved to the city for college and never left.

But as we kept running into each other at book fairs and auctions, I found out Lucas was more interesting than he first seemed. Lucas had an unexpected warmth that made him easy to spend time with, despite occasional awkwardness. He could form a little bubble of shared space that seemed both private and true with nearly anyone, almost instantly. From the first time we met, at a small reception for a rare book fair in Brooklyn, we had an easy rapport, even though we had almost nothing in common. Nothing except books. Lucas was arch and funny without ever being cruel. He was remarkably quick. I wasn't sure if he was intelligent, but he was astoundingly clever. Maybe we liked each other because we could keep up with each other.

Now he would call me looking for books for the library or I would get in touch when I had a book I thought he'd want for his collections. We had a nice little Venn diagram of shared areas of interest: counterculture, bibliographies, and books about books. If he was upstate, near the town where I lived, he'd come by and look at stock and usually buy a few titles. The area had become popular with tourists over the past few years; Lucas made regular visits in the summer and occasional ski trips in the winter. I lived in a small Victorian town a few miles east of the Hudson River, about a hundred and fifteen miles north of the city. Settled by the Dutch, stolen from the Iroquois. I owned about an acre and a half, which held a small house that we lived in and a large barn where I kept my books.

I used to live in Manhattan. I used to live in Brooklyn. I used to live in Oakland. In Taos and Sedona and Phoenix. All that seemed like a lifetime ago.

"Lily," Lucas said. I stood up and he gave me a brief hug. He smelled good, like expensive, masculine soap: sandalwood, sage, clean laundry.

"Good sale?" he asked.

"Yes," I said. "Very good. How about you? Buy anything?"

He had bought plenty: a little sheaf of letters from Doris Lessing to her editor, a rare hardcover on the first European visit to Papua New Guinea, and a bibliography of illuminated manuscripts from Portugal.

"Hey," I asked, "have you ever heard of a book called *The Precious Substance?*"

"No," Lucas answered. "*The Precious* what?"

"*The Precious Substance,*" I said.

"What's the substance?" Lucas asked.

"I have no idea," I said. "But the book is worth a lot of money if I can find it. You know Shyman? He's looking for it."

"Huh," Lucas said.

"Yeah," I said.

A woman across the room was trying to get Lucas's attention and finally he gave it to her. A dealer named Jenny Janes. She was holding up a long, slim book. I didn't recognize it, but Lucas's eyes grew wide at the sight of it.

"I've gotta go," Lucas said. "Think maybe I could help? With the book?"

"Yeah," I said. "Maybe."

Jenny gestured again.

"Dinner tonight?" Lucas said.

"OK," I said.

"Perfect," he said. "I'll text you."

He walked away. Another man approached, a tall, thin man with a sour face, and I went back to work.

3.

At the end of the day I packed up my books, trusted the security guards to protect them from thieves and other dealers, and went to the apartment I was renting for the weekend in Chelsea, a few blocks crosstown from the fair, to shower and change before dinner. Books were a dirty job, one of the black arts, along with witchcraft and printing.

I hadn't planned on dinner so I hadn't brought anything nice to wear. Also, I didn't own anything nice to wear. I put on clean blue jeans and a clean denim button-down shirt. I looked in the mirror. I vaguely remembered that people used to enjoy looking at me. I took off the denim shirt and put on a dirty camisole I'd slept in the night before. Better. I put a cardigan, also dirty, over the camisole, put on a swipe of lipstick that would probably be worn off before I got to my entrée, put a big fat parka and wool hat over it all, and walked to the restaurant Lucas had picked out in the West Village.

It was dark. The sidewalk was wet and slushy, while the air was sharp and clear. Lucas had picked a jewel box of a restaurant on West Tenth Street. It was down a few steps. Lucas was waiting for me at a table by the window. A waitress was smiling as she took his drink order. They flirted a little.

I went inside. It was warm and perfectly lit with warm yellow light. Lucas stood up to kiss me on the cheek. His own cheek was warm and dry. I knew he was paying for dinner, or his library was, and I ordered steak and good wine.

"Lily," he said. "You look beautiful."

I didn't agree, but thanked him nonetheless. Over dinner we gossiped about the fair and the book world in general for a while before we got to talking about *The Precious Substance*. At the book fair, in between customers, I'd poked around online for the book. There was surprisingly little on the internet about it, and none of it useful. On a blog about rare books, *The Precious Substance* was on a list of books that may or may not be real. It was in a Reddit discussion on magical books that had ruined people's lives, with no explanation given. I found out that its full, correct title was *The Book of the Most Precious Substance: A Treatise of the Various Fluids and Their Uses,* and that was about all.

On one obscure occult forum called Dark Triad, there was a small discussion that included someone who claimed to have actually seen a copy.

I happenn [sic] *to know one of the richest men in the world. He swears, up and down, that his fortune os* [also sic] *due to the practices in a book called THE BOOK OF THE MOST PRECIOUS*

SUBSTANCE. But he will not share his copy with me. Does anyone know where I can find one? Or have one I can borrow?

One response: *Ha, yeah. It's the rarest, most sought after book in the entire bibliography of the occult. So no, asshole, I don't have one you can borrow.*

That in itself was strange. It was 2019. Generally, you could type the name of the rarest alchemical text into Google and download a PDF of it to your phone in about five minutes. Not this book.

"I don't think Shyman knows anything about it at all," I said.

"Doesn't sound like anyone does," Lucas said.

Then I realized why Shyman had asked me, of all people, for help: I was a rare generalist in a world of specialists. If Shyman had known for sure that the book was about the occult, he could have called up Jonathan Fracker in Rhode Island. If he knew it was about ships, he could have called Sonya Rabinowitz in Bodega Bay.

He had no idea what it was about. That was my outstanding quality as a bookseller: I was a dilettante.

"I'll ask at work," Lucas said. "Poke around. Someone should know."

"Cool," I said. "Call me if you find anything."

"I will," he said. We paused for a minute before he asked: "So. How's…? Is he…?"

"The same," I replied, as quickly as I could. "How about you? You seeing anyone?"

Lucas said, "Yeah. I'm dating this woman at school. A professor."

I figured that meant Lucas would sleep with her a few times and then find an excuse to never speak to her again. As far as I could tell, that was how all his relationships went. When we first met I thought it was a phase he was going through. I knew he'd been married, briefly, long before we knew each other, and it hadn't worked out. At the time, I'd thought he would soon be married again—he was handsome, bright, friendly, and somehow always seemed to have money. But now I knew all his relationships were brief. There was a fear of depth in Lucas, a resistance to real connection. In truth, that made him a little more attractive, to me and I suspect to the women he dated. All the fun, none of the vulnerability.

"Cool," I said. "What's she teach?"

"Math," Lucas said. "Like weird math philosophy stuff."

"Cool," I said again. "She must be smart."

"Yeah, incredibly smart," Lucas said. "How's upstate? Other than—"

"OK," I said. "I'm thinking about opening a store. The town is getting kind of fancy, as you know."

The waiter refilled our wine and brought our steaks. The steak was just how I like it: pink in the middle, a spot of red in the dead center, almost crisp on the outside. It was the best meal I'd had in ages. I felt the tension in me start to unwind a little.

"Did you hear about May Baron?" Lucas asked. "Found a *Gatsby* in a thrift shop in Ohio."

"Oh, Jesus Christ," I said. "May, of all people. How's your steak?"

"Excellent," Lucas said.

I guessed Lucas was a good cook. I'd sold him a few cookbooks over the years, and you could just see him in the kitchen, throwing together a little Italian-type meal—something green and bitter, some lean protein with lemon, something starchy with butter. Jazz on the hi-fi. A woman leaning against the counter drinking wine and eating an impromptu amuse-bouche. She'd be between thirty and forty and a catch: attractive, accomplished, sane, sense of humor, some free time, some money. Single. Childless. Ideally family-less altogether. It wouldn't be as attractive if she were busy with the actual living of life—birth, death, children, old people, illness, bodily woes. Within ninety to three hundred days he'd be making up a reason to leave her.

Lucas and I finished dinner and went outside together.

"Cab?" Lucas said.

"No thanks," I said. "I'll walk for a little— Oh, we forgot to talk about work."

"Oh, right," Lucas said. "I'll walk with you for a while, if that's OK."

"Sure."

We walked north on Seventh Ave. It was slushy and cold. A typically unpleasant New York winter. The leftover snow was hanging around in dirty little dregs; the air was sharp and cold. Lucas walked close to me and brushed against me a few times as we walked, coat against coat. I couldn't tell if it was intentional or not. Lucas had always been a little flirtatious with me. I figured he was like that with everyone. I would be too, if I were him. Why not open every door? Might get a lady. Might get a tiger.

The first time I'd met Lucas, he told me he'd read everything I'd ever written—one book, six short stories, eight personal essays. I felt a little rush of something forgotten and valuable. Later, I learned that moment wasn't as meaningful as I'd imagined: Lucas was extraordinarily well read. But at the time I'd felt pleased with myself, especially after Lucas and I talked for a while. I liked him: He was strange and funny and bright.

Then that year's girlfriend—a smart, interesting woman who worked in an art gallery—came over and put her arm around Lucas and, with perfect friendliness and charm, introduced herself to me. I liked her right away. I soon realized Lucas had a new girlfriend every eight or twelve months, and he soon realized that I didn't really want to talk about my old life as a writer, and after that first conversation we stuck to rare books and book dealer gossip and got along very well.

I would not have believed it, if you'd told me that night, when I met Lucas, that I wouldn't publish anything again. That five years later, my life would be exactly the same.

Intentional or not, the tiny points of contact between us as we walked down the street had a strong effect, fueling a little spark of desire in me, and an equal one of sadness. I moved away from Lucas and pushed both feelings away.

"We're looking to expand in bibliographies," he said. "I'm pretty much buying everything I can in books about books. Also, a student pointed out to me that our travelogues are pitiful."

"What kind of travel?"

"Firsts," he said. "Early stuff."

I knew he didn't mean first editions, but accounts of the first person from one place to visit another: first American in Nigeria, first Nigerian in France, and so on.

"Nice," I said. "Come by my booth tomorrow after the first hour or two. I have a few things—I'll put them aside for you."

We talked some more about his wants and desires. When we reached the corner of the block where I was staying, Lucas thanked me and we said good night and kissed on the cheek. His face was warm and soft and forgiving. Maybe it was my imagination, but

I was almost sure he hesitated for a sliver of a moment before he turned away. I chalked it up to awkwardness.

"See you tomorrow," I said brightly, and I turned and left before I felt anything else.

I walked back to the apartment I'd rented. It was a little one-bedroom, pleasantly messy and comfortable, crowded with textiles and pillows and wall hangings from Asia and Central America. In the apartment I poured myself a glass from a bottle of good wine that likely was not intended for me to drink, changed into a T-shirt and pajama pants, and got into bed with the wine to watch a TV show about sex cops on my laptop.

Before I fell asleep, I called home. Our nurse, Awe, answered.

"Hey, Lily," he said. He was from Nigeria and had a soft accent.

"How is he?" I asked.

"The same," Awe said. "Very peaceful."

"You need anything?" I asked. "Can I do anything?"

"Get a good night's sleep," Awe said. "Don't worry about us."

After I talked to Awe I watched the cop show and drank more wine, usually a powerfully soporific combination, but that night I couldn't fall asleep. I was thinking about the money I was going to get from the book—if we could find it. I imagined going to the ATM and seeing those numbers line up, zero after zero after zero. I imagined paying off every bill. Giving Awe a raise. Buying a few little gifts for myself—maybe a new face cream from a department store, not a drug store. A new reading chair for the living room.

I never worked with other dealers. I never went chasing after ridiculous books. I never counted money before it was in hand. My life was practical and narrow and tightly confined.

It was like the book already had me, and was leading me exactly where it wanted.

4.

Almost as soon as I got to the fair the next morning and started setting up my table, Jeremy Goodman, another book dealer, came over
and asked if I'd heard about Shyman. I figured he'd found the book
without me. No one ever talked about Shyman.

"No," I said. "Hear what?"

"He was mugged last night," Jeremy said. Jeremy had thinning
hair and wore khaki pants and a pink button-down shirt. A good
Upper East Side Ivy League boy gone to seed.

"He's OK?" I asked.

"He's dead," Jeremy said. Jeremy specialized in New York history.
Knew every inch of the city like his own hands. "Someone killed
him. Right near the Weather Underground house. Eighteen West
Eleventh Street."

"Oh, God," I said. "Wow. Oh my God."

Jeremy looked like he'd been crying. I wasn't crying. I was

unhappy. I was not happy to hear Shyman was dead. But I'd spoken to him only about a dozen times. It was sad in the abstract but there was no need to pretend I was devastated over it. I wasn't going to suffer from the lack of Shyman's presence in my life.

"His sister got his books," Jeremy said, teary-eyed. "I heard she's going to try to sell them as a lot. If you want to bid."

He pulled a napkin from his pocket and blew his nose.

"Well, I'll think about it," I said. "Probably not really my area."

"OK," Jeremy said. "Be well. Take care of yourself. It's hard on all of us."

An hour later Lucas came by my table. He already knew. After we said hello and what a horrible, shocking shame it was about Shyman, neither of us spoke for a moment.

"Goodman is already ready to bid on his inventory," I said.

"Jesus," Lucas said.

Neither of us spoke for another moment. Then I said, "I wonder who his buyer was for that book?"

There was another silent moment. Then Lucas looked away and said, "Didn't Shyman have a girl who worked for him sometimes?"

"I think she did his books," I said. "I mean his financials. His bookkeeping. I don't know if she actually handled books."

"Still," Lucas said.

"Huh," I said. "She might know something."

"She might," Lucas agreed.

Lucas went back to shopping for his library and I went back to working. I sold a good two-hundred-dollar hardcover about ships to a man I'd known for years, a collector named Al. Al wore shabby clothes and had hair that stuck out at the least appealing angles possible and wore big dirty glasses and always, always, had a big wad of cash in the pocket of his wrinkled, stained pants, usually ten grand or more. Transportation collectors were a type.

Around lunchtime Lucas came back to my table with four chicken tacos from a truck parked down the street, two for each of us. The taco truck was a book fair tradition; all the booksellers ate lunch there, and sometimes breakfast and dinner. Most of them, like me, lived in cheaper places, and meals in New York City could kill your weekend profits.

It was too cold to eat outside, so we ate in the lobby of the community college. It was crowded and loud, the linoleum floor doubling the footsteps and chatter.

"You know," Lucas said as we were finishing the last tacos, "we might as well keep looking for it. The book. Without Shyman."

Of course I'd been thinking the same. High six figures. Maybe seven. A million dollars on the table.

"Well, we'd have to find the client," I said. "And the book."

"True," Lucas said. "I think we can, though."

I thought about it. A million dollars. A million dollars and, maybe more enticing, something to do.

Once life had been fun and adventurous and full of surprises. I'd had money, but I never cared about the money. Not for its own sake. What I'd loved was what money could make happen. Money could buy you things, but more so, buy you time: time to travel, to write, to read, to walk, to have sex.

That was a long time ago. Lately it seemed like everything worthwhile was in short supply: time, money, sex, even books. I had thousands of books in my house and never found anything I wanted to read. I would stare at the shelves of books like a hungry person staring into an open refrigerator and wait for something to speak to me. But nothing ever spoke.

"Yes, I think we can," I said, and our fate was sealed. Five stupid words. Five stupid words said in haste, on impulse, with little thought behind them past *This sounds fun.* In the years to come I'd think of that moment often: the fluorescent lights, the loud room, the shiny linoleum tile, beige speckled with a different beige. Lucas, putting the last bite of a chicken taco in his mouth. Then he crumpled the paper that the taco had been wrapped in into a ball and tossed it into a trash can a few feet away. He made the shot. We looked at each other. He smiled, and I smiled back.

Now I think of that moment, combing through it for insight, for thought, for an intelligent decision. But I never find any. Just a lonely woman unwilling to admit how lonely she was, grabbing at something bright and colorful as it floated by.

And maybe if I looked closely, just around the corner, I would see a darker current, a stronger force, pulling agreement out of my mouth. *Yes, I think we can.*

But that was all far in the future. Back at the book fair, Lucas and I were excited. We were going to find the book. First, or at least concurrently, we needed to find the buyer.

And in order to find either of those, we had to find the girl who worked for Shyman. That turned out to be easy. That afternoon I saw a woman at Shyman's table, packing his books into plastic milk crates. She was about thirty, hair in a long, thick, braid, with a Walmart-ish rural outfit on—badly-fitting jeans, awkward turtleneck, unfortunate sneakers. I went over to her.

"Did you work for Shyman?" I asked.

She nodded and tried to look sad.

"Yes," she said, in a slightly theatrical voice. "You know he's dead."

"Yes," I said. "I know. I heard. He was mugged?"

"That's what they say," she said. "I mean, the police. They're the *they*. They told his sister and she called me and asked me to come down here and get his stuff. It's not what I usually do. I don't work with books. I mean, I like books. I like spy novels. But I'm a book-keeper. I'm like an accountant, but I'm not an accountant at all. I used to help him mail things, and keep track of orders. But there was no one else to get his things, so."

"Right," I said. "Of course. How's his sister holding up?"

"Well, they weren't close," she said. "He also had two kids. Adults. They also weren't close."

"Was he close to anyone?" I asked.

The woman frowned. "Not that I know of. Just you guys."

"Us guys?" I asked.

"The other book people," the woman said. "That's as close as he got to closeness."

"Well, he'd asked me for something before—before last night," I said. "He asked me for help with a book yesterday morning."

She stuck a handful of books into a box. She was too rough with them. For a minute a streak of sadness rushed through me—the last hands to touch those books had been Shyman's. Everything that was his was now no one's; everything he'd seen and felt and knew was now gone.

It passed.

"He'd asked me to find this very expensive book," I said. "And I've already started working on it. I would love to get it to the buyer if I can figure out who it is. Of course, his estate would get the lion's share."

"His *estate?*" the woman said. "That's a grand way of putting it. *The lion's share would go to his estate.* That's fancy. Well, I'm sure his sister will be happy to hear it."

"I hope so," I said. "It could be a lot of money for her. But I don't know who the buyer was."

"Who?" the woman said.

"The buyer of the book," I said. "If you could help me figure out who wanted to buy it, we could all, um…" I was going to try to say *fulfill Shyman's last wishes* but I knew I couldn't sell it. "…profit from it."

"Well," the woman said. "I don't know anything about it. Here—"

She tossed a little notebook at me. It was five by three, fat, spiral-bound, used, and a little dirty.

I caught the notebook.

"Are you sure his family won't want this?" I asked.

"Oh, yes," the woman said. "No one else will want it. No one else will even know it's gone."

5.

Back at my table, I flipped through Shyman's notebook, but nothing jumped out at me—on each page were notes like "Carl at 3," "Second/best ed," "Philadelphia," along with dates, phone numbers, and page notations. It was too much to figure out on the fly, and so I put it aside and spent the rest of the day selling books.

Late in the day Lucas came by my table again. He had another dealer, Betty French, with him. The way he led her to my table reminded me of a cat bringing home a finch. *Look what I found! We need this! Aren't I clever!*

"Hey, Betty," I said.

"Lily," she said. "Your table looks great. SO good."

Which was exactly what she would say, because Betty was elegant and sophisticated and attractive and dead inside. She'd been an art history professor for the first half of her adult life. At fifty she'd inherited a large collection of rare art books from her boyfriend—

Betty would probably say *partner* or *lover*—when he died of lung cancer. She started selling them because she needed the money and found out the work suited her and her heart was broken and she had nothing else and no one else to love. And here we were. She was still very kind.

"Let me know if you see anything you like," I said.

"Everything," she said, graciously, about my mediocre little collection. "Lucas said you were working on something with Shyman. It's absolutely horrible. Do they know anything more about it?"

"I don't think so," I said. "I mean, I think it was just, you know, a mugging. I'm not so sure there's anything to know. But, yeah, I was looking for a book for him. We'd made all the arrangements except the important ones—I don't know anything about the book."

"Well, I might be able to help you out," Betty said. "We had lunch yesterday."

I was surprised by that—elegant Betty and shlumpy Shyman. Books made for strange bedfellows. Although loneliness was probably more to the heart of it than books. Loneliness was what linked us all: loneliness made you both a book person and a bedfellow. And a strange one.

I made a noncommittal sound of encouragement like *"Really?"* or *"Oh,"* and she went on:

"He told me about a new client he had. He was excited. He asked me about a couple of the titles he was looking for. I didn't know any of them. Military stuff doesn't interest me."

"Do you remember the titles?" I asked. "Was one of them something like *The Precious Substance?*"

She shrugged. "Maybe?" she said, trying to be helpful.

"Do you know who the client was?" Lucas asked.

Betty cocked her head and frowned. "A man in Connecticut," she said. "That was what came up about him. That he was a man, and he lived in Connecticut. And he had a lot of money to spend. Are you going to the funeral?"

"Of course," I said, because I now realized I'd dug a hole in which we were all friends. "If I can make it. Maybe I'll see you there."

Betty and I exchanged a few more words of sadness and appreciation for Shyman and she returned to her own booth. Lucas and I went back to Shyman's little notebook. None of it made any sense. Lucas asked if he could take it home to look for leads. I said sure.

The fair ended that night. Lucas left at five. He had a little glint in his eye.

"So we'll talk soon?" he said, with a little smile that indicated something like fun. "We'll find the book?"

Suddenly it all seemed silly. Like something from a movie. A lost book, a dead bookseller, Lucas and his fake smiles and hidden awkwardness, his veneer of sophistication—ridiculous, all of it.

"Sure," I said. It was almost funny. "We'll talk soon."

After I closed up, I had dinner alone at an Indian restaurant in the East Village, the only remotely affordable restaurant I still knew of in the city. The restaurant was cheerful, with bright decorations hanging from every possible surface: tinsel, Christmas lights, fake flowers. It was also empty and lonely. I had two books with me and I didn't read either of them; instead, I read dismal news on my phone.

The next day I had nothing to do. I added up my totals and

expenses from the book fair and delivered a few packages around town—books I'd promised to mail but might as well deliver myself as long as I was here. Then I went shopping. First I took the subway to the thrift shops on the Upper East Side, where I was almost certain to find a few modern firsts. Not glamorous, but potentially profitable, and relaxing. I liked skimming through the messy shelves and the satisfying feeling of finding something good. After a few hours I had a first edition of an early Louise Penny, two old illustrated medical books from the 1840s, and an armful of photography books: nice two-hundred-dollar surveys of Diane Arbus, Vivian Maier, and Helmut Newton.

When I couldn't carry a single book more, I stopped by a small bookstore on Seventy-Seventh Street for a break. The owner, Elena, was a friend. I walked in and checked my bags with a girl at the counter. My arms were rubbery and sore. I looked at Elena's books, most of them in antique cases with glass doors on them, all the better to justify their insanely high prices. Only fair—Elena's store was in the most expensive neighborhood in one of the most expensive cities in the world.

Just then Elena came out of her office. She was unattractively tall—there was nothing wrong with her height, which was about six three, but she hunched her shoulders, which made her back look bent and put her face and neck at the worst possible angle—chin out, neck doubled, chest sagging. Her nose was big and matched by her forehead, with cheekbones and chin lagging far behind. But there was much that was appealing about Elena nonetheless; a happiness that shone out from a deep dark point inside. She wasn't really a book person. She knew as much as any of us but she hadn't chosen the business.

She'd inherited the shop from her parents, along with the building it was in. She lived on the top floor, had the shop on the first, stored stock in the basement, and rented out the two middle floors for thousands and thousands of dollars. Elena was a real New Yorker. As long as she had her annual pass to the Natural History Museum and a monthly Metrocard, and her Gristede's stayed open, she was happy.

"Look at you," Elena said, affectionately. "How was the fair?"

Elena was wearing a long, shapeless black velvet dress and thick black tights and silver and blue snow boots that looked like they were meant for walking on the moon. But when it came to everything other than herself she had beautiful taste. The store was elegant and warm and felt magical, like something from a Victorian novel, a place where Edith Wharton and Edgar Allan Poe might have browsed.

We caught up on gossip and news.

"I heard about Shyman," she said. "Horrible. They take his wallet?"

"I don't know," I said. "You know, before he died, he asked me to help him with something. With a book. It's a real mystery, actually."

"Really?" Elena said, eyebrows raised. I knew she read mystery novels for fun—the kind that take place in Ye Olde New Amsterdaam, with Inspector Wittenbrier and a Lady Widemouth, who happen to run into a peculiar fellow named Benjamin Franklin.

"Actually," I said. "Actually. It's a book I never heard of. I think it's called *The Book of the Most Precious Substance*."

"Huh," Elena said.

"I was hoping to find it," I said. "For his family. He said he had a seven-figure offer for it. Six or seven figures. But I don't know what the book is and I don't know who the buyer is."

I'd already figured out that his family didn't know about the book and didn't care about Shyman and there was no need to cut them in. I knew Lucas would feel the same way.

Or, maybe, this: The book had already led me to believe that the wrong thing was right, and the right thing wrong.

"Well, maybe I can help," Elena said. "There's not an infinite number of people out there willing to pay a million bucks for a book."

"But here's what I can't stop wondering," I said. "If they're really a book person, why ask Shyman?"

"Mm," Elena said. "Maybe the buyer didn't know anyone else who sold expensive books. Maybe that was their only other interest—the kind of stuff Shyman sells. *Sold*."

"Good point," I said.

"Well, I don't know the book," Elena said. "But I bet Archie does."

Archie was Elena's husband. He was retired from an academic job and also a native New Yorker, from a famously smart family of intellectuals and writers. Elena promised she would talk to Archie, who was out on a buying trip (one far more upscale than mine—visiting a collector with a vineyard in Sonoma), and would let me know if he had any information.

We said our goodbyes and I got my bags and left the shop. I checked my phone. Lucas hadn't texted. I couldn't quite justify staying in the city any longer.

It was time to go home.

6.

I started the drive back home feeling a little excited about it all—Lucas's attention, the money we might make, the book itself. I felt the excitement rise in myself, and I spent the rest of the ride back home pushing it back down. Lucas was only interested in making some money. Which we probably wouldn't get anyway, because the odds of us finding the book, and then finding the buyer, were about zero in infinity. Then he'd drift away, all the excitement would be gone, and there I'd be again, in a cold farmhouse in upstate New York.

I got home to my cold farmhouse. It wasn't so cold. Awe was in the kitchen, making soup.

"Hey, Lily," he said. "How was your trip?"

"OK," I said. "Not bad. How is he?"

"The same," Awe said with a smile. "He's in the garden, getting some sun."

I left my books in the car for now. I'd unpack tomorrow or the day after. Awe would offer to help and I wouldn't let him, knowing his back was strained enough. I put down my bag and went out to the backyard.

It was a sunny afternoon, warm for upstate in February, about fifty degrees. My husband, Abel, was in his wheelchair. He was clean and well dressed like always. Awe took excellent care of him. The sun was on Abel's face, which was slack and expressionless.

I pulled a lawn chair over to sit next to him.

"Hi, honey," I said.

He didn't say anything. He hadn't said anything in years.

"I'm back from New York."

His expression didn't change.

"It was a good sale," I said. For no particular reason, I acted as if he not only could hear me and understand me, but that he cared about the idiotic, mundane details of life—details he'd never cared much about to begin with.

I'd met Abel when I was thirty-two and he was thirty-eight. I was on the book tour for my first book, *Beauty*. San Francisco. I wrote the book when I was twenty-seven, twenty-eight, and twenty-nine and published it when I was thirty-one. I didn't know if it was any good. I still didn't. I knew I'd done my best and I couldn't do any better.

I was living in Brooklyn. I'd lived in a few cities by then. I didn't have a home and I didn't miss having one. I was from nowhere in particular in the Southwest. We moved every few years. Every time my father got fired for drinking, my parents blamed it on the town, somehow, and we would start packing: Bakersfield, Tucson, Scottsdale, Sedona, Taos. My mother would find the hippie neighborhood and sell the beaded jewelry we made, and whenever possible find work in a stable. She loved horses. My father did whatever the town's shit job was—chicken processing, janitorial, medical waste—because that was what he could get by now. My father had been a composer and a piano player with a few semesters at Berklee under his belt. Getting kicked out of Berklee was the original step down, and there'd been another few steps down each year since. My father was a man with huge, unrealistic dreams and absolutely no acumen for everyday life. What he had in abundance was alcoholism, grandiosity, and maybe manic depression. My mother had studied English at Boston University before she looked for someone to ruin her life and found my father. My parents were both terrified of trying to improve our lives, long sapped of the strength for any more risk. But they approached failure with cheerful bravery, making every move and step down seem like a new adventure for as long as they could. My mother had a fatal heart attack during the year I was finishing *Beauty*. My father drank himself to death before the year was over.

I'd gone to college in Los Angeles, left after two years to travel around the country with a boyfriend, dropped him in Portland, moved to Savannah, moved to Brooklyn, and written a book along the way. I thought I was dreaming when a big publisher with deep pockets wanted it. I'd been working at a coffee shop on Fifth Avenue in Brooklyn, making lattes—apparently not very good lattes, given the reaction—for assholes.

The book was about a painting and a bunch of people who wanted it, fought over it, and sacrificed everything they had to get it. Book sales had started off strong when the tour began in New York. By the time I got to San Francisco, two weeks later, I had what

I'd never imagined: success. The reviews were coming in and they were almost all strong. By San Francisco I was inching my way up the bestseller list. In New York, thirty people had come to see me read. In Chicago, seventy. In San Francisco, there was a crowd of more than a hundred at City Lights, and we added another night in the Ferry Building. Critics liked the book. Readers liked the book. Most surprisingly, other writers seemed to like it. Emails of praise came in every week and then every day, some from people I'd grown up reading.

I loved every minute of it. I loved the travel, the attention, the people I met, the money I made. I loved knowing—or imagining, because I was wrong—that for the rest of my life I would make a living doing what I loved most: thinking, reading, and writing. I'd had enough shitty times to appreciate every minute of the good, and I took my good luck with gratitude and joy. I'd grown up in a house where food stamp day was cause for celebration, and a thrift-shop book was a major purchase.

I read the first half of the first chapter to the crowd at City Lights in San Francisco and then took questions. The questions were always the same and they were never interesting. Then I signed books for an hour and some friends from college—Sophie and Mark, both of whom had graduated and had teaching jobs now—took me out to dinner with a few of their friends. One of those friends was Abel.

Abel met us at an Italian restaurant on Columbus Avenue. He was there first, waiting outside, leaning on the wall near the door, reading a book called *The Philosophy of Sex*. I thought, *That is the most attractive man I've ever seen.* Abel was about five ten and had a face like a fighter—chiseled, sharp, but damaged, with a nose that had been broken twice (once in a fight, once in a motorcycle accident). His eyes were big and round and pale blue, and his hair was dark blond in the summer and light brown in the winter, thick and short. He wore a gray button-down shirt and black work pants under a tweedy overcoat, and he leaned against the wall as if he owned the world. He looked like James Dean or Cary Grant; a man you would see in black-and-white and think, *They don't make them like that anymore.*

I had no idea he knew Sophie and Mark. When I realized he was having dinner with us my stomach jumped.

"I read your book," Abel said over dinner. His voice was like honey over gravel, and I felt a pleasant rush of blood to my nether regions when he spoke. "I was surprised. It was good."

Abel was not exactly famous, but a highly renowned writer of academic theory and criticism and obscure histories. People said he was a genius. Later, after I read his books, I agreed.

Over dinner we ignored Sophie and Mark, who were easy to ignore, and talked about things we loved—lost books, road trips across America. We shared a vision of life: adventure, experience, shutting nothing out and making everything real. We talked about roadside motels and Waffle Houses and buying mescaline in Utah and picking fruit in Florida. After dinner we went to a bar and got drunk on whiskey and ended the night making out in a corner of the bar like teenagers. His kisses were erotic and demanding, always asking for more, always unexpected, always surprising.

San Francisco was the end of the book tour, for now. I had a flight booked for New York the next day. I rebooked it and spent the day with Abel instead. We ate Vietnamese food in Oakland's

Chinatown and then went to bookstores in Berkeley and then went to his place, a big loft in Oakland, and made love for the first time. The sex was good in every way. Being with Abel felt right. It felt like being under warm blankets on a cold morning. It felt like home. That night, he slept with his arms around me, and we fit together as perfectly as a jigsaw puzzle. I'd enjoyed sex before, but I'd never enjoyed actually *sleeping* with anyone before. We slept together like that nearly every night for the next five years.

Soon the book would climb higher on the bestseller list and they'd put me back on the road. For now I had nothing to do and nowhere to go, so I moved my ticket again and stayed in Oakland for a few weeks with Abel. We would lie around his apartment and smoke and have sex and read. We would walk around San Francisco and Oakland for hours talking about art and books. Eat cheap delicious food, kill a bottle of wine, go home and have sex for hours. Once he made me come so hard I cried. I was convinced then, and still believe now, that those weeks were as good as life gets.

Abel had done more in thirty-eight years than most people had done in lifetimes. He'd published two books: a biography of an Argentinian philosopher I'd never heard of and a book about the history of cars in American literature. He'd played guitar and been in four bands. He said he had no talent for music, and he was right, but he had enough passion and technical ability to make up for it. He'd traveled South America on a motorcycle; he'd gotten two PhDs; he'd been married twice; he taught at Berkeley in academic disciplines I didn't understand (cultural studies, semiotics); and he was also a painter who'd occasionally shown work in upscale galleries.

Abel was from upstate New York. His parents were in a small, strange religious movement similar to Quakers. They were decent people, but distant and odd. They loved everyone in the abstract. Individuals, less so. Abel rarely saw them, with years elapsing between visits. Like me, he had no siblings. He had six tattoos when I met him and got six more after.

We'd each, finally, in a lifetime of being the odd one out, the overambitious one, the one who refused to be quiet, the one who aimed too high, too strange, found a best friend.

All my friends loved him. All his friends loved me. A few months after we met, money was coming in. I'd sold so many books that my agent had gotten my publisher to cut me one check and then another months ahead of the royalty schedule. With my wealth I paid a mover to pack everything up in Brooklyn and I moved in to Abel's loft in Oakland. It was a loft like people lived in in the seventies: huge, raw, messy, full of books and art and strange furniture. We had sex until we were both sore and then we'd wait a day and have sex again.

We went to London together and interviewed each other at a conference. In Paris, Abel took me to a private club and introduced me to my favorite writer, an obscure experimental novelist named Lucien Roche, and we stayed up talking until morning. Lucien was wild like an elf or an imp, impenetrable and completely charming. In Marfa I bought Abel a painting and he bought me a pair of cowboy boots. In New Orleans we rented a car and drove until we hit the ocean, where he went down on me on the muddy beach as the sun came up. In Los Angeles we got in a fight on Sunset Boulevard about a friend of mine he didn't like and made up on Venice Beach.

We settled down to life in Oakland. I had money. I had Abel.

I started my next book—*Labyrinth*. He was working on his third book, an analysis of the role of the CIA in twentieth-century entertainment. He would never finish it. Life was so good, I could hardly believe it was real. We both expected to become less passionate, to fight more, to take each other for granted as time went on. But we never did. We developed routines and schedules, but we continued to astound each other, and to amaze ourselves with our own ability to love. Neither of us had believed we had it in us, this capacity for rapturous, uncomplicated, unconditional love. As it turned out, we had everything we needed.

We were people who thought all things were possible. We were sure we could do anything: write, paint, make art, spin gold from straw. Even fall in love and stay in love.

And then, five years after we met, Abel mixed up the coffee and the tea.

It was afternoon. If we were both home we always had coffee after lunch. We used an Italian stovetop espresso maker and good strong espresso from North Beach.

I'd just finished a telephone interview with a French radio station and was about to get back into *Labyrinth*. Abel was grading papers. He made the coffee and brought me a cup.

It was thin and light. I sniffed it.

"Is this tea?" I said.

What spooked me wasn't the tea. What spooked me was his reaction. A blank, howling horror passed over his face, draining everything that I knew as Abel right out of it. I couldn't imagine what he was feeling. I still can't. The look passed. He went back to the espresso maker, unscrewed it all, and sure enough, he had put loose tea in instead of coffee.

He looked in the coffee maker as if it were playing a trick on him. Again that haunted look passed over his face. I felt a chill up my spine.

We both shook it off. He made coffee, correctly this time.

Next was a burned chicken, left in the oven too long. A bath left running that flooded the bathroom and the loft downstairs. Then there was a missed class. Bills unpaid, or paid incorrectly. It was all so unthinkable. It just wasn't possible, so we both kept pretending nothing was happening. We pretended and pretended until Abel got lost coming home from school.

It was toward the end of the spring semester. His last class ended at three thirty. Usually he'd be home around four or five. Our life was not strictly regimented and metered. We came and went as we pleased. It was no big deal if he went for a meal or a walk or some shopping after class. But five came and went. Six, also. Then it was seven.

We did as we pleased. But we called each other. We talked to each other. We didn't let each other worry.

At eight, Abel came through the door. His face scared me. There it was again. The blankness. The void. This time, a wide-eyed fear was added to it.

I wasn't mad. I was terrified. I asked where he'd been.

"The trains," he said. "The trains were all... The trains don't make sense anymore."

Then I knew this wasn't just a bad day. In a moment of clarity, I saw that this was the start of a bad life. Inside, I shook, terrified.

I pushed the clarity away, and told myself things would be fine.

Everything would be fine. But nothing was ever fine again.

Abel seemed angry. I calmed him down. Agreed with him that they'd changed the BART. How stupid. How unfair. Finally, he settled down and ate some dinner. He went to bed early.

I stayed up late, looking on the internet for a neurologist.

The first neurologist didn't know anything. Neither did the second. Wait and see, they said. The third took a long series of blood tests and piss tests and prescribed vitamins and minerals. None of them helped. Abel was up and down. Most days he was exactly as he'd always been—brilliant, witty, energetic. But the bad days got worse, and more frequent. And he didn't seem capable of seeing how he was changing.

I talked to his parents. *That's a shame,* they said. *We'll pray for him.* They checked in again every six months or so after that. They always said they were praying for him. They never offered to visit, or send money, or help in any way.

I kept my hopes up. I thought a lot about the future, a future where we would look back at this awful year as a distant memory. *It was terrifying,* I would say, when we started hosting dinner parties again. *I didn't know how it would turn out.* I would say this with Abel, sharp and well, by my side, nodding in sympathy, in gratitude. I played this scene in my head over and over again: while we waited for late doctors, while I lay next to Abel as he started to toss and turn at night—sometimes now making strange noises in his sleep—when I would look up from my work and see him sitting in a chair, looking confused, doing nothing. *Just get through this,* I told myself. *It will all be over soon.*

But it didn't end. It never ended. Like Alice falling in the rabbit hole, we kept falling, and falling, and falling. Abel slipped further away every month. Our friends slunk away, one at a time, inch by inch. I was terrified every day. He had good insurance through the university, but it didn't matter. The medical system was a mess. No one cared. No one kept track of medications or tests or diagnoses. I kept thinking someone who actually knew what they were doing would step in and take control. Like one of those TV shows where the feisty, if dickish, doctor takes control and digs his teeth in and doesn't let go until he has an answer. Instead, we got sent from one department to another with the wrong charts and incomplete prescriptions, always met with shrugs and smugness, often scolded for having done exactly what we'd been told to do by another department.

I was entirely alone in trying to get Abel well. Somehow, through a series of turns I would trace over and over in my head, trying to figure out what I'd done wrong, I'd ended up one hundred percent responsible for his life. It was all on me. I'd never been responsible for so much as a houseplant before. Now I had to learn about swallow tests and medication half-lives and—soon—pressure-sore prevention and UTI avoidance. Everyone I encountered in this ugly trip down seemed surprised that I was surprised.

"These things happen," one psychiatrist said, with a tone that implied I should have known this. *These things happen!* I'd made the mistake of pretending we were all human, and failed to hold back tears during a medication consult. The psychiatrist was about my own age, with a slim gold band on his left ring finger. "It's all very unpredictable. But we have to live with what's happening now."

"Do they happen to you?" I asked.

He looked away, said nothing, and then we talked about meds

and pretended my embarrassing moment of human suffering had never happened.

It was amazing how quickly everything fell away. Extraordinary that two lives, especially such happy, charmed, productive lives, could crumble so quickly. It wasn't as if we'd been greedy. It wasn't as if we'd aimed too high and been burned by the sun. We'd had our work, a little money, and each other. We were grateful. We appreciated what we had. We tried to be generous. I was a creative person, but I could never make any moral or symbolic sense of our story. We had so much luck, and then so little, and throughout it all it seemed like someone, somewhere, must be laughing at me—but I could never figure out who.

Life shrank, and distorted itself into something ugly. What had been a great adventure was now a grotesque maze, where I was stuck, entirely alone. *Labyrinth,* the title of my next book, now seemed like a horrible joke. And no matter where I turned, no matter what I tried—new drugs! new doctors! positive thinking! mantras!— I never found my way out of that dark labyrinth again.

We kept going to doctors. Abel kept going downhill. It was a year before we got a name. Early-onset dementia. But that was a description, not a diagnosis. The source was unknown. He was losing his mind and no one knew why. Later, other doctors would call it early Alzheimer's, just to call it something. Others called it dementia NOS, for "not otherwise specified." And one kind and honest neurologist admitted that nothing made sense, there was no reason for anything, and some things are so ugly and so rare as to have no words. He charged eight hundred dollars an hour for this truth.

There was no cure. Recovery was not possible. Medications might slightly slow down the progress, but nothing would make a real dent in it. There were no clues in any scan, no spots on his MRIs. No real diagnosis at all.

I didn't tell Abel. The doctor, in a fancy building near Union Square in San Francisco, told me the diagnosis alone in his office. I went back out and told Abel the doctor said it was high blood pressure and stress. After that, Abel forgot about the doctor and never asked about his health again.

That night I told Abel I was going out for drinks with a friend. Instead, I walked out of the loft, around the corner, sat on the curb, and cried for hours.

I'd lied to the doctors and said we were married. No one ever asks you to prove things like that, and soon after we were. We got married in City Hall, a grim, sad legal ceremony in case anyone ever did ask me to prove it, so I could keep talking to his doctors and dealing with his finances. I wasn't sure Abel knew where we were.

"We're getting married," I kept saying. "We're really married now."

He kept nodding, just like he did when I made his breakfast. He rarely spoke now.

The medications made him worse. I stopped giving them to him. We went to acupuncturists in Chinatown, a functional osteopath in Los Angeles, a witch in Arizona. I spent hours on the internet, reading about cures in Sweden, special diets, magic herbs. I tried all of them. Abel still got worse.

We went through money like it was water. Neither of us wrote another book. Abel could now barely read a cereal box. He'd taken medical leave from the university, but time was running out. I had to terminate his employment, which meant both that he had no money coming in, save a few hundred bucks a year in royalties, and that I had to pay his insurance going forward. Only one person from the university bothered to find me and drop me a note, a young woman Abel had mentored into a professorship.

I don't know what to say, she wrote. *Sending love.* Maybe she really did send love. If so, it got lost in the mail.

The one saving grace was that after the first few months, Abel didn't know what was going on. The first part of him to go was the part that might have known what he was losing. He slept a lot, puttered around the house, watched movies. He rarely got angry or sad. He just got *less.* He never seemed to miss himself.

I, on the other hand, did miss him. I missed him a whole lot. I had no one who I would consider anything like a family, and I had nothing else that mattered. Not the way Abel mattered. The only thing I wanted was the thing I would never have: I wanted Abel back. And as far as I could tell, I would want that for the rest of my life.

After another year, Abel spent most of his time sitting in an armchair and looking out at nothing, barely speaking, unable to bathe himself or prepare a meal. We were running out of money. My book still sold, but sales had slowed down to a barely profitable trickle. Every month the rent loomed larger and larger. And living in the city was dangerous for Abel. He couldn't leave the house without getting lost. The only time he got angry with me was when I tried to put an ID bracelet on him.

"I'm not..." he said over and over again, wrenching his arm away from me. "I'm not..."

Whatever he thought he wasn't, he was.

There weren't a lot of options for Abel's care. Long-term care homes ranged from *unaffordably expensive* to *not really long term because you wouldn't live much longer once you checked in.* There wasn't much in the middle. Best-case scenario, he'd get decent care and wouldn't know where he was. Or he could get pneumonia or flu or bedsores and die alone before I found a cure. Which I was going to do, if it took the rest of our lives.

Two years in, it took all of Abel's will to finish a sentence. I scraped together all the money we had left, sold nearly everything we owned, and bought the property in upstate New York. It was a house Abel knew. It had belonged to his cousin, and Abel used to spend time there when he was a child, so there would be some familiarity in the older, less-damaged parts of his brain. It wasn't the town he grew up in, which was closer to Cleveland than New York City. This town—soon to be our town—was about three hours from the city without traffic. The cousin sold it to me at a good price. Our mortgage would be half our rent in Oakland. We'd be near the cousin, and Abel's parents, and other cousins who I thought might want to be near him. Might want to help. As it turned out, they did not. People do not like to be around people like us. His parents visited once a year or so, the other relatives less. But the property was big and fenced and Abel could wander all he wanted without getting lost and, as I'd hoped, he did remember his way around the house in his muscle memory—although within a year he wouldn't remember much at all. Soon after that, he'd be wheelchair-bound and it wouldn't matter anymore.

This time I didn't hire movers to pack the house. We couldn't afford them. All our money was gone, spent on cures that didn't cure, writing days where nothing was written, and a new house neither of us wanted. I packed myself. A few friends came over to help. Most of our friends had dropped us since he'd fallen apart. Of course they had. At least they helped us exit their lives, forever, as seamlessly as possible.

Every day my heart broke more and more and then one day I realized there was nothing left to break. It was all broken. In the years since Abel's diagnosis I'd lost my last living relative, an aunt. I inherited five thousand dollars and a condemned trailer in Sedona. All the love I'd had in the world was gone.

We packed everything into one truck and paid a man to drive it across the country. That was when I started selling our books. I couldn't afford to move any but the most valuable, most beloved titles. Then, when we got to New York, we ran dry and I had to sell those, too, and my career as a book dealer was born.

The town upstate was pretty and fragrant and buzzed with visitors in the summer; the rest of the year it was cold, isolated, and unfriendly. The house was cute enough, a little farmhouse from the turn of the century, but I never had the money or the will to really make it my own. It wasn't really a home. Just a place we lived.

Once we were settled upstate, I tried to start writing again. I had plenty of time, and I'd been well into my next book when Abel got sick. But writing took feeling and passion and inspiration, and I had none of those things now. I didn't especially want to live anymore, let alone feel anything. Every once in a while I would sit at my desk and open up my manuscript and look at it. Then I'd think, *Why am I doing this?* No one had less to say than I did. I'd thought I'd found happiness. Had anyone ever been more wrong? My old work was dead. In the unlikely event I was able to come up with something new, it would be too gruesome to read.

Every time, I'd close the computer again and move on.

Sometimes I would wake up in the middle of the night and have to convince myself, all over again, that it was real. My career was gone. Abel was gone. Sometimes I thought I was crazy. Of course none of that had happened. I was still in California, still in the big solid platform bed Abel had in his loft, warm bodies under heavy comforters, cold bay fog seeping in through the windows, holding each other for hours, a complete universe of two.

But every time, it was real. Every time, I was in bed alone.

I'd now known Abel sick longer than I'd known him well. He'd said his last word three years ago.

"Sandwich," he'd said, looking at a bowl of soup.

He did not speak again.

7.

Back home, I tried to put *The Book of the Most Precious Substance* out of my mind and forget about it. My life was here, upstate. It wasn't so bad. People had it worse, that was for sure. I needed money, but chasing after this book was not a particularly wise or logical way to go about getting it.

And Lucas was something I'd avoided for years. I'd developed a kind of resentment of people who were attractive and looked like they had sex and maybe even enjoyed life. There wasn't really any reason I couldn't date. It wasn't like Abel would be jealous. But I was married. I loved my husband. I didn't love anyone else, and I didn't think I ever would. And I wasn't at all interested in facing the potentially ugly landscape of dating in my forties: looks fading away, career now a dirty and demanding one, responsible for a husband who was now a full-time job. I'd had a few sexual and romantic encounters over the years. They were awkward and unskilled and messy and did not encourage me to seek out more.

What life had for me was this: my house, my books, Abel, and Awe. Three years ago I'd found Awe through a service. He lived in the house with us and provided full-time care for Abel and coordinated his own little crew of floaters when he needed a day off. Roughly thirty cents of every dollar I made went to Awe. He deserved more. He was one of the most generous people I'd ever met, and I couldn't ask for a better partner in taking care of my husband. Awe was fifty-five. He'd come to America at forty-six. He'd been an accountant in Nigeria. Then his mother died from cancer, and his wife died of malaria. After that he moved to the USA, sponsored by his daughters, who'd gone to Stanford and NYU (neurology and experimental theater, respectively—the daughters were apparently very close despite their differences). The plan was for Awe to start a new life in America. But, overwhelmed by grief, he became a drunk instead. When he sobered up, he was offered free training to become a home health aide through an immigrants' aid organization, and he grabbed it. He still hoped to become a CPA again. He walked to an AA meeting in town painfully early every morning, before Abel woke up. His relationship with his kids was rocky after years of drinking and disappointments, but they now spoke regularly, and his connection with them was improving every year.

We got by. And if some days that didn't feel like enough, if some nights I found myself dreaming—well, I had more than most people. It was enough. It had to be.

I settled back into my life at home. There were books to mail, emails to answer, errands to run, a sink that needed a new washer, and a mountain of laundry to get through. I made a few calls about *The Precious Substance*—a customer who I knew collected in the occult, another I knew was fairly knowledgeable about alchemy—and texted with a few other booksellers. No one had heard of it. I looked through a few bibliographies I had, and then bought a half dozen more, but it wasn't in any of them.

It was a dead end.

My second day back, my neighbor Jeremiah came over for tea, as he did a few times a month. Jeremiah had moved up here to work on an apple orchard one summer in between semesters at NYU in the seventies and never left. We traded books and apples. Other than Awe, Jeremiah was the only person who would look Abel in the face and acknowledge that he existed. On the rare occasions that other people came over, they skittered around him as if he were an ugly new piece of furniture, one they were withholding comment on.

"Here's my boy," Jeremiah said, as he usually did when he saw Abel. I had no idea what it meant but he said it with great cheer. I made coffee and put out supermarket cookies for us. We talked about Jeremiah's farm and TV we'd watched and books we'd read and the disastrous state of politics local, national, and global. Jeremiah was an activist, and sponsored the local Black Lives Matter chapter, but he was also a Christian and an optimist. He believed, although he rarely discussed it, that there was a force for good in the world that was stronger than any other force extant. This force was mysterious, and often thwarted, but in the end, it would save us all, whenever we stopped getting in its way. I didn't agree. So far, my life was proof his theory was false.

When Jeremiah left, I knew I was unlikely to have another visitor until he came back. I called Abel's doctor, Dr. Richards. I'd been trying to talk her into trying a new medication for Abel. It was a precise mix of hormones that would block one thing and encourage another and had been suspected, in exactly two cases in Australia, to reverse dementia. Dr. Richards didn't like it when I called about new treatments we could try for Abel. Neither did any other doctor, which was why I switched every few years. At first they'd be willing to try that drug or supplement I'd read about or heard about or found on a message board. Then maybe they'd go along with the second possible treatment I wanted to try. By the time I got to the third possible treatment, our relationship would invariably be over.

"I think you need to accept what's going on here," Dr. Richards said. There was the twist, and here we were only on our second little experiment. I'd gone through maybe thirty trials since Abel had gotten sick. I didn't plan on stopping.

"It's highly, highly unlikely that your husband is going to improve," she said.

"I know that," I said. "But it isn't impossible."

"Practically," she said. "One out of a million."

"Right," I said. "One out of a million. I want to give my husband every chance to be that one."

"One in ten million," she said.

"The same principle applies," I said. "There are more than ten million people who have had dementia. So those odds aren't bad."

"There really isn't any evidence behind it," she said. "There were two people who showed results."

"But what's the harm?" I asked. "If he gets worse, we stop. What could possibly go wrong?"

"I don't want you to get your hopes up," Dr. Richards said.

"I won't," I said. "But I don't want to give up hope altogether. That doesn't seem like a fruitful path."

"Hope can be deceiving," Dr. Richards said. "Hope can be addictive, like a drug."

"So can despair," I argued.

Dr. Richards relented and wrote the prescription, begrudgingly. We both knew I'd be changing doctors again soon. I didn't like her anyway. Like with so many people, even doctors (maybe especially doctors), there was the constant implication that I'd done something wrong, as if the situation Abel and I were in was the result of bad decisions we'd made, a chain of selfish and foolish mistakes that had dropped us here. If this had happened to *them,* well, surely they would have found a way out. They'd find a cure, have better insurance, have a real family, and, most of all, never be so stupid as to get sick to begin with. Or marry a sick person.

Awe made a chicken stew for dinner. He cooked most nights, usually Nigerian food, sometimes Chinese. Other nights I'd cook or we ate leftovers or snacks. I rarely ate out, saving the luxury for when I traveled for book fairs. Neither of us was a particularly interesting cook. Dinner was always fine. Exactly fine, and never any better.

After dinner I went back to the barn to catch up on work. The barn was semi-finished with a half loft and a peaked roof about twenty feet high. I'd lined it with bookshelves and set up a little office for myself in the back and a worktable in another corner for cleaning, repairing, and packing books. It was hot in the summer and cold in the winter and always dusty, but it was entirely mine, and I always relaxed a little when I stepped through the doors. No one came in but me and the occasional trusted customer. A few hours later, I went to bed with a glass of wine and a cop show on my laptop. I found my mind turning to Lucas again, to the book. I had an extra glass of wine and half of a sleeping pill and shut those thoughts up.

The next day Awe wasn't feeling well—he got headaches, occasionally, which made him half blind—and I told him to go to bed. I parked Abel in front of the TV and sat on the sofa with my laptop to catch up on emails. I hadn't been alone with Abel in so long that I'd forgotten how much work it was to take care of someone who did absolutely nothing. After ten minutes I needed to wipe some spittle off his face. Then it was time to spoon-feed him a cup of protein shake, which took close to forty minutes. The doctors kept warning me that he might lose the ability to swallow soon, which would open the door to a whole new gruesome world of feeding tubes, but, miraculously, we weren't there yet.

I went back to work for five minutes. Then Abel began making a strange sound, in between groaning and crying, and his face looked pained. I checked him for any potentially painful spots, found none, and tried to rearrange him into a more comfortable position anyway. He was heavy, and moving him up in his chair took all I had. I remembered a time when we fucked in the car in the parking lot of an oyster joint in Bodega Bay. We were so in love we couldn't wait. It seemed impossible now that someone once loved me so much they wanted to see me come in the backseat of a Ford. Finally I got him peacefully adjusted, and he quieted down.

Then I started to cry. I never got used to it. Never got used to seeing Abel like this, never got used to missing him, never got used to dealing with his complicated, frightening body.

I gave up trying to work and sat with Abel and watched TV for the rest of the day, fussing over Abel as needed. *It could be worse,* I told myself, which was the only way I could bring myself back around in moments like this. It was a perverse little routine. *You could be homeless. You could be in a car accident and lose your arms, both of them, altogether. You could be a refugee. There are people right now who have no face, because someone threw acid at them and melted their face off. Someday, you might look back at when you lived in this nice house, with Awe to help, and think:* I didn't know how good I had it.

By the time Awe got up, feeling better, I was numb again. I skipped dinner and drove into town and walked around for the rest of the evening, looking in stores, getting a cup of tea in the café, feeling nothing, mind largely blank, flooded with relief that the afternoon was over, unwilling to think about the night and day ahead.

Life went on. I started watching a new TV show about cops in a different sex crimes unit. It was dull and erotic. I sold a few good books and a dozen dull ones and one I could hardly stand to part with, a little Hanuman Books title by Cookie Meuller. I looked into renting a shop in town, like I'd talked about with Lucas, but it would be harder than I thought: I could rent out my perfectly livable barn, where I stored my books now, for more than I would pay for a storefront, but I would need a couple of months' rent upfront for the storefront, which I didn't have right now. I was good at what I did.

I earned a good living for us. But there was Awe's salary, insurance for all of us, medications and medical devices and physical therapy, and all the new treatments to try. Every month I was behind.

Life went back to normal. It was what it was. But after seven days home, when I'd resigned myself again to the dull ache of my life upstate, the phone rang, and it was Lucas, and we started the whole thing in earnest.

8.

I was having breakfast in the kitchen with Abel and Awe. Which meant I was eating the poached eggs on toast I'd made for myself exactly as I liked them (medium eggs, crisp toast) and Abel was sitting next to me, doing absolutely nothing, looking at nothing, while Awe blended a broccoli puree.

My phone rang. I checked it and saw Lucas's name. I felt a jolt that took me by surprise. I'd known Lucas for years. We talked on the phone a few times a year. Nothing had changed, or so I told myself.

But I didn't pick up. It didn't feel right to talk to Lucas in front of Abel. As if I really had a husband, and as if Lucas were really interested in me for anything other than light friendship and mild flirtation and the money we might make together. As if, as if.

After breakfast the sun came out and Awe took Abel out for a spin around town, as they did most mornings when the weather was nice. I checked my internet sales, packed up five books to mail, then made a few phone calls about titles I was trying to track down for buyers. Right before lunch I called Lucas back from my desk in the barn.

"So," Lucas said with a little drama, after we exchanged pleasantries. "I have news. Do you know Leo Singleton?"

"I know who he is," I said.

Leo Singleton was one of the top rare book men in New York, which made him one of the top men in the world. I'd seen him at events and book fairs, but we'd never met.

"He's a friend," Lucas said. "Not a good one, but a friend. We had drinks last night, and I asked him about *The Precious Substance*. He doesn't have a copy. But he's *seen* a copy."

"Wow," I said. "And? What did he say? Does he know where we can get one?"

"Not exactly," Lucas said. "But he knows quite a lot about it."

"Such as?" I said.

"I want you to hear it from him," Lucas said. His voice had a little tease in it. "It's bonkers."

"OK," I said. "Sure."

Looking back, I don't understand why I said that. *OK. Sure.* Nothing could be less like me than to say, *OK. Sure.* I was someone who questioned. I was someone who probed. I was someone who looked under rocks and peeked into medicine cabinets. But now I believe the book had its own story, a story it was writing the whole time. We were only characters in it, with no more choice than characters in a novel.

Two days from now was the first night of the upscale antiquarian book fair in the Park Avenue Armory. Lucas made plans for us to meet Singleton at the fair in the evening and take him out to dinner nearby.

"This is going to be exciting," Lucas said.

"If you say so," I said, a little sarcastically, and we said goodbye. But he was right. The truth was, I was already dreaming about what might happen next.

The next two days I again worked to tamp down, and eventually kill, the butterflies that were flitting around my stomach and my thighs. I sold books. I cleaned the house. I took care of Abel.

That afternoon I took the train into the city. It was the middle of the day and the train car was nearly empty. An elderly man by the door and a young couple, maybe in their early twenties, across and a few rows up from me.

I was reading a new book on degenerative neurological illnesses. It was boring as sin and I knew everything in it already, at least everything that I could understand. I put the book down and looked around the train car. My eyes fell on the young couple across the car. The car had seats facing both ways, and they were facing me. They were sitting close, whispering and kissing. At fifteen feet away I could almost feel the warmth coming off them—sexual heat but also closeness, intimacy, the bliss of anticipation and memory. A world of pink glow they'd created that nothing would pierce. That, at least for this moment, would protect them from the cruelty of the world.

I got up and switched cars.

9.

Dark nights in New York sometimes felt interchangeable to me; each winter bled into the one before and it felt like I could turn a corner and be in 1999 or 2004. But when I ran into Lucas on the steps of the armory as we were both heading in, the night felt specific in a satisfying way. It wasn't any of those other nights; it was, undeniably, tonight. Lucas kissed me on the cheek and asked about my trip and said nothing untoward or unusual, but his eyes were bright and he kept one hand lightly on my arm after we cheek-kissed, and kept his arm there as we walked up the rest of the stairs and into the armory. I'd dropped off my bags at my hotel and changed into a decent dress and a pair of ankle boots.

The antiquarian fair in the armory was exactly like the book fair a few weeks ago, except entirely different. The most expensive book at the fair downtown had been a hundred and fifty grand. The most expensive book at this fair was 1.5 million, and Singleton, who we

were meeting, was selling it. It was a sixteenth-century Italian astrol-
ogy text with spinning movable parts.

The Park Avenue Armory was once a real armory; now it was
a club for gentlefolk to host events like this: book sales, orchid shows,
ladies' auxiliary meetings. It was a Queen Anne masterpiece, with
high ceilings, stained-glass windows, and shiny mahogany trim on
every wall, windowsill, and staircase. Instead of rickety tables, the
book dealers had lavish convention-style displays. In the ten minutes
it took us to find Singleton, I saw a William Blake manuscript, an
exorcism manual from 1555, and a first edition of *Ulysses*. It was
almost enough to make books thrilling again.

I recognized Leo Singleton right away. He was tall and thin,
about forty, and had short hair that looked as if he got it trimmed
every week. He wore a slim dark gray suit that was elegant without being the slightest bit square, a crisp white shirt, and a dark
tie. He was talking to a customer, or a potential one. The customer
was a very round man, bald, wearing cropped black pants, black
boots, a large silk black T-shirt, and small, circular, red-framed
glasses. I couldn't hear what they were talking about, but Singleton's face was pleasantly animated, eyebrows in constant motion,
smile moving around his lips as if he was sharing a delightful,
conspiratorial secret.

Singleton held up a finger at Lucas and me: *Wait.* We nodded.
Singleton had two other men working for him and both were busy.
His booth was wide, and at a prime location, probably the most
expensive in the fair.

We looked at his books as we waited for Singleton to wrap up
with the man in the red glasses. We were surrounded by the kind

of books most people wouldn't see in two lifetimes. A Chinese *I Ching* from 1400. An alchemy scroll from the 1600s. A book of "receipts"—recipes, household formulas, and spells, this one heavy on the spells—from the late 1500s.

"Now, that one was supposedly owned by Elizabeth Báthory."

I turned around. Singleton was standing behind us, looking over our shoulders at the same book. He had a little smile that was wry and mischievous.

"I couldn't prove it, so I couldn't include it in the listing. But I have good reason to believe it's true."

"Not exactly a ringing endorsement," I said.

"Lily Albrecht," Lucas said. "Leo Singleton. You have a mutual admiration."

Singleton smiled and took my hand. "I've heard you don't like it when people do this, but I'm one of your many fans. I'm so glad to meet you."

I never knew what to say in that situation, so I did what I always did and changed the topic.

"I'm a fan of yours," I said. "I don't think I've ever seen a collection quite like this."

"I hope not," Singleton said. "I'd be heartbroken. Let me show you something."

He walked us to the other side of his booth and opened a glass case. He took out a leather-bound book a little larger than a modern hardcover, but much older. I guessed early 1800s and American for reasons I couldn't immediately put into words. Spend enough time around books—or anything, really—and you'd move from words to intuition. Some people called it a smell, or a feeling. You just knew an interesting book when you were near one, and you could guess the provenance before your conscious mind could piece it together.

Singleton opened the book for us. It was a handwritten journal from 1845. I couldn't read the handwriting clearly enough to make out much more.

"It's from Boston," Singleton said. "It's the very explicit diary of a libertine. She was a radical who was raised on a free-love and free-thinking commune in the Berkshires. It's the only one, although I made a copy for myself."

I'd always been fascinated by the utopian communities: Oneida, Lily Dale, Brook Farm. It was one of many topics Abel and I had planned to write a book on together. The secret history of utopian communities in America. The aesthetics of Las Vegas. The simultaneously inclusive and exclusionary history of American popular music.

"It's like a cross between *Fanny Hill* and *Moll Flanders*," Singleton said. "An extraordinary woman." He looked at me. "Like yourself."

Like I used to be, I thought. I forced a smile.

"Come on," Lucas said. "We have reservations. And Leo has a story for us."

We walked to the restaurant, four slushy blocks away. Lucas and Singleton caught up on gossip from their shared world of highly expensive books and the people who buy and sell them. The restaurant was off Fifth Avenue, around the corner onto a residential street. The exterior was brownstone and the inside was dark wood and low lights and a lot of candles on white tablecloths. When we walked inside, the young hostess smiled at Singleton and Lucas the way people used to smile at me. She showed us to our table.

I looked at the menu, counting up the exorbitant prices in my head with anxiety. Sixty-dollar milk chicken from a very specific farm in the next town over from mine upstate. Forty-five-dollar sea bass. As if reading my mind, Singleton ordered a two-hundred-dollar bottle of champagne.

"Obviously I'm picking up the bill," Singleton said. "Wine is a hobby."

"We'll see about that," Lucas said. "I'm pretty sure it's my turn."

I relaxed. They could fight about the bill all night. I got a twenty-four-dollar salad of preserved peaches and fresh ricotta and mint to start and the forty-five-dollar sea bass for my entrée. I thought of Abel back home. Awe would have fed him his nutritional formula, or a chicken and broccoli puree, hours ago. Now they'd be settled in front of the TV, maybe with a blanket over each of them. Awe would have sports on, or a cop show. Abel seemed to follow the colors and the shapes with his eyes, sometimes.

"So what do you know about *The Book of the Most Precious Substance* so far?" Singleton asked, snapping me back into the present. He had a slightly amused look on his face. I was about to find out why.

"Almost nothing," I said. "Frankly, I have a client who's interested in spending a lot of money on it, and I need a lot of money, so I'd like to find it."

Singleton laughed at my bluntness.

"Well," he said, "I'm guessing your client is either a magician or a pervert. And I mean both of those terms with the highest respect."

We all laughed. I surprised myself by being a decent liar.

"He's anonymous," I replied, as if I knew who the buyer was. "As far as I know, he's both."

"Well, I'll tell you all I know," said Singleton. Our appetizers arrived. My salad was meticulously arranged on a plain white plate, sweet peach halves skinned and dotted with freshly made ricotta, just-picked mint, and tiny drizzles of honey and olive oil. Lucas got beef carpaccio and Singleton got a salad of tiny beets and their equally tiny greens, sliced raw and tossed with olive oil and lemon and Maine sea salt.

"Three copies are known to exist," Singleton said. "As far as I know, they're identical. They're from 1620, but they aren't printed. They're hand-copied. I spent some time with the copy now in Amsterdam, its original home. People call that one the Frankfurt copy, because it lived there for many years. That's where I encountered it. Originally there were five, but two were destroyed over the years: one in a fire in London in eighteen-something, one ripped apart by monks in Mexico City in seventeen-something. Of the three remaining, there's the Frankfurt copy, now in Amsterdam; the Rockefeller copy, rumored to once be owned by him, which I don't think is true, now I think in Paris, although frankly I'm not sure; and the copy in Los Angeles, which some people call the Huntington edition, having been part of the Huntington Library in Pasadena for a few years in the 1930s. All in private collections. Very private."

"Do you know who owns them?" I asked.

"Yes," Singleton said, with a tone that made it clear he wasn't going to tell us. He poured me the last of the champagne and ordered another bottle. "So: 1614. A man in Amsterdam named Hieronymus Zeel— Well. Let me back up a bit. You're familiar with Aleister Crowley, right?"

Lucas and I both nodded qualified nods. Anyone who was into

books knew a Crowley first edition could make your month. Beyond that, all I knew was that he was a magician—or magickian, or magus, or whatever you might call someone who cast spells and talked to ghosts.

"Crowley," Singleton said, "was the world's leading authority on sex magic. And it's rumored that he learned everything he knew about it from *The Book of the Most Precious Substance*."

"Well," I said.

"What's sex magic?" Lucas said.

"Oh!" Singleton said. "Well, what it sounds like, basically: the art of using sex to, as Crowley defined magic, effect change in accordance with one's will. Or something like that. There's different schools. For example, in Tantra, the male withholds the sexual fluids to build up his power. Conversely, in Western Occultism, it's common to visualize one's desire at the moment of orgasm. There's also ways to invoke deities and demons, although I know less about that. Satanists might fuck on an altar to prove a point. Wiccans use sex to bring male and female polarities together. And that's just intercourse. There's a whole other world of it around, say, queer sex, or kink."

"Wow," Lucas said. "I guess I sort of knew that that existed."

I definitely knew that it existed, but not much more. Singleton had just doubled my knowledge on the topic. I'd read a few occult books and occasionally tried to read tarot cards as a teenager, but my knowledge didn't go very deep. Abel had been more interested in the Dark Arts, but only in the context of fakes, forgeries, and hoaxes. He was sure it was all bullshit. It was a rare point of dissent for us— I wasn't so sure. I'd had some coincidences in life, and some strokes of luck, good and bad, that seemed awfully precise. I didn't exactly believe in anything. But I didn't believe in nothing, either.

"So: *The Book of the Most Precious Substance,* 1614," Singleton went on. "A man in Amsterdam named Hieronymus Zeel is the author, or so we think. He was a chemist and an alchemist. Robert Fludd, the alchemist and engraver, is our primary source of knowledge about Zeel. He considered Zeel a friend and wrote about him extensively. It's believed that a lost book of Zeel's was the inspiration for Fludd's famous rose."

I knew that rose, a famous etching, often reproduced. Seven layers of petals represented the seven bodies of man, from spiritual to physical. Or the seven planes of existence, from heaven to hell. Or something like that.

Our entrées were served. My sea bass was crusted with fresh green herbs and hazelnuts. Lucas had ordered duck with early morels and lion's mane mushrooms. Singleton got three tiny rare lamb chops plated on a bed of mashed, yellow, buttery-looking potatoes.

"Zeel is also mentioned in a few contemporary letters and diaries," Singleton continued. "Hans Hanson, a fellow alchemist in Amsterdam, was found dead in his house at the age of thirty-three. On his desk was an unfinished letter to Zeel, calling him a 'wicked man with the heart of a pig.' A priest—can't remember his name—wrote, 'Of all the men in Amsterdam, the most clever and the most vile are unfortunately the same: Hieronymus Zeel.' There's been a few explanations floated for this reputation: one, that he was involved in black magic, which he most certainly was; and two, that he was a bit of a con man, which he also certainly was: selling fake minerals and potions. Both were common enough back then. And now, I guess.

Anyway, yes, it's believed, due to a good, but not definitive, amount of evidence, that Zeel wrote *The Precious Substance.*"

"Why isn't it more famous?" Lucas asked.

"Ah," Singleton said. "Interesting. The book, all five copies, has had very few owners through history, and for whatever reasons, none have chosen to make it public. As far as I know, it's never been reproduced. Zeel made the five original editions, and that was that. Your only chance of reading it is to get your hands on an original copy, and then you better know Latin. The Frankfurt copy...Well. I'll start from the beginning."

"Please do," Lucas said.

"Magic has always been of interest to me," Singleton said. "I started with Crowley, as expected. Then I went to Oxford, where I found a group. A magical order. The group claimed to be ancient—they all do, but most of them aren't. A bunch of rich young men who tried to summon demons and talk to angels for fun."

"Does it work?" I asked.

"I'll defer to my superiors," Singleton said. "I'm just a bookseller. I will say, though, I've seen some remarkable things. Things I wouldn't believe if I hadn't seen them. So I worked with this group in Oxford for a while. They had some rituals that weren't half bad. Funny to see some of them in the papers now, running companies, sitting in Parliament. I've had other experiences, too. So I'd always bought and sold in that area. My best sale—not my most lucrative, certainly, but my most interesting—was finding an original tarot deck, handmade, from the seventeenth century, in an attic in Lyons. Sold it to an heiress for close to a million dollars. Those cards paid for my little place in the Hamptons. Of course, I held on to them for some time before I sold them. Very finely drawn, with unusual illustrations."

We were all getting a little drunk now.

"You read cards?" I asked.

"Poorly," Singleton said. I was starting to see that while his modesty wasn't entirely genuine, it wasn't exactly false, either. He just wasn't interested in competing.

"So what'd they say?" I asked.

"Well," Singleton said, "I will say those cards helped me make an important decision. And I think I chose well. Anyway, Crowley published much of his own work, as I'm sure you know. Occult people are, generally, book people. Sorry, I'm a little drunk. It's a fascinating area to sell and collect.

"So I'm in Frankfurt. I'm in a client's hotel room. I wish I could tell you who. This is, my, over ten years ago. He's got the whole top floor of a very nice hotel. Now I have to go back again—I was in Frankfurt on another sale. A CEO had sent me out there to pick up a very rare grimoire that had just gone on the market. Later he asked me to pick him up some SS memorabilia—that was his last day as my client. That's my limit. But before I knew about *that*, I actually sort of liked the man. Anyway, it was a handwritten book of spells from an occultist who worked in the 1600s. I was in Frankfurt, and I had my hands on the book, when I get a call from *another* client. A musician. How he knew I was in Frankfurt, I still don't know. A lot of these types know each other, you'll find, so perhaps he'd heard from the other man."

The waiter brought another bottle of wine and dessert: rose and pistachio ice cream, vanilla-orange meringues, and a plate of tiny white and dark chocolates in unusual flavors: violet, pecan, lemon blossom.

"These types?" I said.

"People who buy multimillion-dollar occult books," Singleton explained. "There's less than a dozen or so of them—closer to ten, really—and they're always competing for the same books. Plus they're always throwing spells at each other. It's all very petty and ridiculous. Until you remember that these are some of the wealthiest, most powerful men on earth.

"In any case, the musician calls me, ranting and raving that he needs a translator immediately. Latin. He knows I know it well enough. This is a man who'd spent over half a million dollars on books the previous year, quite a bit of it with me, so I was inclined to do him a favor. Besides, I liked him. I still do.

"So I go to his hotel room and it's…it's a spectacle. Now, when I say *musician* and *hotel room,* I think that gives you an idea right there. Empty champagne bottles, pill bottles, room service plates stacked up, clothes and guitars strewn about. A glorious mess. He'd been living there for a few weeks. This man is also a pretty serious student of the occult. I mean, you'd guess a passing interest in Satan and goats, but you wouldn't imagine him to be a scholar. He is. He's also a practitioner. He attributes his success to a meeting with a particular dark entity. There's also books stacked everywhere—old, new, some quite ancient and bound in leather, some cheap paperbacks.

"I meet him in the sitting room. He's got a copy of *The Book of the Most Precious Substance,* and the person he bought it from gave him a rough translation, but he wasn't getting any results. He wanted me to retranslate. Which I did, and I found his mistake—"

"Wait," Lucas said. "What mistake? What results? What was he actually doing?"

Singleton smiled. He lifted the bottle of wine. Somehow it was empty again.

"Brandy?" he said. "Should we?"

"A drop," said Lucas. "The tiniest drop. You choose."

"Yes, but then you really have to let me pick up the bill," Singleton said, "because I'm getting us the best."

Lucas and Singleton bantered about the brandy some more. They ordered, our drinks came, and Singleton started again.

"So the book," Singleton said, "is the most precise, and most effective, grimoire of sex magic ever written. It guides the reader through five steps, each corresponding to a different bodily fluid, and along with it, a specific symbol and a word. Occultists are very big on correspondences. It's one of many highly unnecessary hobbies they like. They're very into theater. Back to the hotel room—"

"No, wait," I said. "Back to the book. What does it actually tell you to do?"

"Well," Singleton said, "I only had time to read the first four chapters. The book is…Things happen when you're around it. I wouldn't be surprised if things start happening when you even think about looking for it."

"What kind of things?" I asked.

"Things," Singleton said opaquely. "Chapter one is about sweat. It was written for a cis man and woman—other pairings are possible at various points, but you do need specific fluids. The main thing is intent. Both parties are to focus on what they want. And there's a word. It's ████████ for the first operation. First you clearly picture what you want as you generate 'the sweat produced from unfulfilled desire.' Then you touch that sweat, charged by your own

70

energies, on a symbol in the book, and you say the word. That's the first step. You're to do this until 'the gates open.'"

He used his hands to put quotes around the words.

"So what does that mean?" I asked. "What gates open?"

Singleton smiled a flirtatious, knowing smile.

"You'll know," he said. "You'll be ready for the next step. 'The fluid of female desire.'"

It wasn't until much later, in hindsight, that I realized how naturally Singleton switched to *you*. At the time it seemed like the generic, impersonal *you*. Now I think he meant *me*, in particular. As if it were a given: Lucas and I would find the book and do the rituals. As if it had already been written somewhere and Singleton was just reading it aloud.

"But what are you doing with these fluids?" Lucas asked.

"You seal a seal," Singleton answered.

"Seal a seal?" I repeated.

"For lack of a better word," Singleton said. "More correspondences. There's the word, the fluid, and the seal. I guess you could say *anoint* the seal."

The tablecloth had a piece of white paper over it, now spotted with food and wine. Singleton took a pen out of his pocket and drew an odd shape on the paper. It was simple enough, but somehow when I looked at it, I couldn't quite parse it out. It was a star, but it seemed to be shifting on the table; I told myself it was the wine, but no matter how many times I counted, I couldn't tell how many points it had. Underneath the shape he wrote a word. As with the shape, unless I was looking right at the word, I couldn't exactly remember it. It wasn't in any language that I knew, and I suspected it was no known language at all, but it was simple enough to spell and pronounce. Or should have been, but I couldn't seem to wrap my head around it. I chalked that up to the wine too.

"It's funny," Singleton said. "I spent days with the book, but that's the only one I can remember. The book has a way of not being captured."

"What do you mean?" Lucas asked.

"You'll see," Singleton said, without following up. "Anyway, to seal the seal: You'll each put a drop of fluid on the seal," Singleton went on, somewhat drunk. "You're feeding it. Giving it power. The book both gives power and receives it. You give the seals power. You can use the seals, but the seals will also get power from you."

"So what's after sweat?" I asked.

Singleton smiled.

"The book calls it 'the nectar of the woman.' Next is the 'life-giving seed of the man.' After that is the one not everyone knows about. What the book calls 'the Most Precious Substance.' 'Only one man in a thousand will be able to draw it out of the woman, and only one woman in one hundred thousand will allow it to be drawn.'"

"So what is it?" I asked.

"'When the woman's pleasure reaches a crescendo,'" Singleton continued to quote, using a tilted voice so we knew he was quoting verbatim, "'there will be a wave like the ocean, violent and forceful, but sweet and delicious when it crashes.'"

"Oh!" I said.

I'd heard of it. I knew it was possible. But I'd never actually seen it. It had never happened to me. My sex life with Abel had been as good as I'd known it was possible to be. But there was never a violent and forceful wave like the ocean.

"Oh!" Lucas said. "My ex-wife used to…I mean she…I have some experience with that."

"Well," Singleton said, "to your credit. So, back to the hotel room. I stayed there for the first day and translated the first two chapters. Took about ten hours for a rough translation. My Latin is rusty but I've got the basics in my head and a laptop for the rest. So I translate, and as I do we're ordering food, discussing magic, my client is pacing around the room. About three hours in, the most beautiful woman I've ever seen in my life comes out of the bedroom in a pair of tiny underwear and a T-shirt. Barely notices me—until she sees I'm translating the book. Then we have a long conversation about karezza, another form of sex magic. She was highly knowledgeable, quite a scholar herself. I think she was a PhD student, if I remember right.

"So I translate for ten hours, go home, sleep, come back the next morning. Apparently they'd completed the first two tasks, all good. They each had a specific goal, which I ought not to disclose. But his was material and hers was very personal. I don't think they meshed. Magic is always much stronger when the partners share a goal. I translated the next two, they completed the third that night, all was well.

"Then they got to the fourth. The Most Precious Substance. Not to brag, but I've rarely found it insurmountable myself. Some women do seem to create it more easily than others. But it isn't as if it's hard labor to try."

A quick, erotic image of Singleton working on the fourth step flashed into my mind.

"However," he went on, "these two were at an impasse. Three days went by. Once the pressure was on, neither one was at their best, and it all started to fall apart. After much consultation, none of which produced results, my customer was kind enough to ask me if I would step in and help. The young woman liked the idea as well."

"So did you?" I asked.

"Unfortunately," Singleton said, "I was needed back in London. And practicing magic with people creates a certain bond. I wasn't sure how bonded I wanted to be with him. Her, though...But it wasn't in the cards."

Singleton blinked and got a look on his face and you could tell it wasn't idle bragging: He was skilled.

"So did they get what they wanted?" I asked. "Does it work?"

"They did not," Singleton said. "They couldn't complete that act. Would it have worked if they had?" He shrugged. "It depends on what you believe, I guess. I'm no theologist. Just a bookseller with hobbies. Anyway, that copy is now owned by a rich media man in Europe. My client sold it soon thereafter."

We'd been at the table for three hours and we were all winding down. Singleton had paid the bill while we weren't paying attention, leading Lucas to promise the next dinner was his.

We bundled up and walked out and stood outside the restaurant, the cold air refreshing after the warm meal. After the luxurious food and the alcohol and the company of two smart and attractive people, the city was friendlier, the lights prettier, the muddy slush more like white snow. I thanked Singleton, sincerely, for the best meal I'd had in years.

"Anytime," Singleton said, taking my hand. "I'm sorry to embarrass you again, but I think you're an enormous talent, and now I think you're a wonderful person, too. If there's ever anything I can do to help you, I want to do it."

Impulsively, I hugged him goodbye. He slid one warm hand around my waist. Again I had a brief erotic image of him, working toward the Precious Substance with his impish smile, as his cheekbone pressed against mine.

We all said good night with warm goodbyes and more thanks to Singleton, and then we parted ways. Singleton walked east. Lucas and I stopped for a moment before walking west. But then Singleton turned back toward us.

"Yes," he said. "It works."

"What?" Lucas said.

"Magic," Singleton said. "To answer your question from earlier. Sorry, I'm a little drunk. It works. But the tricky thing is, it never works exactly how you expect. People think they're smart enough to summon up some entity or make someone fall in love with them and have it all turn out for the best. But they *aren't* smart enough. Whatever it is that usually decides our fates—Gods, luck, random chance—it's smarter than us. It's always smarter. Magic works, but it's an exercise in irony, sometimes a dangerous one. Be careful."

He turned and walked away. I watched him until he turned a corner, his head slightly down, collar up, gait a little crooked after all the wine.

I looked up. Lucas was looking at me. On his face was amusement, excitement, and something else. Something I'd forgotten about. Something I hadn't thought about in so long that it took me a moment to recognize it.

"Come on," he said. "I'll walk you to your hotel."

We walked down the cold New York street together, close, bumping against each other as we walked. This time I was sure it was intentional. Each time we touched I felt a little warmer.

I felt myself sliding into dangerous territory. I knew I should stop. I *wanted* to stop.

I also knew that I wasn't going to. It felt like I'd been hungry for years, and here was a ripe apple, ready to bite.

"So what do you think?" Lucas said.

"I think we can find it," I said.

Lucas stopped, put his hand on my arm, firmly, and stopped me. I turned to face him. There was that look on his face again.

"No," he said. "What do you think of us?"

And then he put one hand behind my head, gently, firmly, pulling my head up and back, and kissed me. I hadn't felt lips against my own in so long, it was as if I'd never been kissed before: the sensation felt entirely new and strange and thrilling. After a moment I felt his tongue testing my closed lips; with no effort from me, they parted.

Lucas pulled his head away. It was like tearing myself away from a warm bed on a cold morning. I was surprised that he wasn't awkward at all. When it came to sex, Lucas was utterly confident.

"Next time," Lucas said. "Sweat."

And he walked away, leaving me breathless and cold, and wanting warmth. Wanting sweat.

10.

I slept restlessly that night, head full of Lucas and Singleton and the book. I woke up with the sun at six. I made a bad cup of double-strength coffee in the shitty little hotel coffeemaker. It tasted better than it had any right to and I knew it was my mood, not the coffee. For the first time in a long time, I was excited about the day ahead.

A spark had been lit in me. I could have snuffed it out, as I'd done many times before.

Instead, this time, I fanned it into flames.

I opened the window to the cold, gray city outside. This morning it seemed more welcoming than usual. Ordinarily I would have called Awe right away. Instead I texted him.

Busy morning. All good?

He wrote back right away: *All good. Peaceful night.*

Let me know if you need anything, I texted back. He wouldn't need anything. He never did. All Abel needed was to be cleaned and fed and propped up comfortably. Everything else we did to him was for our own amusement.

While I was texting Awe, an email came in. It was Elena from the bookstore on Seventy-Seventh Street: She'd told me her husband might know something about *The Most Precious Substance,* and now she said he did know something: *He's pretty sure he knows the book. And he's almost sure he knows who's looking for it.*

My heart jumped a little. We emailed back and forth and I agreed to meet her at her shop at four. I texted Lucas and told him about it. He would also be at the shop at four.

You looked beautiful last night, Lucas wrote after we'd made our plans.

It was the wine, I wrote back flippantly. Flippant was the exact opposite of how I felt. But I was more comfortable playing a little bit of a game with Lucas than letting him ease right into my life. The whole situation overwhelmed me with anxiety, and keeping him at arm's length went a long way toward quelling that anxiety. Sex and everything that hovered around it hadn't been part of my life for years. I'd shut the door to that part of myself so tightly I rarely even thought about it. I told myself I didn't miss it. Now I wasn't sure what would happen if I opened that door.

I took a shower and got dressed and had a terrible, free hotel-lobby breakfast. Then I did something I hadn't done in months, maybe a year: I took the day off. Spending a day in New York City without spending a lot of money was hard, but I'd lived here once and I knew it could be done. Museums and movies were expensive. Art galleries were free. I looked online and came up with three exhibits in Chelsea I'd like to see. The sun was out and the slush was melting and I walked to

Chelsea and saw two very bad shows and one very good one. The two bad shows were painters; the good one was a photographer from the 1950s whose work had just been discovered, or rediscovered, or reappraised. Her photos were strange and magical views of Coney Island and Times Square. For lunch I got two slices of pizza and a Coke from a good place I knew on Eighth Avenue. If you ever forgot that money did not buy what mattered in life, New York pizza would remind you. After that lunch I was sleepy and needed a pick-me-up, so I found a café near Elena's store and settled in with a good cup of coffee and a paperback I'd been carrying around with me, with the intention of reading it "in my free time," for months. A rare departure for me, it wasn't about neurology—it was a novel written by an old friend, one I'd lost touch with a few years ago. Most friends had fallen away over the years. Either they'd started avoiding me, as if my grief and bad luck were contagious, or I'd started to avoid them, unwilling to give them the chance to disappoint me. Besides, too much time around normal people made me feel like an alien, unwanted and ugly, fluent in a different language.

Four o'clock came soon and I walked to Elena's, feeling something I hadn't felt in so long, I could hardly name it. As I was opening the door to her jewel box of a shop, I remembered what it was: excitement. Anticipation.

Lucas was already at Elena's when I arrived, helping her authenticate a set of old prints.

"Of course!" Elena was saying. "Well, you sure know your watermarks, kiddo." She looked up and saw me. "Lily, what doesn't this man know?"

When Lucas saw me, he smiled. This was what his face looked

like when he saw me now, I realized with a pleasant start: happy, excited, and a little lustful. I tried to remember the last time I made someone happy. Probably one of the caregivers when I gave them a surprise afternoon off.

Lucas wrapped one hand around my waist for a quick, intoxicating second before pulling away. If Elena noticed the extra spark, she didn't let on. We stood around her sales counter, next to a glass-faced cabinet of first editions. Elena put the prints away and smiled, very pleased with the gift she was about to give us.

"I talked to Archie," she said. Archie, her husband, shared some overlap in clientele with Shyman: rich old men who bought first-edition biographies of Churchill and outdated books of maps that showed the lines men killed each other over.

"He says half of them are into that voodoo stuff," Elena said, eyebrows raised. "The military guys. The business guys. They buy Anton LaVey, they buy Manly P. Hall. But he said there's only a few people with both the interest and the—"

"The money!" a man's voice boomed. We all turned toward the voice: Archie was walking down the staircase from their apartment upstairs. "They all want to run the world. Once they start making money, they become scared of losing it. Once they get power, they're even more scared of losing *that*. So they turn to anything—witches, astrologers, good-luck charms. But there's also quite a few who were in the Dark Arts when they were first starting out. Credit all their success to Pan or Lucifer or guardian angels."

He reached the counter, where we all listened, enthralled. Archie was older than Elena, and nearly a foot shorter. He had white hair and a big sharp nose and walked with a cane with a rabbit carved on the top. He looked a little like an elf, maybe one that had never left Manhattan.

"Now," he said, "I hear you're looking for *The Book of the Most Precious Substance*. That's a rare one. Only two copies known to exist."

"Two?" I said.

"We heard three," Lucas said. We exchanged a look.

"Whoever told you that didn't know about the fire," Archie said. "Terrible. Johann Van Welt, the Dutchman, had one of the three copies. Lost it in a fire just six months ago."

"Van Welt had a fire?" Lucas asked. "Jesus. Is the whole collection gone?"

"Who's Van Welt?" I asked.

"The fire wasn't in his library," Archie answered Lucas. "It was in his temple. And to answer your question"—Archie looked at me—"Johann Van Welt owns most of the television stations in Europe, eighty percent of the radio stations, and half the movie theaters. He's also a book collector: military, media, the occult. He bought his copy of *The Most Precious Substance* a few years back. Half a million, a good price then and now. Bought his copy from a musician who I'm not allowed to name. A big rock-and-roll star. I brokered the sale. Some clients, as you all know, value confidentiality above all else. Some, like Van Welt, like to brag."

I noticed the way Elena looked at Archie. Proud. In love. In a quick moment I saw their past and their future: love, support, growing old together, tending to each other's bodies as they twisted with age. *Fuck them both,* I immediately thought, before I shut myself up. I didn't really wish them ill. I was just jealous.

"So the fire was where?" Lucas asked.

"His temple," Archie said. "Johann is the second type—started with the occult young, believes it got him where he is today. Thinks he owes his loyalty to what he calls 'the darkness at the center of all things.' Some people call it Satan, some people call it chaos. He calls it The Dark. Johann and his kind believe that you can get to know that darkness, befriend it, work with it. There's rules, of course. You can find them in any Llewelyn paperback at the corner shop. And once you're committed, it might not be up to you when to break that commitment. None of this modern-day no-fault divorce. Not for devils and demons!"

Archie laughed. I laughed with him. I was still pretending I didn't believe. Still pretending that I hadn't begun that marriage, from which no divorce was possible.

"Johann moved to Crete. Thought it was sacred ground for The Dark. Supposedly there's an entryway to hell on the island. A portal. In Crete, Johann bought an abandoned church and turned it into a temple of filth. He brought two books with him: a Bible to shit on, presumably to prove his loyalty to the forces of darkness, and *The Book of the Most Precious Substance*. I'm sure you've heard by now about the nature of the book," Archie said. "The steps? The substances?"

"Somewhat," Lucas said.

"A little," I said.

"Oh, please," Elena said, affectionately. "Do you guys really want to hear this?"

"Oh yes," Lucas said.

"Absolutely," I agreed.

Archie smiled with a look of triumph and went on: "There's five steps. Five fluids from the human body. Each brings growing levels of power. The final step is the most powerful: It involves blood from a beating heart. A human heart."

Lucas and I looked at each other. Suddenly it was all much less sexy. Much less fun. But just as quickly, Archie let out a laugh and pushed any seriousness away.

"I don't know anyone who's actually done it," Archie added. "Even Johann stopped before that. Although he did try with the closest thing to a person."

"A dog?" Lucas guessed.

"A monkey!" Archie said with glee. "Bought it from a lab supply company. The main thing about the book is, you need a partner to go through the stages with you, and they must be an equally devoted student of the arts. Not easy to find! Johann found one in…Well, I suppose I can tell you. You might know her name. The famous witch, Bella Donna."

The name rang a bell, and an image came to mind: a big woman, older than me, frizzy purple hair, bright eyes, died recently. The gears in my mind turned and yes, I knew her books. She'd written a dozen or so books on witchcraft, some popular paperbacks still in print, some more esoteric, published by small presses. Her early first editions were worth money. Maybe she had lived in Salem. I had a quick memory of her on *Donahue* or *Sally Jessy Raphael,* defending her craft.

"Bella Donna and Johann loathed each other, you know. Bella Donna was a green witch. Believed in the Sacred Feminine, the earth is a womb, all of that. Johann's favorite hobby is raping the earth and pillaging the townsfolk. All he ever wanted was power and money.

But they each needed a partner, and so they did the work together, all in one night. Began with sweat, moved on to all the rest, then they got to the blood.

"Now," Archie went on, "as I said, they were in what Johann called his temple—an old abandoned church he'd bought in Crete, desecrated, and set up as his own little Satanic playroom. Pissed on all the crosses, sex toys in every corner, sexual fluid sprayed around as thoroughly as he could get a gang of Cretan boys to spread it. Bella Donna brought in all her herbs and powders and potions. His goal was supreme financial power. Hers was saving the earth. Hard to believe two brilliant magicians could be so stupid as to think they wouldn't create a disaster. Imagine: two older people, neither in particularly good physical shape, full of loathing and sexual excitement, candles everywhere, probably on fifteen different drugs, herbs, and poisons each, each supposedly, with a room full of spirits and demons around them, drawing the substances out of each other, one at a time, over a long day and night.

"Then Johann brought out the monkey. He—the monkey—had been in a cage all night, growing, one would imagine, ever more excited by what he was watching. Or, perhaps, terrified. Maybe both. Johann and Bella Donna were, of course, in a complete, intoxicated haze of sex, drugs, and magic. Johann tried to drag the monkey to the altar. Bella Donna started to have second thoughts when she saw how Johann treated him. She'd thought it was going to be a peaceful death. They fought—all of them. The monkey grew agitated, and escaped Johann's grasp. Bella tried to save him. In the process, someone knocked over a candle, then another one.

"By the time they realized, it was too late. The whole temple went up in flames. Johann got out. Bella didn't. Neither did the book. She died that night. Her family tried to sue Johann. Of course, they were laughed out of court."

"What about the monkey?" Elena asked. She looked genuinely concerned about him.

Archie came over and kissed Elena on her jawbone. She smiled.

"That, my dear," he said, "no one knows. Maybe he's still alive, dancing on the beaches of Crete, laughing at us all."

Lucas and I looked at each other. First he laughed, then I did, then Archie and Elena joined in.

"So," Lucas said, "do you think Johann is our buyer?"

"Oh no," Archie said, wrapping an arm around his wife. "He's done with *The Book of the Most Precious Substance* for a good long while. No, I think your client is a man named Oswald Johnson Haber the third."

"Who?" I said.

"Wow," Lucas said.

"Who?" I said again.

"One of the richest men in New York," Archie said.

"Which makes him one of the richest men in the world," Lucas said. "I mean, top couple of hundred, at least." Lucas knew things like that: lists of rich men, where other men stood in their boys' rankings of cash and power and influence, who was in and out of the billionaires' club.

"What made him so rich?" Elena asked.

"Money," Archie said, definitively. "He inherited a few million, and knew how to make it multiply. I'm not sure he's your client, but I don't know who else it could be. He bought from Shyman, collects in all the relevant fields—occult, war, history—and there's rumors."

"Rumors?" Lucas asked.

"Rumors," Archie said, in a way that made it clear he wasn't going to say more. "Do you have the book?"

"No," I said. "But we will. We know where to get it."

Archie nodded. "Good. I'll give him a call. See if he wants to meet. I'll let you know."

With profuse thanks, Lucas and I left their shop. We stood on the cold dark street and looked at each other.

"Come over for dinner," Lucas said.

The sun was going down and the city was twilight-purple. I should have gone home. I should have gotten my head together, at least, and gone back to my hotel room. I should have been buying and selling books, answering emails, making a living.

Instead I said yes, and went back to Lucas's place.

11.

Lucas's apartment was exactly like I imagined it would be. The building was from the 1910s and had a doorman and an elegant, if shabby, lobby. Lucas exchanged a few friendly words with the doorman, who seemed to adore Lucas, and we took the elevator up to the third floor out of five. A bland carpeted hallway led to a door with the usual four good locks on a New York City apartment, even in this era of rare break-ins. The door opened to a charming, elegant, masculine space.

It was small, being Manhattan, but not tiny. Nothing in it was cheap. There was a decent kitchen, a bedroom, and a living room big enough to hold a little work area with a desk. And, of course, the whole place was lined with bookshelves, custom-built from the look of them, that snaked through the living room, the halls, and even into the bedroom.

"You're finally here," Lucas said, taking off his coat and emptying his pockets. "I've wanted to have you over for years."

I put my bag and jacket down on the sofa.

"Why?" I asked.

"Because I like you," he said, smiling a little. "Wine?"

He poured us each a glass of sparkling wine and looked through the refrigerator. I looked at his books. Lucas's collection was pretty extraordinary. He had an entire case of New York City history, another entire case of books on the history of printing, two cases on biographies of writers, plus shelves and shelves of light literary thrillers and popular nonfiction—books with TED Talk–ish titles like *How Bacteria Wrote History* and *What Money Wants*.

"What are we having?" I asked.

"Steak," he said, digging through the refrigerator. "And… mushrooms. Maybe with salad, if these greens are fresh."

I offered to help and he turned me down. When I'd seen enough of his books I sat at the kitchen counter, which doubled as a bar, and watched him cook, like I'd always imagined him doing with other women.

"Here, try this," he said. He brought a spoon up to my mouth. I took it before he could feed me. It reminded me too much of Abel.

"Delicious," I said truthfully. It was mushrooms, sautéed in garlic and some kind of booze. "Can I ask you something?"

"Of course," he said.

"How do you pay for this place?"

Lucas laughed. "See, this is why I like you, Lily. Most people would have danced around that question for weeks. I had an inheritance from my father. He died fifteen years ago. He worked on Wall Street. He did all right financially and died earlier than expected, unfortunately. When he died there was a decent lump sum, which paid for most of this apartment, and an annuity."

He brought me another taste of mushrooms, handing me the spoon this time. Lucas caught on quick. He was always highly attuned to the people around him, especially women. I didn't think it was fakeness, just a subtle, unspoken ability to please that he made the most of.

"But the annuity runs out soon," Lucas said. "I guess I can live off of what I make at the library. But it'll certainly be different. Now, if we can find the book…"

He lifted up his wineglass in an optimistic toast.

"Aha," I said. "I knew you needed money, but I couldn't figure out why."

"That's not the only reason I'm looking for the book," he said, turning back to the stove. "I've been trying to get your attention for years. Now that I've got it, I'm not letting it slip away so fast."

I didn't know if I believed him. I also wasn't sure I cared. All the better, in fact, if he was lying. The question of whether I was actually single or not was equally unaskable and unanswerable. Whatever was going on between Lucas and me would be much easier if neither of us was looking for disruption. Just a few light encounters to enjoy while they lasted.

Lucas turned the stove off, crossed the kitchen, and kissed me again. I thought about how a second kiss was different from a first. It was both less—less hesitant, less surprising, less of the thrill of the new—and more: more promising, more exciting, more indicative of what was to come.

Lucas moved his hands down and around, exploring. I stopped

thinking. Good sex wasn't only the presence of pleasure; it was the absence of all other thoughts. I was wordlessly aware that I had been thinking twenty-four hours a day for what felt like years. Thinking, scheming, plotting, planning, and trying. Always trying. My throat felt tight just imagining it all. There was enormous relief in letting it all go, knowing full well all my thoughts would be there waiting for me when this sensation passed.

It was remarkable how quickly I responded, after hardly thinking of sex for so long. How quickly we forget—but even more quickly, we remember.

Lucas made a soft sound like a moan. He pulled himself away and whispered in my ear, "Are you sweating yet?"

I swallowed. "Not yet," I said.

He kissed my neck. I felt my breath get deep.

"Now?" he said.

"Uh-uh," I said.

Lucas took his hands and his mouth back, smiling like the cat who ate the canary. This was what he liked, I saw. Building up desire. Being wanted.

"Then it'll have to wait," he said. "'Cause our dinner is cooked."

I didn't take the idea of casting spells seriously. I thought of it all as a flirtation device, a ruse for physical contact, like an adult game of truth or dare. Or so I told myself. Now I wonder: Did a part of me, some hidden streak of intelligence, know what I was doing? That soon, right after our lovely and sophisticated little dinner, I would be opening a door that I would be powerless to shut?

Lucas set the table elegantly and unpretentiously, with sturdy white plates and yellow napkins. Over dinner we talked about books in general and *the* book in particular. We traded stories we knew of other ultra-rare titles and where they'd been found. An Edgar Allan Poe sitting in an attic. A copy of the Declaration of Independence stuck in a picture frame. An unknown Christopher Smart poem used as a bookmark. We knew some of those stories were true. We also knew that some were fabricated to cover up gray-market sales—books sold when inheritors were fighting over an inheritance, books sold while their owners were in the hospital, books that may have been a real book with a fake dust jacket, books where the dates were fudged a tiny bit. These little adjustments were how the business worked. You didn't ask for chain of title and you didn't believe what anyone said.

For dessert Lucas found some vanilla ice cream in the freezer and lemon cookies in the cupboard and put them in pretty, simple dishes. There was an artfulness to everything he did. After we ate we went back to the sofa to get back to work. But we didn't get back to work: instead Lucas leaned over and firmly pushed me back on the sofa and kissed me again, testing what I would allow and how I would allow it.

"You like that," he said. He meant his hands pinned on my shoulders, holding me down. His voice had a hypnotic sleepiness to it that sounded like sex.

"I do," I said. It was thrilling to let Lucas take control—in the kitchen, on the sofa, in the search for the book. Much of my life was a dreary grind in which I was responsible for everything, always. For someone else to take that responsibility, even for a few minutes, was pure pleasure. Lucas kissed me again. When my mouth softened against his, with no effort from me—with something more like the opposite of effort—it was as if that softening had a rippling effect from my mouth, through my face, across my skull, down my neck, through my limbs, and finally reaching down between my legs, getting warmer, warmer, and warmer still.

I wasn't sweating yet. Lucas kissed down my face and neck until he got to my chest. He pulled my hair back and I let out a little gasp. With his other hand he pulled my shirt down, and kept moving his his mouth down, teasing and poking until—

He stopped and pulled away. I looked at him. He ran a finger down my sternum, between my breasts. He smiled.

"Now," Lucas said, "you're sweating."

He stopped, and turned to a large manila envelope on the coffee table. I hadn't noticed it before. Lucas opened the envelope and got out Singleton's sketch of the seal. It was the white paper that had been over the tablecloth in the restaurant where Singleton had sketched the symbol. I hadn't seen Lucas take it.

He rubbed my chest again, picking up a drop of sweat on his finger, and then touched the seal and said the word.

"The back of my neck," he said.

I reached for him and traced a circle on the back of his neck, where a nice fat drop of sweat dripped, and I touched it to the paper and said the word: ▉▉▉▉▉▉▉▉

And there it was. The first act.

When I touched the paper I felt a strange sensation inside of me: an unpleasant, sticky chill, as with an infection. Then the sticky feeling rolled into something familiar and bigger and uglier, almost like shame, or a bad memory I'd tried to forget. It felt like the pressure drop before a storm, or the rumbling before an earthquake.

I looked at Lucas. He had a slightly sick look on his face, and

I knew he felt it too.

"Whoa," Lucas said.

"What—" I began.

Just then, Lucas's phone rang. We looked at each other.

Lucas picked up his phone and looked at the number. He didn't recognize it. He answered anyway.

It was Mr. Grady, personal assistant to Oswald Johnson Haber III. Haber was the man Archie was almost sure was Shyman's customer for *The Book of the Most Precious Substance*.

Neither of us said the words, but we looked at each other and I knew we were thinking the same thought: *It's working already.*

Lucas put Grady on speakerphone. Judging from his voice, Grady was a white man in his thirties who was both obsequious and dignified at the same time.

"Mr. Haber is very interested in the book," Grady said after a few rounds of introductions and niceties. "As I'm sure you know, he's willing to pay top dollar. You can check his bona fides with Mr. Cohen"—he meant Archie—"or any one of a number of book dealers. He's a frequent customer at Bauman. He does a *lot* of business with the rare book room at Argosy."

"We don't actually have the book in our possession," Lucas said. "But—"

"But we can get it," I interrupted. "We'd like to meet Mr. Haber first, though. To be blunt, it's a very expensive book, and we have other offers. We'd like to see for ourselves if it's worth keeping Mr. Haber in the running. No one wants to waste anyone else's time here."

Lucas gave me a look of amazement at my bullshit. He was impressed.

I wanted that book. And, now I know, it wanted me.

"Of course," Grady said. "Of course. I can assure you that he's ready to top any other offer, but I can see why you'd want to hear it yourself, from the horse's mouth, so to speak. Can you come up tomorrow?"

"Up where?" I asked.

"Oh, so sorry," Grady said. "Up to Mr. Haber's place in Connecticut. Pig's Bay. We'll send a car, of course."

Lucas and I pretended we were busy and pretended to hem and pretended to haw and made Grady ask again and then we said yes. We'd come to Connecticut tomorrow and meet Mr. Haber and talk about the book.

The sex in the room had been chased out by Grady's call—and, equally, by my own hesitation. I felt it and so did Lucas. It had been a long time, and while getting used to sex again was exhilarating, it was also overwhelming. Lucas was, as I'd observed, acutely sensitive to the needs of any woman in a fifty-foot radius, and he picked up on my discomfort. We kissed good night and I left.

"Will you come back?" he said at the door.

"Maybe," I said, still keeping up a façade of coolness, of distance.

I walked to the subway station and took the train back to my hotel. I'd been with other men, of course. Plenty before Abel, and a few after. Those were the men I thought of now. The afters. A sordid, shitty, one-night stand at a book fair in Florida with a man who looked good fully dressed but naked was pudgy and unskilled. A brief affair with a friend of a friend that ended when he asked me to go to his kid's school play. My first obligation was to Abel, and my friend's daughter deserved reliable people in her life. Another ruined friendship with a musician I'd dated before Abel and become friendly with again about when Abel stopped speaking. I knew he had a few other women in his life and I thought we might work as friends who slept together occasionally. But after we slept together a few times, he'd stopped calling or texting and never told me why. We never spoke again. And a disastrous, drunken few weeks with another novelist I'd had an ongoing flirtation with for years. He had a world of problems of his own—a bad marriage, depression, a troubled adult son—which I had no room for or interest in. My own problems were all-consuming.

I'd dreamed, on the rare occasions when I let myself dream, of someone like Lucas—someone attractive, sexually interested in me, good in bed, fun to be around, and with no interest in a real, committed, lasting relationship.

I'd dreamed of it and here it was. That didn't mean I was ready for it. Other lips on my body, other hands in my hair—somehow, after so long, Abel was still my gold standard. We had loved each other very much. We also loved sex. Abel was fascinated with the human body. His insatiable intellectual curiosity extended to every inch, hole, and pore of me. In the same way he knew about the history of Situationist philosophy and the economics of cats in the French Revolution, Abel wanted to know all about flesh and how it responded to skin, tongue, velvet, fur, lips. His enthusiasm was contagious. I'd been a good-enough lover before, but Abel inspired my curiosity and my lust. Sex wasn't just better than I'd ever known it could be; it was more interesting. There were tools to explore, sensations to try, tastes and textures to experiment with, states of consciousness to achieve or discard. We weren't monogamous out of obligation. We were monogamous because we wanted each other more than anyone else. We were monogamous because no one else could compare.

But that was a long time ago. I'd kept up a physical relationship with Abel as long as possible. We went from weekend-long trysts, stopping only to eat and smoke, to occasional, but blissful, lovemaking, to brief, nostalgic, encounters on his last few good days. He had his last orgasm a few months before he said his last word. That was not a good day. It was one of the worst—one of the few days where Abel seemed to have some understanding of how sick he was. We'd been upstate for a few months. It was our last visit to a specialist, a fancy neurologist in Albany who ruined my credit when I found out, after the fact, that he didn't take our insurance. He talked about Abel as if he weren't there, tried to get him to answer questions I promised him Abel couldn't answer, and, worse—so much worse—used the words around him I'd been protecting him from for years: "dementia," "decline," "nursing home."

Abel became agitated. The whole ride home, and for the rest of the day, he was trying to do things he couldn't—say hard words, finish sentences, walk by himself. His face was contorted with sadness and frustration. I couldn't bear it. Anything but this. It was all right for me to know what was happening to him, but for years I'd protected him. Now this one awful doctor had pierced the bubble I'd spent years building around Abel.

Finally I got him to take a few Xanax and watch a soothing show on TV. Abel didn't even own a TV when I met him. Now his life was measured out in doses of sitcoms and soap operas. Like a new parent, you think you'll be different: *I will read to him,* I thought at first. *I will always feed him real food. I will never give him dangerous, addictive barbiturates.* But then you have to work and you're broke and you're exhausted and reality is too ugly to live with anymore, so it's Ensure and Xanax and *Friends.*

He calmed down after the Xanax and even laughed at *Friends* a little, which was almost worse than not laughing at it. We went to bed early. This was the last month we slept in the same bed. Soon he would start tossing and turning and occasionally screaming all night, making it too hard for us to sleep together, although a year after that he would stop thrashing and sleep deeper and with more stillness every year, some nights so eerily still I wasn't sure if he was alive. But for now we slept in the same bed. He had no way to express it, but I could tell he was still distressed from the doctor's words. I sat up and straddled him and began to stroke him. His body responded. I kept going until he came, shuddering, with a grunt. He used to always laugh after he came. Laugh, hug me, kiss me, and often after sex he'd get up and make a snack, hungry from exertion.

Now Abel looked straight ahead, face vacant. Then he closed his eyes, rolled over, and fell asleep.

We never did that again.

12.

Oswald Johnson Haber's limo picked us both up at my hotel at ten a.m. The morning was gray and still. Lucas turned the corner at the same time as the car pulled up, and we met at the car door. Lucas wore a nicer version of what he usually wore: blue jeans, a button-down shirt, a blazer, and boots, all under an expensive black parka. Today the jeans were a little more expensive, the shirt less wrinkled, and the blazer was well cut and tweedy.

The driver was an older man in uniform. I'd never seen an actual uniformed chauffeur before. He opened the door for us with a bow and a low "Good morning."

Lucas and I raised our eyebrows at each other and got in the back of the limo. The last time I'd been in a car like this was in Germany. *Beauty* had been popular there, and a year into Abel's illness I was invited to a big festival in Berlin. On that trip to Germany the publisher was happy enough with book sales to take me around in a luxury limo and spring for fancy, futuristic meals in Berlin and Frankfurt. I thought, *I'm still me. I can still travel. I can still have the life I wanted.* Then I got home and Abel had a rash from his shitty caregiver not bathing him enough and had lost three pounds. That was before Awe. I hadn't left the country since. Even Awe needed days off, and his replacements were not as reliable.

I'd sat across from Lucas when we got in the limo. Now he got up and moved next to me. Without speaking he pulled my head back a little and kissed me again.

"I missed you last night," he said. He kissed my cheek, near my ear, and then kissed my ear itself, which was strangely thrilling.

"I," I began. "It's a lot. It's been a while since—"

"Do you want me to stop?" Lucas said, kissing my neck.

I did not want him to stop kissing my neck. Then I didn't want him to stop kissing my neck, then my chest and my breasts. I also did not want him to stop when he slipped his hand down to my thighs and over my jeans to the growing heat between.

But then, when he nudged one hand in the waistband of my jeans, I wanted him to stop. It was too much: too much pleasure, too much closeness, too much of feeling alive after being in stasis for so long. Lucas wordlessly, seamlessly, sensed my discomfort and retracted his hand. I barely had my shirt on when we pulled off the road to a gate. The driver paused for a moment while someone or something acknowledged our presence and the gate swung up to let us in.

Oswald Johnson Haber's house was the size of five or ten regular houses. On either side of the driveway was a row of perfectly manicured trees. Behind them were formal gardens that went on for acres, dotted by concrete urns you could fit a teenager in and marble sculptures of naked women that looked like they'd been stolen from Rome. Beyond the house was a beach and the ocean. I smelled the sharp, cold salt air, one of my favorite smells.

I loved the beach. On the rare occasions I let myself dream, I dreamed of selling the house upstate and moving to the seashore, ideally somewhere warm. All I needed was one good year and for the house upstate to increase a little more in value and I could make it happen. A house in Georgia or northern Florida wouldn't be much more than the house in New York—all I needed was the money to cover the initial expenses, the move, and expensive medical transport for Abel.

After another minute we were at the house and the car stopped. The driver opened the door and Lucas and I got out of the car. A man came from out of the massive front door of the house to meet us. He was about my age and thin and wore a suit.

"Grady?" Lucas guessed.

He smiled.

"Grady," he confirmed.

"Lucas," Lucas said.

"Lily," I said.

Grady smiled, nodded, and did not tell us his first name.

"Mr. Haber is out on the beach. Will you do him the honor of joining him for lunch?"

"Of course," I said.

"Very well," Grady said.

Grady led us around the house to the beach. The air smelled crisp and marine. It was noon, cool and cloudy, sky white and ocean gray. A man in his fifties—Oswald Johnson Haber—stood facing the ocean. He was shooting seagulls. The first time he fired the gun, I jumped. The second time, he hit a seagull and it exploded in a flash of red and white and fell into the ocean.

Haber shot another seagull. Grady stood patiently. I gathered we were supposed to wait too. I waited one minute. Then another. Haber reloaded his shotgun.

Then I nudged Lucas, mouthed *Come with me,* and turned and walked away. Lucas followed, if reluctantly, with great shock.

Grady came after us.

"Lily," he said. "Lucas. Please."

"Apparently he's busy," I said. I got out my phone. "There seems to have been a mistake. If the car can't take us back, I can get us an Uber to the train. What's the address here?"

Lucas looked a little pale, but also excited.

This wasn't just about sex. Or money. The book was already shaping us. Drawing a fuck-it-all-ness out of us. Or maybe it was a fuck-you-ness. Fuck you to the world, fuck you to the rich, fuck you to anyone who stood between us and the book that wanted us.

At the time, it was exhilarating.

"No, no," Grady said. "He's available. He's—"

"I didn't know you were on such a tight schedule," a thick, deep voice crackled from behind us.

I turned around. Oswald Johnson Haber III stood behind Grady, gun in hand, a crooked smile on his face. He was a big man with a big face, weathered, older-looking than he was, with messy white hair. He wore a hunting jacket and khaki pants and big rubber boots. He held a shotgun. It looked old.

"We're not," I said. "I just don't want to spend my day watching you shoot birds."

Oswald looked me up and down, taking his time. He smiled again.

"Come to the house," he said, sounding amused. He had a bit of a New England accent. The rich kind. "I won't waste any more of your valuable time."

"Sounds good," Lucas said quickly, before I could screw it up.

We all went in the house. The foyer was huge, with white walls twenty feet high and a cold stone floor. We walked through the foyer, through a large room I didn't know what to call—it had sofas and chairs and a few large fireplaces roaring with fire, but it was too big to be a living room, and you could see no one actually did any living in it—through another long hallway to the dining room.

In the dining room was a long table with a white tablecloth and three formal place settings bunched at one end—with Haber at the head, of course.

We sat at the table. A butler served lobster soup with foie gras floating on top. I tasted it. It was maybe the best thing I'd ever tasted. Maybe second best was the sparkling white wine served with it, exactly as I liked it, crisp with only the smallest hint of fruit and sugar.

"Wow," said Lucas.

"I believe in pleasure," said Haber. "Life is short. I'm a very lucky man. I can indulge most of my whims. So I do. Except *The Book of the Most Precious Substance*. It's one of the few things I want but don't have. Of course, that makes me want it all the more. But I will have it, hopefully sooner rather than later."

"Why do you want it?" Lucas asked.

Haber frowned.

"I thought you knew what it was," he said. "The book—its methods—can give you everything you want."

"I know," Lucas said. "But it seems like you already have everything you want. Except the book."

Haber's eyes brightened. He already liked me, and now he also liked Lucas.

"Aha," he said. "You aren't stupid. Good. There's one thing I want. Not a thing. A person. Another man's wife. I've wanted her for thirty years. She hates me. But she'll love me. She'll be mine and she'll like it."

I doubted that, but I didn't tell Haber.

"Isn't there an easier way?" I asked.

"I've tried the easier ways," Haber said. "They didn't work. The book gives infinite power. Money and power aren't the same thing, you know. Close. But not identical. Money can be taken away. True power, supernatural power, can't."

"But someone can take the book away just as easily as your money," Lucas said. "I mean, theoretically. I'm assuming neither would be particularly easy."

"You're correct. It wouldn't be easy," Haber said. "But you're wrong about the book. Once you have that kind of power, it stays with you. If you complete the operation. Only a few people have."

As far as any interested party knew, no one currently alive had completed all the steps. Maybe no one since Hieronymus Zeel.

"How far have you gotten?" Haber asked.

"In getting the book?" I asked. "We—"

"No," Haber said. "In the acts."

"We're book dealers," Lucas said.

Haber smirked. I didn't know how he knew, but he knew. The strange quick unpleasantness, the sick chill that I'd felt when we finished the first act, took me over again at that moment. For a quick moment I was convinced those feelings had marked me in some way, some ugly stain Haber could now see.

But the chill passed and I pushed the thought away. He was guessing. Trying to get the better of us.

"Suit yourself," Haber said. "But if you learn anything, let me know."

"Has anyone successfully done it?" Lucas asked. "Ever? All five steps?"

"Of course," Haber said. "Rasputin is the most famous. Supposedly used the Frankfurt copy. John Dee completed the third step right before the Enochian language was revealed to him, but he never got to the fourth. Jack Parsons and Marjorie Cameron completed all the steps before the Babalon Working."

I wasn't sure any of those stories was true, and later I would be sure: none of them was.

Empty soup bowls were taken away, replaced with plates of gem-like fish with sliced pears over little shoots of green.

"None of those people seem to have had a happy ending," I pointed out.

"Very few people know what to do with power," Haber said. "I do."

I had another glass of sparkling wine. I was starting to relax a little. Haber was on his third glass, I noticed, and Lucas well into his second. I didn't like Haber, but I enjoyed his company. He seemed like a terrible person, but he was sharp and surprisingly funny.

"You do know about Hieronymus Zeel," Haber said. "The history of the book?"

"Yes," I said. "But I'm sure you know more."

Haber smiled and took on the air of a wise man, as if *wise* were synonymous with *rich*. He launched into the story.

"Hieronymus Zeel was a con man. Or so he began. He sold snake oils to the gullible bourgeois and travelers who wouldn't come back for a refund. Then one day he pissed off the wrong man: Richard the Crow was a powerful alchemist, a pioneer of the nigredo working, which is where he got his name. Zeel sold him a dram of fake dragon's blood—it's a resin, not an actual blood—and Richard came back with a hatchet. But by nightfall, the con man and the alchemist were the best of friends. That night, Richard showed Zeel how to make at least a few of his cons real—that is, how to really work magic.

"No one knows exactly how extensive Zeel's education with Richard was. But after that, Zeel became a master of the Dark Arts. He continued to sell his snake oils to the stupid and wealthy, but also became a serious practitioner of the occult.

"Then, there was a second meeting that changed his life again. As Zeel continued to study and practice, in every sense of the word, people began to talk, of course. People came to see him in his little hovel on the edges of Amsterdam, to seek out his potions and his knowledge. Word traveled high enough that it reached Princess Isabelle of Luxembourg. She was young and beautiful, but she wasn't dumb."

I hadn't assumed she was, but Haber was reveling in his lecture—and, honestly, so was I—so I didn't interrupt. We'd long finished our fish and been brought ten kinds of cheese, served with fig and currant preserves, then a break for coffee. Now we had a choice of a dozen small fruit tarts for dessert, each with an intricate, abstract design of small edible flowers on top.

"Isabelle of Luxembourg was a fascinating woman," Haber went on. "Her tutor said she had a mind like a man: 'insatiable, and obsessed with vice.' By twenty-two, she'd had close to one hundred lovers, spoke eight languages, knew Arabian mathematics and Chinese alchemy. She'd heard of Zeel and insisted, against the wishes of her family and all others, on visiting his filthy little workshop. It was 1610, or close to it. The princess stayed the night. No one knows exactly what happened over the next twelve hours. But when morning came, the princess and the magician had developed the working of the Precious Substances. And the princess's maid was dead.

"Zeel spent the next year making the five copies of the book. As I'm sure you know, there's now two left. One belongs to the General—"

"General?" Lucas and I said at the same time.

"General, Admiral, whatever he is," Haber said dismissively. "You don't expect me to believe you don't know him?"

"I do not know him," I said.

Haber let out a rueful laugh. "The General says he lost his copy. Don't believe him. And don't tell him you're working for me. He'd burn the book before he'd let me have it."

"Why?" Lucas asked.

"The past is past," Haber said. "It doesn't matter why. And if I find out you've sold the book to the Fool, I'll have you both killed."

He lifted up his glass and had a long sip. I wasn't sure if he was joking.

"What the fuck are you talking about?" I said.

"Don't worry," Haber said. "I like you, Lily. That's the only thing you could ever do to make me kill you."

I looked at Lucas. I was sure we were both thinking the same thing—first, that he certainly wouldn't kill us *today*, and second, that it would be very helpful to know who the General and the Fool were. But we also didn't want to let on how little we knew about the book and its world.

Lunch was over and Haber tossed his napkin on the table and looked at us.

"So," he said. "Are you going to get me my book?"

"I'll be honest," I said. "And I'm only speaking for myself here, not Lucas. I know who has your book. And I know they'll sell it to me, with some persuading."

None of this was true. I was usually a very honest person. But the book had already reached a long tentacle into my head, twisting my thoughts. In a few days, I had convinced myself that I not only wanted the book, but needed it.

There was a steady tattoo in my head: *If we found the book, I could move to the beach. If we found the book, I'd never have to drag a thousand pounds of books to a community college again. If we found the book, I'd never have to go back to that fucking house, never smell those smells or clean those stains again...*

"But," I said to Haber, "I do not have the funds to buy it for you right now. If I was a bigger person, I suppose I would let you and Lucas go on without me, or bring someone with more capital into the equation. I am not a bigger person. And I'm the one who knows where the book is. So if you want the book, I'm going to need a deposit. A large one."

Lucas looked at the table and I could tell I'd jarred him a little, maybe even embarrassed him. He liked to think of himself as a well-off man. And he kind of, sort of was. I was not.

Haber looked at me for a good long minute. Then he said, "All right," and screamed, "GRADY!"

Grady came out from the shadows of the house where he'd been lurking nearby.

"Checkbook," Haber said. Grady reached into a jacket pocket and pulled out a checkbook. I told him to make the check out to Lucas. Haber wrote out a check, ripped it out of the book, and handed it to me.

I took it. One hundred grand.

At the moment, I had five thousand dollars in my checking account, out of which two thousand was earmarked for Awe, two hundred for Abel's medical supplies, six hundred for bills, fifteen hundred for insurance, and fifteen hundred for my mortgage—plus living expenses, gas, and food. Like every month, it added up to more than I had.

"OK," I said. "We'll get the book."

Haber looked at Grady, who wordlessly brought us a new bottle of wine. Haber poured us each a glass. This one didn't sparkle, but like its predecessor it smelled crisp and delicious. I didn't know about wine, but Lucas did, and I could tell by his reaction it was a rare bottle.

We toasted.

"To the book," I said.

"To successful ventures," Lucas said.

"To power," Haber said. We clinked glasses, drank the bottle, and said our goodbyes. Lunch was over. We left.

13.

Silently, Lucas and I both decided not to discuss the book in the car. We trusted the driver enough to nearly have sex in front of him, separated only by a thin opaque barrier, but not to discuss money. We spent the ride chastely staring at our phones and got out of the limo at Lucas's apartment. It was a cold and dreary evening, but we both felt tense after Oswald Johnson Haber III, and decided to go for a walk. Other than my visit to Lucas's apartment the day before, I hadn't spent time in this neighborhood in years. I remembered it as having a handful of good bookstores, and it still did; without discussing it, we walked to one of them.

In the store we made a bee line for the secondhand section. I grazed through the shelves, pulling out intriguing titles to check for damage or edition.

"Who do you think those other people are?" Lucas asked. "The Fool? The General?"

"If they were really talking to Shyman about the book," I said, "they might be in the notebook."

"And," Lucas said, "we now have one potential buyer. Might as well see if anyone wants to bid against him."

I pulled a neat little history of orgies off the shelf, flipped through it, saw no marks and a two-dollar price tag, and handed it to Lucas to hold for me. I'd sell it for forty or fifty. An out-of-print book on a rarely written-about topic was always a sure bet.

"What if Haber kills us?" I said, mostly joking.

"Then none of this will matter," Lucas said, also mostly joking. "I have the notebook at my place. Come over. We'll have dinner and look through it."

I agreed. I pulled another book from the shelf and flipped through: a history of Italian hats and hat makers. Incredibly specific books made for a fun table at fairs, and while they wouldn't sell to just anyone, a costume designer or hat collector would pay a hundred bucks or more for this one.

"I used to love clothes," I said suddenly, apropos of nothing. It was true; I used to spend hours shopping. When I was broke, before *Beauty*, I shopped at thrift shops. Then, when I had money, at boutiques and high-end consignment shops. But when I was broke again, when I lost Abel and my money ran out and I started selling our books, I never got interested in what I wore again.

"Buy yourself a new outfit," Lucas said. "You have one hundred grand in your pocket."

I shrugged. For all I knew it was the last time I'd ever see a check of that size, and it seemed foolish to spend any of it on myself. Awe deserved a bonus. Our hot water heater was ten years old. My car was dying an ugly death.

On the other hand, a new outfit from one of the good thrift shops in Manhattan could be had for less than fifty dollars and a few hours of time. Forty dollars and a few hours that could be spent giving Awe a break, or researching a new avenue to try for Abel, or—

Lucas could see my anxiety mounting. He took my arm and led me toward the cashier.

"Come on," Lucas said. "We're supposed to be celebrating."

I paid for my books, which Lucas continued to carry, and Lucas led us to an Italian restaurant nearby, where we ordered antipasto, a big plate of pasta, and a large salad to take out.

Back at Lucas's place, we ate dinner while we looked at Shyman's notebook. After we ate we sat next to each other on the couch, taking turns with the notebook. I was starting to feel more comfortable around Lucas. Shyman's notes were incoherent and disorganized, the sad leftover words from a life not particularly well spent:

FIRST ONLY

NO RANCH ONLY ITALIAN NO PICKLES

CALL AFTER TEN ONLY

DO NOT DELIVER

Lucas flipped to a recent page in the notebook.

"I've been trying to decipher this," he said, pointing at a jumble of words. Most of the words were hard to read, scrawled in an unsharpened pencil and ballpoint pen. Others were legible, but mysterious:

LIBRO

The Accountant

The Admiral

???l—TG/LA—NO
The Whore
The Prince

"Huh," I said. "Potential sellers?"

"Or potential buyers," Lucas said. "If he had a lead on a copy."

It was possible.

"So I figure Haber is the Accountant," Lucas said. Having met him, I agreed: He loved money and he kept close accounts.

"The Whore would be a woman," I said. "Obviously. And the Admiral is probably the General, whoever that is."

"Singleton said there were only about ten people or fewer who might buy this stuff at this price range," Lucas reminded me.

"So if we look at recent sales," I said, "we can probably find them fast."

"The problem," Lucas said, "is that most of these people spending this kind of money don't do their own buying. They'd use a dealer. They like their privacy."

"Hmm," I said.

"Hmm," said Lucas.

We ate leftovers and thought.

"What if there was a list we could cross-reference sales records with?" I said.

"What kind of list?" Lucas said.

"Well, we could put one together ourselves," I said. "You know who buys expensive books, at least some of them. And even if they buy anonymously, people loan books for exhibits, they give interviews, they trade books. If we scrape together the sales records, the gossip, and what we know, we can at least narrow it down."

We spent the next four hours doing exactly that. It was two a.m. when we were done. The General and the Prince were still a mystery, but we had a short list of suspects for the Fool and the Whore.

I was especially interested in the Fool. Haber wouldn't have been so concerned about us selling to him without a reason. Either the Fool knew something about the book, or he was willing to pay even more for it than Haber was.

Lucas narrowed it down to five men who had the money, the interest, and the pull to buy a million-dollar occult book: two musicians, another East Coast businessman like Haber, and two tech billionaires. Lucas wrote their names on a piece of paper. I went through the notebook with a metaphorical magnifying glass, looking for correlation.

Just before the clock struck three, I figured it out.

Toby Gunn. In Shyman's notebook he was TG/LA. Toby Gunn was a tech billionaire who'd invented something uninteresting and written a book that seemed even less interesting and lived in Los Angeles. Lucas knew Gunn bought expensive books. He'd seen him at book fairs and auctions, even though he did most of his actual buying through a dealer.

In Shyman's notebook, next to "TG/LA," was written "NO."

Lucas and I looked at each other.

"No to buying?" Lucas guessed.

"Or," I guessed, "no to selling. Or to having."

We'd done enough for one night. Lucas put the book down and leaned over and kissed me.

"I like you, Lily," he said again, in a low voice. "I've liked you for a long, long time. And now that I have you, I'm going to try to hold on to you."

14.

I slept at Lucas's that night. He nudged me at seven when he woke up and again at eight when he left, but I pretended to sleep through both nudges. I felt an ocean of anxiety around what the morning might be like, and I didn't want to face any of it. Would we act like lovers? Would we go back to being friends? Better to sleep through it all. Lucas told me to stay as late as I wanted as he walked out the door.

I got up after he left. He'd made me coffee and left me a toasted English muffin, now cold, which I ate anyway, and sent a text: *some things to wrap up at the library, dinner later?* I wrote back: *yes dinner, enjoy work*. It was Sunday. Maybe he'd had some morning anxiety as well. I considered staying for a while and exploring his apartment but that, too, seemed more than I was ready for, so I washed up, got dressed, and went to a café, where I spent a few hours reading about the Fool.

Toby Gunn, the Fool, was, or was imagined to be, a tech genius, and as such he had written a book about how to be a genius like him. It was called *Thinking Outside the Circle.* I flipped through an excerpt online. It seemed to be an entire book of meaningless phrases like "Once you leave the confines of the predetermined circle, creativity can soar to new heights" and "While the circle of expectations confines our creativity, it can also nurture and defend." Apparently it had been a bestseller. His book made me feel good about not having published in more than a decade.

I realized we knew someone in common. The editor at Random House who had published the Fool's book, Allen Bane, was a fan of *Beauty* who wrote me once or twice a year. At first, five long years ago, he wrote to try to woo me away from my old publisher. He was under the mistaken impression that I had a finished book and the publisher was dicking around with it. He sent cute, professionally flirtatious emails about wanting to publish me. I gave him polite answers. He sent more cute notes and I ignored them. Finally, on a particularly bad day, I responded in a rage: I was broke, selling off everything I owned, and my husband was likely dying. A book deal was not in the fucking cards. He could drop it now and move along.

But he didn't move along. Instead, he wrote back a few months later, with an offer to send me a box of books I might like. And then again with a little article he thought I might like. Now he sent books a few times a year and wrote every six or nine months to say hello and ask if I'd read or sold any interesting books. I'd never met him. But somehow, out of everyone on earth, he'd become something like a friend.

Now I called his cell phone.

"Lily Albrecht," he said, after I explained myself, which took a long, frightening moment. I was anxious about his reaction to a near-stranger calling him on Sunday, but he sounded shockingly happy to hear from me. "I finally get to hear your voice. Are you in town? Can I take you out to lunch?"

I felt a ping of regret. Why hadn't I called him before? He didn't want anything from me. He was just a nice man who liked my book and wanted to spend a little expense account money on me. I'd forgotten that I wasn't always a burden. That awful woman calling for a doctor's appointment or to argue about insurance. To some people, I was still the glamorous Lily Albrecht.

"Hey," I said, shaking off my sadness. "It's so good to talk to you. I am actually calling to ask a favor. A big one. I totally understand if you aren't able to do it. And," I added impulsively, "I'm taking *you* out. To dinner. The next time I'm in town."

I knew I couldn't ask Allen to introduce me to Toby Gunn—we weren't in the same weight class. Instead, I asked him to pass on my information to Gunn and let him know I wanted to talk to him about *The Book of the Most Precious Substance* and that I'd be in town the next few days—which was, as of now, not true, but might be tomorrow. Allen said he would write Gunn right away.

"Lily," he said. "I got into this business with the sole hope of being called by my favorite writers and asked to do them a favor. Toby isn't the smartest, but he's an OK guy. It's his privilege to meet you."

"Thank you," I said, because I didn't know what else to say.

"You promise?" he said before we got off the phone. "About dinner?"

"Yes," I said. "I promise." I wondered if I meant it. Maybe I did.

I spent the rest of the day wandering lazily around Soho, window shopping and stopping for coffee a few times to check my email and rest. By five o'clock, there was an email from Toby Gunn.

Hey Lily. Any friend of Allen Bane's. Not looking to sell but if you'd like to check out the precious substance you're more than welcome. Come by anytime—I'll leave word for the assistants in case I'm not around. He left his address in Los Angeles, phone number, and a bunch of ways to contact him on devices or apps I didn't have or want.

Two hours later I met Lucas for dinner at a dark little Greek restaurant in the East Village. I got there before him and got us a table. When Lucas walked in, I noticed a few heads turn. He looked good today. He kissed me on the cheek, deftly, as if a practiced gesture, as he sat down.

"He has the book," I said to Lucas.

"Holy shit," Lucas said.

"He says he's not selling," I said.

"He doesn't know what we're offering," Lucas said.

I handed him my phone and he read the email. He smiled and his eyes were bright.

"We're going to Los Angeles," he said.

I immediately thought of a thousand reasons why I couldn't leave New York. But none of them were true. I'd already put my online sales on hold before I left home. I'd mailed out every pending book, except a few expensive titles I hadn't gotten paid for yet. I'd emailed with the buyers to tell them their book would be delayed and if they wanted to cancel their orders, they could. Awe had just had a ten-day break over the holidays. I hadn't taken a vacation since I'd hired Awe, although I'd traveled for work, and

I strongly suspected his days were easier without me fretting over him and Abel.

Lucas saw me hesitating.

"Lily," he said. "If you don't take this trip, you will never, ever forgive yourself. If for no other reason, you can't walk away from the money. You need it. Abel needs it."

I thought about it. Nothing Lucas had just said was true. I had skipped dozens of potentially exciting escapades over the years and forgiven myself entirely. I didn't need the money, and neither did Abel. I wanted it. But I didn't *need* it.

I should go home. Let Lucas take over the book, arrange a seventy-five/twenty-five split—seventy-five to him for finding it, twenty-five to me for hooking him up. I should pack my bags, take the train back upstate, get a taxi at the train station.

But I didn't even get into the taxi in my head before I was overcome by a heavy depression so big, I hadn't been able to see it before. Like a fish who can't see water. The thought of getting off the train in my gray little town and getting in an Uber, driving through the cold snow to my house to be alone again...

I looked at Lucas. His eyes were bright. He was talking about where to stay in L.A.—we could save money and get a motel by the airport, but we really should stay at the Chateau Marmont, especially as the trip was so short. It was hardly L.A. without it.

"OK," I said. "Book it."

Lucas smiled and bit his lip to stop his smile from revealing too much. He really wanted to do this.

I told myself he was smiling over the money, and I shouldn't take that smile personally. But I did.

Over dinner Lucas booked the whole trip on his phone. He'd already put the hundred grand from Haber in his account, persuaded his bank to expedite it, and wired me half. Now he bought us business-class tickets to L.A. and booked us at the Chateau Marmont. Lucas had plenty of personal, sick, and vacation time coming to him at work, and it was easy enough for him to concoct a story about a family emergency and arrange a few weeks off. I didn't ask what he was going to do about the woman he was dating. I figured she would get a text—the same text I'd get from him someday: *Not your fault at all. You're amazing and you deserve someone who...*

After dinner Lucas wanted me to come back to his apartment. I told him I had too much to do. It wasn't true. I needed some time alone. As always, Lucas understood the not-quite-said part of what I was saying and let me go with no complaints. We kissed goodbye and I went back to my hotel for the first time since yesterday morning.

My hotel room felt strange and cold, but a little more glamorous than it had the day before. I took a long bath and tried not to think too much. I knew I could talk myself out of this trip as easily as I'd talked myself into it.

I called Awe and told him I'd be gone a few days. Maybe a few weeks. I was almost dismayed at how happy he was.

"Lily," he said. "Take your time. You need a break. Enjoy your travels. I'll call you if I need you."

I took a sleeping pill before I could think too much more and woke up at eight to meet Lucas at the airport at eleven. I still wasn't sure I was making the right choice. But when I saw Lucas standing by the gate looking at his phone, I felt a little better. When he saw me coming, he smiled, and I felt like I hadn't felt in years. Not needed. Only desired.

I held back a smile as I met him. I felt...normal. Not cursed, not overly stressed, no thousand-pound weight on my shoulders. I even felt a little happy.

The book already had me by the throat. If only I'd been smart enough to see it.

The flight from New York to Los Angeles was uneventful but exciting. I'd packed bottles of tranquilizers and sleeping pills—my home medicine cabinet was a pharmacopeia of failed experiments for my husband—and I'd popped a small Xanax as soon as I stepped foot in the airport. On the flight we splurged for tiny bottles of champagne and upgraded meals and indulged a few more Xanax; we slept through most of the trip, had a few cups of decent coffee when we woke, and arrived well rested at four to pick up our rental car. I'd always wanted to stay at the Chateau Marmont. The lush hidden driveway was lined with bougainvillea and something that looked like banana trees. Los Angeles was warm and verdant, another planet from the frozen East Coast. The hotel itself was a gothic castle. Half the people in the lobby looked familiar from somewhere—not exactly famous, but not entirely not famous, either.

Lucas checked us in, and a man came around to whisk our bags away and ready our room. Lucas led me to the outdoor restaurant in the courtyard. Mockingbirds and hummingbirds and finches darted among the palm trees and plentiful flowers. We got burgers and more coffee, both of us a little dazed, and then went up to our room to clean up and change and come up with some kind of strategy before we met Toby Gunn. The room was simple and clean and bright.

None of it quite seemed real. Seeing so much greenery in what had, hours ago, been winter, made me feel almost drunk with visual pleasure. As Lucas drove us to Toby Gunn's house in Bel Air, the sky was bathed in a dramatic pink-into-violet sunset. When we reached the address, the property was surrounded by black iron gates. There was an LCD screen to the right of the gates, with no obvious buttons, knockers, or buzzers. Lucas pulled up close to the screen. Lucas touched it and it sprang to life, glowing a wordless pale blue.

"Name?" a woman's voice said. I couldn't tell if it was a real woman or a computer.

"Lily Albrecht and partner," I said.

The gate swung open and we drove up the long cul-de-sac drive. As we got closer to the house we saw cars parked by the front door: a Rolls-Royce, a Bentley, three Ferraris, and a few sports cars that I couldn't name but that seemed to excite Lucas, who knew them all by name, number, and year. The house was a big Spanish-style mansion, probably from the 1920s, with an artful arrangement of tall, slender palm trees out front, lit up by hidden spotlights.

Lucas parked and we got out of the car. In the strange warm wind we stepped up to the massive wooden door and heard a faint click. I tried the brass handle. The door was unlocked. Lucas and I looked at each other, shrugged, opened the door, and entered.

The entryway to Toby Gunn's house had twenty-foot-high ceilings and stone walls and marble floors. Tapestries that looked like they were from the 1500s hung from the walls, showing scenes of unicorns and walled gardens, muffling the noise in the already too-quiet house. A chandelier that was as large as a car hung from the ceiling. I wondered where they got a ladder tall enough to clean it, and then I quickly realized that they would just make a ladder. I was learning the ways of the rich. There was a low beige sofa pressed against one wall but instead of sitting I paced as we waited for someone to greet us, or shun us, or reveal themselves at all. Lucas paced with me, taking my hand and squeezing it as if wringing the anxiety out of me.

Just when the thought entered my head that this was the first time we'd held hands, Toby Gunn, a.k.a. the Fool, came into the room. He walked over and smiled. He looked like he might have been homeless: thirty-something, long beard, hair that was thin on top and long around the sides, wearing an old T-shirt, a hooded sweatshirt, and sagging shorts, all in various shades of dull blue. There was a kind of general uncoolness about him that, combined with his ridiculous book, made it clear why they called him the Fool. There was also a twitchiness to him that made it clear he'd been doing cocaine since long before our flight had landed that afternoon.

He stuck out his right hand to shake Lucas's. In his left hand, he was holding a gun.

"Nice Glock," Lucas said offhandedly, as they shook. This was clearly a rich-boy game of chicken, and Lucas knew exactly how to play. Toby smiled.

"Thanks," Toby said. "Who are you?"

"Lucas," Lucas said, keeping himself surprisingly calm. "This is Lily. We wanted to talk to you about *The Book of the Most Precious Substance*? I think your editor spoke to you?"

Toby gave us a long suspicious look before he broke into a smile.

"Right," he said, recognition dawning. "Well, I'm not selling you the book. But come on up. You can look at it, at least."

Lucas and I met eyes. Of course we wanted to see it.

Toby wore shearling slippers and thick socks, and he walked noiselessly on the marble floor as he turned up the big staircase in the entryway. As we walked up the stairs he tucked the gun away in his shorts. I didn't see it again. Lucas and I followed Toby up the winding stairs. At the top of the second floor the door to the master suite was open. The bedroom was huge and looked like a mid-priced hotel: beige, clean, impersonal. Inside were eight women, naked except for a few scraps of silk and lace lingerie and high heels, lounging on the bed or the hotel-like armchairs. The women were tall and stunningly beautiful and looked bored. They looked at their phones, except for two women who were talking in quiet voices. One woman caught me looking and smiled when we met eyes. Then she went back to her phone.

Toby Gunn waved at the women and walked us down the long hallway to two Spanish-looking wooden doors at the end. They were closed, with a black iron latch keeping them shut and locked with both a large, iron antique hasp with a padlock and a complicated modern lock set into the door. Toby reached into the pocket of his shorts and pulled out a ring with a dozen or more keys on it: a few small, regular keys; two strange new technical keys I didn't understand; and one big iron antique, which he took and used, with some wiggling and finessing, to open the padlock. Then he used another key, one of the technical ones with recesses and dents, to open the modern lock. He pushed the heavy door open, leaning on it with his shoulder. A gust of air with the precise temperature of 63 degrees and 60 percent humidity drifted out. The ideal climate for books.

Toby smiled at us before we headed in. I immediately liked him more; there was a cleverness, and impishness, in his smile.

"Welcome," he said, dramatically, "to the most expensive library in the country. Maybe the world."

We stepped inside. Toby shut the door behind us. The room didn't have many books in it—maybe seventy-five. But he was right; it was likely the most expensive collection in the country, maybe the world. There was an original manuscript of *The Lesser Key of Solomon*. Across the room was a priceless Ripley Scroll in a glass case. Next to it was a shelf of three kabbalistic manuscripts, each open to charts and graphs I couldn't make any sense out of. The bare minimum for this collection, during a recession, might be a couple of million bucks. In a good economy, the sky would be the limit.

And there, on a long, clean white table, was *The Book of the Most Precious Substance.*

I couldn't remember the last time I'd been excited about a book. Ever since I'd stopped writing and started selling our library, books had gone from being the great delight of my life to a fucking drag. Selling books isn't like selling stocks and bonds, where you sit at a computer all day, or selling houses, where no one expects you to hand-deliver a cabin or a condo. Books are heavy and dirty and messy and have strong smells and leave your skin dry and dusty.

With a little sadness, I now saw I'd come to dread and resent books, every last one. It was a loss. Opening a book had always been like opening a window into a new and mysterious world. When I was a child my books were my best friends. I pored over my picture books, memorizing every line of every drawing. When I moved on to chapter books, I saw that words could illustrate even more than a drawing. In my mind's eye, I could see the exact picture a book painted for me: Times Square with a cricket, a pig's pen with a spider web, a peach so large that it was its own sweet, sticky world. I wanted to be a writer before I understood what a job was. Books had been the most lasting, profound relationship in my life. I'd long bought and sold a few books for extra money. But once I'd started selling them out of desperation, not luck or love, I'd come to wordlessly feel like even my love of books—like everything else I'd loved—had turned on me and become ugly.

Until now. *The Book of the Most Precious Substance* was small and slim, octavo size. It was bound in old, battered pale leather—calf's or lamb's skin. It was laid open to a page near the middle; a full-page woodcut illustration of the fourth act. I hadn't expected it to be illustrated: The drawing was crude but had enough style to capture the enthusiastic determination of the man and woman engaged. The paper was vellum, likely made from the skin of a newborn calf. It was slightly translucent and seemed to glow in the soft light of the library. Next to it were three pairs of white cotton gloves. The oils from our skin wouldn't immediately fuck the book, but over time could add wear and tear.

Was it my imagination, or did I feel a hum around the book? An appetite? Here was the source of all this trouble. Or all this delight, really. I had to admit I was having more fun than I'd had in years. I was neglecting my home, my husband, my business. Neither my home nor my husband nor my business seemed to miss me too much.

I knew it wasn't true, but it felt like I would keep doing this for the rest of my life—follow the book around the world with Lucas, with more sex and more money and more adventure at every step. I'd never return to that house upstate, which I now saw I hated. Never wanted to see—

"Lily."

I looked up. Lucas and Toby had their gloves on. Toby, jittery and excited, was looking at me.

"You're the expert," Lucas said. We were both experts, of course, but one of us had to go first. It was a nice little kick of respect from Lucas to ask me to authenticate. I put my gloves on, carefully closed the book, and looked at the binding. The pages were sewn and the cover was leather pasted over wood, as expected. All good.

I opened the book. The endpapers were marbled in faded pink— the paper would have been skimmed over a tub of water with ink floating on top to make the effect. I turned to the first proper leaf: It was blank, as was the second. The third was the frontispiece, with the long version of the title and some abstract decoration around it. Other than the illustrations, which were block printed, the book was handwritten, and whoever had written it had exquisite script. It had probably been written in black ink, but now it had faded to a mid-toned sepia. I could barely read the antiquated writing, and of course it was in Latin. Neither Lucas nor I could read Latin particularly well, but I knew some Spanish and some French and Lucas, even better, was nearly fluent in both of those and Italian. Together, we could muddle out enough to make sense out of most of it.

Lucas looked over my shoulder and translated the frontispiece:

"The Book of the Most Precious Substance; by a Citizen of Amsterdam. Concerning the Substances of Man and Woman and

Spirits Held Within. A Treatise on Various Fluids and Their Uses."

I turned to the next page. The first chapter began.

"The Liquids of Skin," Lucas translated. Below it were instructions—basically the instructions Singleton had given us about finding a drop of sweat, saying the word, and anointing the symbol, which was on the next page. There was another crude illustration of a man and a woman. The man was touching the woman's sternum, the woman had her finger on the back of the man's neck, just as Lucas and I had done. It gave me an uncomfortable, dark feeling. It passed. Chapter two was "The Female Nectar," third was "The Male Seed," and fourth was "The Most Precious Substance." It was all exactly as Singleton had described.

But when I got to the last pages of the text, where the fifth step should have been, there was nothing. Just torn-out stubs.

We both looked at Toby. He looked at us.

"Oh," Toby said. "Shit. I thought you knew. This isn't a complete copy."

"Wait, what?" Lucas said.

"Really?" I said at the same time.

"I thought you knew," Toby said again. "You don't know the story?"

"Actually, no," Lucas said. He seemed pissed.

"You don't need to get angry," Toby said to Lucas. "I wasn't going to sell it to you anyway."

"You didn't hear our offer," I said.

Toby shrugged. "Look around. I don't mean to be crude, but I paid cash for this place. And the cars. I know it isn't always easy to tell who has money and who's faking. I'm not faking. I have money.

What could you offer me? *A million dollars? Five million?"*

He said "a million dollars" with a bit of an accent, as if there was something funny about it, a child scared of the bogeyman on Halloween.

"That's what a decent party costs," Toby said. "Sorry."

It was worth the trip to see the book. Of course, with no real prior knowledge of it, I couldn't precisely authenticate it. But, intuitively, it felt right. It smelled right, literally and metaphorically. The paper, binding, ink, et al. were perfect. It was written by hand, as described. If it was a fake, it was a very good one, made not long after the original, and it would still be useful in authenticating any other editions we found.

I asked Toby if I could take photos of it.

"Fuck no," he said. "But take notes if you want."

I found I found a notebook in my purse and Toby gave me a pencil from a drawer in a side table. No one would open a pen in the same room as these books. I wrote down the details that would help me compare the other copies, if and when we found them: the paper, the size, the precise leathers used on the binding and the boards. I also sketched out the symbols and the words for steps two through four.

Like when Singleton had sketched the first symbol on the table, I both could and couldn't see the shapes in front of me. The third one was like a rectangle, but with extra sides. The fourth was a kind of sphere, but a sphere that somehow came to a point at one end. The magical words for each step, likewise, should have been simple enough, but somehow were hard to read and even harder to make sense of, seemingly having both too many letters and not enough at the same time.

Before we left, Toby went to one of the sparsely filled book-shelves and found a gray clamshell box made of cardboard covered with acid-free paper, the type it was typical for collectors to keep fragile books in, and handed it to me.

I opened it, expecting something rare and valuable inside. But it was a stapled-together stack of printed copy paper. I looked at Toby.

"It's a reproduction, obviously," he said. "The original is very fragile. I don't let anyone see it. But you can keep that. I can print out another."

"Thanks," I said, confused. "But what is it?"

"It's the story of what happened to the last pages of the book," Toby said. I thanked him again and we all left the rare book room and walked down the stairs together.

Before we left, I asked him a question. We were standing in the high-ceilinged foyer.

"What did you want?"

Toby looked at me. "What do you mean?"

"With the book," I said. "You have money. You have power. What did you want that you didn't have?"

"Everything," he said.

"Everything what?" I asked.

"Everything everything," Toby said, a strange dullness on his face. "People lie, you know. They say they're happy with a few million. They'll say they're happy with a *billion*. It's bullshit. No one's happy with that. How could they be? Everyone wants to be the best."

"The best at what?" I asked.

"I want to be number one," Toby said. "I want to be the richest, most powerful man on earth. Most people won't say it out loud, but everyone wants it. Everyone."

I didn't want that. But I pretended to agree, thanked him again for his time. Lucas did the same, and we left.

I knew exactly what I wanted. Whether the book would provide, I still had no idea. But it had nothing to do with wealth or power.

Driving away from Toby's house was the first time we realized we were being followed. It was a black Mercedes, a fancy car back east but commonplace in Los Angeles. It was easy enough to see that it was following us: The hills where Toby lived were fairly deserted, and the Mercedes kept pace with us but never got too close, staying a good twenty yards behind every time we stopped.

"You see that?" I asked Lucas.

"Yep," he said. "You think it's Toby?"

"No," I said. "We don't have anything he wants."

"Haber?"

"Maybe someone working for him. Or the General, whoever he is."

"Well," Lucas said, "I think we have to lose this tail."

He looked at me. We both smiled. Of course, neither of us had ever *lost a tail* in our lives.

Lucas drove east on Sunset and kept driving. The Mercedes kept up with us until we got into crowded, hellish Hollywood. Lucas was a good driver and skidded through traffic, taking us past the Chinese theater and the wax museum and through thousands of tourists and the people who preyed on them. The Mercedes got farther and farther behind us until, after a few nonsensical turns and lane changes and loops, we couldn't spot him anymore. Just to be sure, Lucas drove away from the crowds again and up a long, narrow canyon to the Valley. No one followed. We had, indeed, lost our tail.

Lucas seemed excited by the chase. When we finally circled back to our room, he ordered us steaks from room service and opened a half-size bottle of champagne from the minibar.

"To progress," Lucas said.

After dinner we started to kiss. After a while, I stopped and opened the notebook where I'd sketched the next three steps.

But when I opened my notebook, I gasped.

"Look," I called to Lucas.

He came over and looked. Somehow, when we'd opened the champagne, a few drops had dripped into my bag and onto the paper I'd sketched on, ruining my images of the third and fourth steps. All we had was the second.

That night we completed the second act. We'd achieved the fluid before—quotidian female wetness—but we didn't have the seal or the word to make it official.

I touched the book and said the word first; Lucas followed a moment later. I happened to look at the clock when Lucas got up to anoint the seal with my fluids. It was 2:55 a.m.

When we did, we both felt something flip, or twist, or tighten inside. The room seemed to get darker, then the light seemed to shift altogether.

"Ugh," I said.

"Oh," said Lucas, looking confused. "Oh."

I closed my eyes and I saw a woman's face, round and young, looking at me as if through a window. Her face was plump and she wore a strange tall, pointed hat.

I opened my eyes and shook my head. It passed quickly, and neither of us was really sure if it had happened at all. Or so we told ourselves.

The next morning, there was a strange, clipped voicemail on Lucas's phone from a man who called himself Admiral Masters, asking us to call him about "a certain book."

It was the General. We never found out how he got Lucas's number. He called at 2:58 a.m.

15.

After breakfast we called the Admiral back.

"This is Admiral Mason Masters in Washington, D.C.," he said. "I've heard you have *The Book of the Most Precious Substance*. I'm interested in verifying that."

"OK," I said, playing it cool again. This was starting to be fun—strange and wealthy men barking instructions at me, and me ignoring those instructions. Not a bad hobby. Lucas had woken me up with coffee and a hot croissant. He was the kind of lover who went out early to get fresh baked goods before his partner got out of bed. Cliché, but appreciated. After we ate we'd listened to the Admiral's message.

"Well?" the Admiral said. "Do you have it?"

"Who is this again?" I said. "Sorry. Didn't catch the name."

The Admiral made a noise in between a grunt and a sigh.

"MASTERS," he said again. "Admiral Mason Masters, U.S.

Marines."

"Oh," I said. "OK. So you have the book? Or you're looking for it?"

He made the same grunt-sigh sound.

"I'm looking for it," he said. "And whatever the Accountant offered you, I assure you I can offer you more."

"Well," I said, "that's a very interesting offer, thank you."

"So?"

"And I'll let you know if we have a copy for sale," I said. "Thank you for your interest."

I hung up.

"Fuck," Lucas said. But his eyes were bright and excited. He loved this.

My phone rang.

"Hello?" I said, feigning innocence.

"I'm going to put you on the phone with Maria," the Admiral went on, as if I hadn't hung up on him, and as if I had any idea who Maria was. "She's going to send you a first-class ticket to come to Washington to talk to me about the book. We'll meet at oh-eight-hundred hours, Wednesday. Suitable?"

"Two tickets," I said. It was Tuesday. "I have a partner. And make it later."

"Very well," he said. "Wednesday at thirteen—"

"At five thirty," I said. "Text me your address and we'll be there at five thirty in the afternoon. And I'll text you at this number to tell you where to send the tickets, and which flight."

"Very well," he said, and hung up.

We booked a flight that left Los Angeles at seven a.m. the next day and landed in Washington at three. We had twenty hours in Los Angeles.

"What should we do?" I said. I felt restless and guilty and a strong drive to do something useful. I had convinced myself this trip was OK because it was work. But I was shaking up my life in a way that, if I let myself think about it, felt painfully uncomfortable. It was taking me away from the life I'd built around Abel.

"We're going to the beach," Lucas said.

I started to protest that we should meet with rare book dealers, maybe visit the Huntington Library or the Getty to see what we could learn. But Lucas had already made calls to the Huntington and the Getty and plenty of other book-related joints, with no luck. Two hours later we were walking on the Venice boardwalk. We stopped at a boardwalk café for burgers and a few bottles of beer and then a few more. Why not? I'd texted with Awe that morning; all was well at home and no one seemed to miss me. The day was ours, until seven a.m. tomorrow, and no one knew where we were or what we were doing. So why not eat burgers, get drunk, buy a cheap beach towel, and loll on the sand, warm even in March? Why not fool around on said towel in a deserted corner of the beach until Lucas reached his hand into my jeans and made me come for the first time with him, come so hard I had to bite the towel to stop from making too much noise? Lucas was a very, very good lover. He brought me close and then stopped, leaving me hungry and strained; brought me close again and then bit my lip, hard, sending shocks between my mouth and my thighs; and then finally made me come so hard it shook me deep in my solar plexus. After, we dozed on the beach for a while and then, when the sun was going down, woke up and had Japanese food and sake for dinner on Sawtelle Boulevard.

Back in our hotel room, we started to fool around again. I hadn't had full penetrative sex for a few years. I reminded myself that I used to be good at this. We began with me on top, but a few minutes in, I was suddenly at a loss at how to proceed. I'd entirely forgotten how it was supposed to work. Was I supposed to go back and forth? Up and down? Eye contact? Noise? Should I really be doing this at all? Lucas sensed my obvious hesitation—he could hardly miss it—and sat up and wrapped his arms around me and turned me over so he was on top. Now it all came back to me, and I could tell from his half-closed eyes that everything was fine. It felt wonderful, but also a little painful and dangerously strange at first, as if I might break wide open. Soon he said, "Fuck, fuck," and then he pulled out and came on my stomach and my breasts and my chest.

He rolled over and sighed, content. He looked at the pleasant mess he'd made on my skin.

"Sorry," he said. "I should have asked."

"I like it," I said.

We fell asleep, naked and warm, and slept until our alarm went off at four thirty. Missing the flight was out of the question.

I called Awe again on the way to the airport. Everything at home was fine. As suspected, he sounded a little easier without me there moping around. I looked at Lucas, who was driving our rental car. He was a good driver, self-assured, calm, assertive, light grip on the steering wheel. He had the kind of forearms women stared at: strong, trim, a little black hair under the pushed-up sleeves of a button-down shirt.

"Are you having fun?" Awe asked.

"No," I said. "I mean yes. But this is work. We're going to find this book."

A quick tight look passed over Lucas's face.

Why didn't I give up after Los Angeles? Why didn't I turn around and go home? Because I wanted the money. Because there was nothing for me at home. Because I wanted to keep having sex with Lucas.

And, I now believe, because the book itself was pulling me toward our inevitable future, all three of us—Lucas, the book, and me—already locked together.

Driving to the airport, Lucas and I were slightly worried about whoever had been following us the night before last. But neither of us knew how to travel under a fake name or cover our tracks or anything like that, so we just booked the tickets under our real names. Our one concession to privacy was that Lucas changed and rebooked the tickets twice at the last minute—first to a later flight, then to an earlier one—which got us a thorough going-over from security, but maybe bought us some time from whoever had followed us through Los Angeles. Maybe.

On the plane I read the stapled papers Toby had given me. It was a Xerox of a translation of a passage from a minor alchemical text from 1655, *The Emerald Peacock*.

> *The seeking of the secrets of metals is a most dangerous search. If you should find the end, all riches are yours, except the one most rare, the only gem worthy of desire. This emerald most rare cannot be bought with gold or sold for silver, nor can it be achieved by magic or alchemy. No man can give it to another, but anything*

*may inspire a man to create it for himself. But once
seen, no other beauty can ever compare. The wise man
searches only for this. The foolish man searches to turn
lead into gold, hoping to buy that which no gold can
ever buy.*

*In Amsterdam there was a man who knew the secrets
to give a man and woman anything they desired. The
man and the woman only had to participate in the
five most wicked and degraded acts, culminating with
taking the life of a third, or one of the two, if heartless-
ness led one to steal all the spoils. He put these secrets
in a book which he copied only five times, and never
copied again.*

I didn't know what the rare emerald was, but for the rest of it,
obviously he was talking about steps of *The Book of the Most Precious
Substance*. I hadn't found any of it particularly degrading thus far,
but I probably had slightly looser morals than a seventeenth-century
magician.

I also didn't know that the final act could be completed with just
one participant. Two could begin, and one could end.

*A husband and wife who I will call Adam and
Eve, whose names were nonesuch at all, were very poor
bakers, and through many turns of providence found
themselves in possession of one copy of this book. After
the first act, they found many people came to buy their
bread, and their income increased. They bought many*

fine things, and gave none to those in need. After the second act, a distant relation was killed at war, and they inherited a sum equal to two ounces of gold. They built a new oven and a new chimney, and gave nothing to their other relations, who also were in need. After the third and fourth acts, many more riches came their way, through strange and extraordinary circumstances, and still they shared nothing with those who were hungry. They showed off their fine clothing and plentiful meat and no longer baked at all.

With great merriment and no thought to their Lord, they set in motion plans to hire a new servant girl, with no family of her own, in order to use her life to accomplish the fifth act, the most wicked of them all. They made such preparations as necessary, and the night came for them to complete the terrible act, with a fine shard blade acquired just for this loathsome act. To the husband's surprise, the wife and the servant girl turned the weapon on him, and tried to use him as the sacrifice, and gain all the wealth in the world for only themselves, and indulge in sinful acts with broomsticks, as they were now witches, and had no need for men or God.

The husband fought the women, killing them both, and was left alone with his book and his riches. But, in the curious ways of life, all was taken from him. First his bakery was lost to a fire. Then his fine house was taken by another man who laid claim to his land through an inheritance. Then his gold was taken by a relation of his deceased wife, who rightfully claimed it for his own. After some years, this man had nothing but his book, which was worth very much, and he decided to sell it for food, as he was now living on scraps and filth, and sleeping in a barn with swine. But before he sold this book, which he sold to me, he ripped out the last chapter and burned it in a fire, losing for all time the exact nature of the fifth act.

"Let no man suffer like I did," the man said, "at the wicked, wicked hands of witches!"

I thought blaming the lesbians for his fate was a stretch, but the moral of the story was well taken. I put the pages away; we were landing at Dulles.

But on our way into the fancy hotel Lucas had booked for us, I made sure to give the first homeless woman I saw a twenty-dollar bill. She was about my age, weathered, mumbling to herself on the corner just before the hotel driveway.

"You don't know what you're doing," she said, to herself or me or who knows who. "You don't know nothing at all."

She was right.

16.

Our hotel room in Washington was sleek and modern. The minibar was stocked with two cute cans of sparkling wine, chocolates, and local potato chips. You could tell Lucas was used to money because he always ordered room service and never thought twice before dipping into the minibar. He ordered us sandwiches and coffee and we quickly ate, drank, and got ready for our meeting.

I knew why Lucas wanted the book. He wasn't interested in testing the bounds of reality. Sex was common enough for him, and he didn't have to resort to an alchemical scheme to get it. He wanted the book because he didn't want to give this up—first-class flights, good hotels, meals in the best restaurants. He wanted money. And more than that, I suspected, he liked the sense of self that went with it. It was one of the few things I didn't like about him, but I wasn't sure how deep it went. And besides, I was happy to find things not to like about Lucas, reasons we would never really work as a couple—

he was too into money, he was too square for me, he wasn't creative. His flaws helped maintain distance between us. As of now I had no expectations for a future together after we found the book, and I didn't want to develop any expectations.

The Admiral lived on an upscale, tree-lined block in a nice part of town. We were eleven minutes late ringing his doorbell, which the Admiral used to great effect when he opened the door with a noticeable lack of a friendliness.

"You're late," Admiral Masters said in a stern voice. He was bald, Black, taller than Lucas, and wearing an immaculate uniform. I didn't know anything about the military, but later Lucas explained to me it was a dress uniform, worn for effect. Lucas was interested in things like that.

"I've been waiting," the Admiral went on.

"I apologize," I said. "We're flying back to New York tomorrow. If you ran out of time today, we can come back next month."

He frowned.

"No," he said. "Don't do that. Come in."

Lucas introduced us all as we went inside. The house was bland and dated. It looked like it had been expensively redone about twenty years ago and meticulously maintained since then. The Admiral walked us through a wood-paneled hallway, past a farmhouse-style kitchen with Mediterranean pottery on the counter and a spotless, chintz-upholstered living room, and into his office. The office was masculine and slightly ridiculous: a large dark wooden desk, big leather chair behind it, paintings of ships and horses on the walls, and two smaller chairs, for Lucas and me, in front of the desk.

We all took our assigned seats. The Admiral's chair was, unsurprisingly, a good half foot higher than ours. No beverages were offered.

"So what can we do for you?" I asked the Admiral.

"You know why you're here," he said. "I heard you have a copy of the book."

"Which book?" I asked.

"Don't play games," he said, clearly annoyed. *The Book of the Most Precious Substance.*"

The Admiral scowled. I saw a small smile start to play around Lucas's lips. He was seeing through the bluster and the uniform to see a man just like us: greedy and a little desperate. A man, maybe, we could use.

"Oh, *that* book," Lucas said. "We actually have a confidential client, and are not at liberty to—"

"Oh, shut up," the Admiral said. I laughed. He glared at me. "Everyone knows you're working for the Accountant. And everyone knows you have the book."

"We do not have the book," I said. "But we have access to it."

"Access?" the Admiral snorted. "Access? What kind of horseshit is that?"

"I don't know," I said. "I wasn't aware there were multiple types. I was under the impression that *you* had a copy for sale."

He scowled again. "My copy was stolen. I want it back. That's why you're here."

Lucas and I looked at each other and back at the Admiral. This was news to us.

"Who stole it?" I asked.

"The Whore," he said.

"Pardon me?" I said.

"Don't be coy," he said. "That won't work with me."

"Then stop dropping hints," I said, "and tell me who stole the book from you, and what you want from me."

The Admiral scowled again and stood up. I thought he was going to leave, but instead he started to pace around the room. He looked lost in thought for a moment, like he was making a decision. Then he stopped, presumably having decided, and looked at us.

"I'd like a cup of coffee," he said. Then he called out: "MARIA."

We heard a bustle, and a moment later a middle-aged, thin, put-upon-looking woman in sweatpants and a pilled cardigan and running shoes came in to the room. She raised an eyebrow at the Admiral.

"Coffee," he said. "For three."

Maria nodded and left.

The Admiral dropped some of his forceful, intimidating fakeness.

"Lady Imogen Southworth," he said. "You know who she is."

"I do not," Lucas said. I shook my head, equally ignorant.

"I don't believe you," the Admiral said. "But I'll indulge your little charade. Imogen Southworth is a…" He frowned, overwhelmed with the task of putting the Whore Lady Imogen Southworth into words. "She's a woman who lives in Paris. A lady. I mean, technically. She is *not* a lady in the colloquial sense of the word. You know, I presume, what the book is about?"

"Roughly," Lucas said.

Maria entered with coffee in plain white cups, a small white bowl of sugar cubes, and a paper carton of half-and-half on a tray. The Admiral stopped talking until she'd put the coffee on the desk and left. I took a sip of the coffee. It was weak and awful, like Nescafé.

The Admiral put three sugar cubes and a large pour of half-and-half into his cup.

"So you know about the acts," the Admiral said.

"We know the idea," I said.

"Well, then you can imagine our relationship," he said bluntly. He avoided eye contact, slightly embarrassed.

"Let's go back a little," I said. "How did you know each other?"

"Never mind that," the Admiral said quickly. "We had mutual goals: using unorthodox techniques to achieve certain metrics."

"That's the worst description of sex I've ever heard," I said. Lucas laughed. The Admiral did not.

"It isn't *entertainment*," he said. "It's a tool of warfare."

"So how did you say you met this whore?" I asked.

The Admiral glared at me. "There are some of us with certain interests who talk, mostly online. We aren't friends. There's no romantic imaginings here. We're…colleagues."

"Colleagues in what?" I asked.

"In power," the Admiral said, without hesitating. "That's the only thing we have in common. Power. We all want more of it."

"Why?" I asked.

"Why do *you* want it?" he shot back.

"That wasn't the question," Lucas said. "And we aren't looking for power. We're looking for money. We're book dealers. We're doing our job."

If the Admiral picked up on the dishonesty in Lucas's answer, he ignored it.

"I've devoted my life to the study of power," the Admiral said. "Not for myself. Power for good. For the good of our country, our government—"

"*And* yourself," Lucas interjected.

The Admiral looked at Lucas long and hard.

"People like you," the Admiral said, "don't know the meaning of the word *sacrifice*."

Lucas wasn't wounded. He knew exactly who he was: a man who was good in bed and good at picking out wine and was usually the smartest man in the room—he sure was now—and had likely never thrown a punch in his life.

"True," Lucas said. "So let's sum it up: You, a selfless scholar of power, want the book. We, craven booksellers, know how to get it. So if you seriously expect us to sell it to you, you need to get in our good graces. And the only way you could possibly make me like you at this point is to help me get the book. So I can sell it to the Accountant."

The Admiral swallowed his anger.

"There are two copies left," Admiral Masters said. "The Fool in Los Angeles and the Whore in Paris. I want the book," he said. "Whatever the Accountant is offering, I can top it."

Of course, we knew the Fool's copy wasn't complete. That meant one copy was left that even had a chance of being complete, and now we knew who had it: the Whore, Lady Imogen Southworth.

"I doubt that," Lucas said.

"Try me," the Admiral said. "Looks can be deceiving. But you can't let Imogen know I'm the buyer. She'd rather burn the book than sell it to me."

"Sell it to you?" I asked. "I thought she stole it?"

"You find the book," the Admiral barked. "Let me worry about the rest of it. You'll get a fee, don't worry."

The Admiral wrote Lady Imogen's name, email address, and phone number on a piece of paper and pushed it across the desk toward me. I took it.

"I expect to hear from you shortly," the Admiral said as we left. "Good day."

We went back to the hotel room and I immediately sent an email to the Whore, Imogen, at the address the Admiral had given me. All the excitement of the past few days was catching up with me. I was exhausted, but wired. I was staring at my phone, searching for the book for the four-hundredth time. Nothing new popped up. We went over the strange meeting with the Admiral. He certainly didn't seem to have half a million bucks lying around, and neither of us believed a word that he'd said. We didn't so much think he was lying so much as we were sure he was deranged.

"You need a massage," Lucas said.

"I don't like massages," I said.

"I don't believe you," Lucas said. He called the spa and in fifteen minutes a woman was knocking on our door. The truth was, I hadn't had a massage in years. I felt a little annoyed with Lucas and oddly protective of the quirks I'd developed over the years since Abel had been sick—defense mechanisms and poverty adjustments that I'd tried to mold into a personality. *I don't like massages. I don't want to wear makeup. Writing doesn't interest me anymore. I don't think about sex anymore. Nice things aren't important to me.*

The masseuse was named Nellie and she was a tiny, very strong woman of few words. She set up a table near the foot of the bed.

Lucas told me to go first.

In the bathroom I took off my clothes and put on the plush white hotel robe. In the bedroom, Nellie turned around discreetly as I took off the robe and slipped under the sheets of the massage table.

Lucas's phone rang.

"Can you take that outside?" Nellie said, annoyed and authoritative. "She needs to relax."

Lucas left to wander around the hotel. I lay facedown on the massage table. Nellie put her hands on my shoulders.

"You're incredibly tense," she said.

"I know," I said defensively. I wanted to say, *Let's see how fucking tense you'd be,* but I held back.

"It's not an accusation," she said. "It's an observation."

I tried to relax. She pushed and prodded. *I don't like massages,* I thought. *This is a waste of money. Is Lucas paying for this? Am I?*

She continued to knead and poke and I started to feel emotional, almost angry. *Why am I doing this? Why does Lucas think he knows what's best for me? Why does he—*

Then Nellie pushed deep into the left side of my neck and I felt a little sick, and suddenly I let go of something I didn't know I'd been holding on to for years. I felt tears come to my eyes. Whatever it was, it was hard to let it go.

"It's OK to cry," Nellie said. "You have a lot of dark energy. You need to let it out."

I couldn't have stopped if I'd wanted to. I was crying, hard, and I couldn't stop, as Nellie continued to work on my neck and shoulders. I was crying for myself, for Abel, for the utter fucking unfairness of life.

Lucas came back in.

"She's not done," Nellie snapped. "Go."

Lucas did as he was told. Nellie rubbed deep into the soft flesh where my skull met my spine and I cried fresh tears. I wasn't only sad—I was angry. I still felt lost in a dark, terrifying maze. And I was furious at the world for leaving me here.

But now, maybe, with the book, there was a way out.

She slowly wound down her massage and my tears subsided. Finally she was done.

"Thank you," I said.

"Drink water," she said. "Take care of yourself. I hope you feel better now."

I did. I took a hot bath while Lucas got his massage. When Nellie was gone, I came out of the bathroom. I was ravenous for Lucas.

"Don't put your clothes back on," I said. At the end of it we were spent and again we fell asleep naked and exhausted.

I woke up to the sound of someone banging on the door. It took me a minute to figure out what the sound was. Lucas was gone.

"Who is it?" I called out. "We don't need service."

The banging didn't stop.

"Police," a loud woman's voice yelled back. "Open the door immediately."

I sat up and threw on pajama bottoms and a T-shirt. Then I opened the door. Immediately.

It was a woman and two men, all in their forties, all in suits. The woman was Black and the two men were white. They brushed past me and came in the room. Each was armed, with guns bulging under their suit jackets. No one had their gun out.

"Sit," the woman said. She pointed at the table. I sat. She told me her name was Detective Frank. I told her I was Lily Albrecht. She told me she knew that already.

"Who else is here?" she said.

"Lucas. I mean, I don't know," I said groggily. "My friend is staying here with me, but I don't know where he is right now."

"Get her coffee," Detective Frank said judgmentally. One of the men called for room service. Detective Frank sat at the table with me.

"Admiral Mason Enterprise Masters was found stabbed to death in his house this morning at six a.m. Body was found by his housekeeper," she said, after coffee had been ordered.

"Holy shit," I said. "Maria?"

Detective Frank and the two men all looked at each other, as if to say, *See?*

"I was there yesterday," I said.

"I know," Detective Frank said. "Why?"

"I'm a book dealer," I said. "He asked me to come. He was interested in a book."

"What did you talk about?" Detective Frank asked.

"Books," I said.

"What else?" she said. They all looked at me with suspicion. No one would get on an airplane and go to someone's house to talk to them about *books*.

"The book," I said, "is worth half a million dollars at a minimum."

"Oh," Detective Frank said. The men nodded. They didn't understand books. Everyone understands money.

I told them a very short version of the story: Lucas and I were book dealers, a colleague died, we were helping fill some of his orders—for the good of his family, of course—and Admiral Masters, hearing we had a way to a very rare book, had called us to D.C. to make us an offer to fuck the other buyer and sell to him instead, although I had no idea how he planned to pay for it, and strongly suspected he planned to steal it, if I gave him the chance. While I told them about it, the coffee came. Detective Frank and I each drank two cups. The two men looked on. Apparently they were of a much lower rank and coffee wasn't in the cards for them.

"Would you say this is a common occurrence in the book world?" Detective Frank said.

"No," I said. "But not unheard of, either. There's probably a hundred books worth as much as this one, and when one is available for sale, it tends to generate drama."

"What's the book about?" she asked.

"War," I said. "Power."

"Like Machiavelli?" she asked. "They're nuts for that. That and the *Art of War*. Every scene in D.C. has a copy. *White* D.C.," she clarified.

"Scene?" I said.

"Murder scene," she said.

"Oh," I said. "Yeah, kind of like that."

Just then I looked up and saw Lucas in the doorway. He was holding two big cups that I guessed were lattes and a bag that likely held croissants. He looked, understandably, confused.

"My friend," I said. I gestured to Lucas.

Detective Frank turned around and looked at him. He looked good. She looked back at me with a raised eyebrow. She was impressed. Then I relaxed. I could tell she didn't really think we'd murdered anyone. She was just trying to put together the Admiral's last day.

"Hi," Lucas said. There was no situation his charm couldn't rise to. "Hello. What's going on?"

"Someone killed Admiral Masters," I said. The detectives looked at me, slightly annoyed. Apparently they'd wanted to say it.

"Admiral Masters was murdered at approximately four a.m. last night," one of the men said, reasserting control of information.

"Jesus," Lucas said. "We left there around six."

"She told us," Detective Frank said, *she* being me. "Come on in. Sit."

Lucas came in and sat at the table. He gave me my latte.

"Sorry," he said to Detective Frank. "I didn't know you'd be here."

"That's OK," she said. "I didn't expect you to bring me anything." But she looked at the lattes wistfully.

"Murdered," Lucas said. "Are you sure?"

"Well, he was stabbed in the back," she said. "So yeah, pretty sure."

"Jesus," Lucas said again. I felt sick. Until that moment, it had seemed abstract. Now it seemed very tangible and real. A man was dead, and it might, in some way, be related to me.

But how? Had Haber sent someone to take out his competition? Had the Whore heard we were looking for her book?

I thought about telling Detective Frank about how we'd been followed in Los Angeles. I looked at Lucas. Maybe he was thinking the same. If he was, we both silently decided against it. That would complicate things, and stand between us and the book.

"Does he have any family?" Lucas asked. "Who found him?"

"Never mind about that," Detective Frank said.

Maria, I mouthed. Lucas nodded.

The woman and men asked us more questions about what time

we came and left, if any money traded hands, if we knew anyone in common with the Admiral, and how he'd found us. We explained that we didn't know how he'd found us, and we answered their other questions as best we could. We were honest enough. We didn't have much to hide.

After another hour we gave them all of our contact information and we were done.

"Don't leave town for a few days," the woman said. "We might have more questions."

We said we wouldn't. Then, that afternoon, we got on a plane to New Orleans, and left town.

17.

New Orleans in March was clear and cool. Lucas booked us in a hotel in the French Quarter that was as modern as anything in New Orleans could be: In the Victorian lobby was a sleek desk with blue lights underneath and big, soft white chairs. In the hotel restaurant we had fried pickles, upscale po'boys, and iced coffees.

New Orleans was Lucas's idea. We were both freaked out by the Admiral's murder and whoever had been following us in Los Angeles. Maybe his death was related to the book, maybe not. Neither of us was so self-important as to think anyone was looking to murder *us* in particular. But still, it was getting a little spooky.

The next logical step was to fly to Paris and try to see Imogen, or stay in D.C., as we'd been asked. Instead, we bought last-minute first-class tickets to New Orleans, where Lucas had a book dealer friend—Paul Krakhour—he thought would likely have useful information about *The Book of the Most Precious Substance*. Lucas had texted with Paul on the flight to let him know we'd be coming.

We finished our po'boys and walked to Paul's place. New Orleans seemed like a movie set, or a location from a fairy tale. The light, the colors, the smells, the music—none of it seemed real, especially contrasted with the dreariness of my regular upstate existence. I'd been here before, once for my own book tour and once for Abel's. Abel's books, dense and hard to read, only sold a few thousand copies each, but he had a small, devoted club of fans who would show up anywhere to see him.

"Now, first," Lucas said as we walked out of the French Quarter and into the Faubourg Marigny, "I didn't really tell you about Paul. You're going to loathe him."

We both laughed. I liked that Lucas knew me well enough to know who I would loathe.

"Paul's from some suburb in New Jersey," Lucas said. "You know, malls and the Olive Garden. He's very dramatic. Talks a lot, and loudly. Drinks too much. But he has a good soul. Always picks up the check. Anyway, he's a book dealer, and a good one, specializing in religion, folklore, and magic. I've bought from him before for the library."

"So he knows about the book?"

Lucas had been texting with him throughout the day, and now another text popped up. He read it and reported back.

"Well," Lucas said, "he said he has a story for us. He's quite the storyteller."

"In a good way?" I asked.

"Mm," Lucas said, noncommittally.

Paul lived in a big, faded-blue rundown house outside the Quarter, peppered with seemingly dozens of strange additions and alternate doorways, each with jury-rigged wiring flowing around to the power lines above. Huge bushes I couldn't name sprouted up irregularly around the yard, and a giant live oak had sent its roots under the porch, causing a ripple in the floorboards. In New Orleans, nature was always in charge. We walked around the house, chose the door that seemed front-ish, and rang one of four doorbells. After a minute the door was answered by a young woman, maybe twenty-five, in a tie-dyed lace-trimmed slip that was a few sizes too big and slipping off her shoulders. Her hair was plain and she didn't wear any makeup except bright red lipstick. She smiled.

"Hi!" she said. She looked at Lucas. "Are you Hayden?"

"No," Lucas said. His cheeks turned a little pink. "Hi. We're here to meet Paul? I think he's expecting us?"

"Oh, sorry," the young woman said brightly. "Come in! I think Paul's in the kitchen."

The main layout, excluding the additions, was shotgun-style, one room leading to the next. The first room was a living-room type space cluttered with thrift-shop furniture, piles of books and magazines, and full ashtrays. But despite the obvious lack of money, it felt good. It looked like people actually lived here, and liked it.

A second room was designed entirely for sex. There was a large bed with a black satin fitted sheet on it, a few pillows, and bedposts with ropes already attached. Against another wall was a large frame with cuffs attached where a person might be affixed. Next to it was a dresser and above the dresser was a pegboard; hanging from the pegboard was a sex-shop-worthy assortment of paddles, crops, and the like. Unlike the rest of the house, this room was clean and neat.

The next room was a large dining room/work area—a big table took up most of the room and clearly served as communal workshop more than eating space. A man in his thirties, prematurely gray at the temples, in blue jeans and a black button-down shirt sat at the table, peering at a computer and frowning. He ignored us as we passed through the room into the big kitchen, messier and friendlier than the previous two rooms, where a man stood in front of a stove, stirring a giant pot of audibly bubbling red beans, and two women sat at a table, sharing a joint and chopping vegetables.

"Paul," Lucas said. The man stirring the red beans turned around and smiled broadly. He was maybe thirty-five, as were the women chopping vegetables, and he wore a silly outfit: pants with lots of pockets and loops, for a painter or carpenter, a T-shirt with suspiciously deliberate-looking holes in it, and no shoes or socks. He wore a porkpie-ish hat and had a mustache waxed into exaggerated perfection.

"Lucas!" he exclaimed. He came over and engaged in a complicated handshake with Lucas, and then a warm hug. Lucas seemed happy to see him. Seeing the person you were fucking talking to a stranger put that person in a sharp relief, as you saw them through this new person's eyes. With Paul, I saw a sweetness in Lucas I hadn't noticed before. I liked it.

"This is Lily, my friend and business partner," Lucas said. Paul gave me an enthusiastic handshake and introduced us to the two women at the table. The girl in the slip had gone. I noticed Lucas look around for her. In that, too, there was a kind of sweetness. Lucas obviously found the girl attractive.

"This is Caitlin and Rose," Paul said. Caitlin and Rose both smiled and waved. Rose, in a black dress, was slim and Black with dark skin and a perfect face of makeup under short, precise, hair; Caitlin, in a loose flowered top like a flour sack over ragged blue jeans, was chubby and white. They both, like Paul, had genuine smiles and something else, something I couldn't name—a shininess to them, a healthiness.

"Come," Paul said. "The books are in the guesthouse."

The kitchen had a back door and we all walked through the messy yard to a small house, about four hundred square feet, at the other end of the property. The small house was locked up well; it took Paul three keys to let us in, and I noticed all the windows were tightly gated.

Inside I saw why: It was a small, pristine, jewel box of a library, maybe five hundred books, each precisely shelved on dark wood bookshelves. In the middle of the room was a desk in the same dark wood with a laptop and stacks of more books on top. A few chairs and a few library carts, also full of books, took up the rest of the room.

The books themselves were extraordinary. Most were in three areas: New Orleansiana; books about books (always the booksellers' favorite); and magic of all kinds: witchcraft, hoodoo, voodoo, tarot, stage magic, and, most of all, sex magic. By now I recognized some of the names: Alice Bunker Stockham, Paschal Beverly Randolph.

Paul left us alone with the books for a few minutes while he went back in the house to make us a pot of tea.

"Wow," Lucas said.

"Wow," I agreed, looking around at the books. Then I realized we weren't talking about the same thing. I was talking about the books:

Lucas was talking about the girl in the slip and the room with the satin sheets.

"So what is this place?" I asked. "Some kind of a sex commune?"

"Yes," a voice behind me said. I turned around. Paul had reentered with a tray holding an iron teapot and three small ceramic cups.

"It is indeed a sex commune," Paul said, putting the tea down on the table. He shut and locked the door behind him before he went on: "Really, an intentional community. We call ourselves Krewe D'Amour."

"Soo..." Lucas asked, vaguely.

"So," Paul said, answering the unasked, obviously present question. "There are nine of us. We do as we please, but we have certain commitments to each other—kindness, care, radical honesty. If you want to leave, you leave, but if you stay, you really stay. No one tells anyone else what to do, beyond setting their own boundaries. We're very big on consent."

"Huh," I said.

"Huh," Lucas said.

"We're having a party tonight," Paul said. "Screened guests only. You're both welcome to stay if you like."

"Lucas would like to," I said quickly, before he could demure. "I'm a little tired. I might go back to our hotel."

"As you like," Paul said. Lucas looked at me. I shrugged. I knew he was into the girl with the slip, and I suspected he was fascinated by the whole place. For me, a sex party sounded good in the abstract, but pretty distasteful in the material realm—I was still slightly overwhelmed by kissing.

"So," Paul said. "*The Book of the Most Precious Substance*. As I'm sure you know by now, it's a real white whale—maybe three copies are left? People ask for it all the time. I always tell them to forget about it. It isn't going to happen. I know a little bit about it—"

"How?" I asked.

"Because it's a legend," Paul said. "And because I've seen it. As you likely know by now, Johann Van Welt owned a copy for years—"

"We do know," Lucas said. "The fire."

"Exactly," Paul said. "So this was a few years before that. A customer came to me about buying a copy. Specifically, he wanted me to make an offer to Johann. A very large offer."

"Was it Haber?" I asked. "Or the Admiral?"

Paul gave me a sharp, amused look and said, "The better part of bookselling is discretion. I think Oscar Wilde said that."

Haber, I mouthed to Lucas. He nodded.

"So," Paul went on, "Johann agreed to hear the offer, out of politesse. I sold him a lot of books, and the buyer, the want-to-be buyer, was in the same general social circles as Johann. I'm not sure if they actually knew each other, but they knew plenty of people in common. So he let me look at the book and authenticate it in person next time I was in Europe, which was a few months from then, and hear the offer."

Paul refilled our tea cups. He was easy to laugh at, with his silly pants and ostentatious sex life, but he was a good storyteller, and we were rapt.

"At the time Johann was a very, very wealthy man. He was not always very kind, and he has never been well liked. I would say he was lonely, but I'm not sure he wanted anyone around. His house looked like a mausoleum. Concrete floors, everything gray, not one photo or personal item anywhere. Like an unfinished hotel. His fortunes have diminished somewhat since then, although he's still doing fine. More than fine.

"As you've probably noticed"—Paul glanced around the room—"I am very, very into magic. So I wasn't going to let this book slip through my hands. They—Johann's guys—set me up in a room at Johann's with exactly one table, one chair, concrete walls and floors, and no windows. The first time I go to look at the book, I bring my cell phone and take a few pictures. Specifically, pictures of the symbols. There's a funny thing about the book—I'd always thought it was myth, but now I'm not sure. It doesn't seem to like being reproduced. It also doesn't seem to like being memorized. I usually have an excellent memory—magic encourages it. And I snapped a few pictures with my phone. For backup.

"So I get home that night, right away I try to draw the symbols while they're fresh in my mind, and somehow, they're not there. I had them firmly committed to memory and then they just…weren't. It was as if I'd been…not exactly drunk when I looked at the book, but as if I'd been under the influence somehow. Acid, DMT, something like that. So I get out my phone, open up to the pictures, and my phone dies. Immediately. I take it to the shop—it's dead, nothing can be recovered, and the photos hadn't been backed up yet.

"So the next time I brought in an actual camera, with a little memory thing in it. But the photos didn't come out. The pictures were there in Johann's house, then at home they weren't. Johann must have known what I was up to by this point. I'm sure there was surveillance in that room. Either he didn't care, or knew it wouldn't work. The third time, the last time—I was pushing my luck already,

I really had no need to see the book a third time—I brought two film cameras. Disposables. I knew this was my last chance with the book. Johann wasn't going to sell it, and he was indulging me by letting me come and look at it so I could promise my client I'd tried—and, of course, he knew I wanted to see it. But, honestly, I think he had another motivation too, which I'll get to in a minute.

"So on my last visit I took in the disposable cameras and shot two rolls. By now you won't be surprised to know that most of the pictures came out black—"

"Most?" I interjected.

"Most," Paul said, with a little smile. "We'll get there. So *most* of the pictures were black, and, again, I couldn't exactly remember most of what I'd seen. Now, here's why I really think Johann let me look at the book: The next day, he called me. He *never* called me himself. I always, always went through one of his employees. I met him in person maybe four or five times in the ten years I'd been selling to him. But I picked up the phone and there he was. He said he was calling to thank me for a special book I'd sold him, this old book on traditional French witchcraft. We chatted for a few minutes and he asked how I'd enjoyed *The Precious Substance*. Now, we talked about books, but we never talked about magic itself. That would have been—well, too intimate, I guess. We certainly weren't, and aren't, friends. So this was strange. I kept it very businesslike, thanked him for the chance to view it. And then he asked me all these detailed questions about the points. What did I think of the transcribing error on page fifty-two? What did I think about the repeated paragraph on page thirty-six? I have no idea if these points were accurate, by the way, because I remembered none of it, which I told him.

I was very honest. And of course that was the real reason he was calling—to find out my reaction to the book. He said something noncommittal like 'Yes, that happens,' and we got off the phone."

"You said most of the pictures didn't come out," I said. "Some did?"

Paul's face brightened. He'd been waiting for us to ask.

"One did," he said. From a drawer in his desk he pulled out a printed snapshot. It was a blurry, dark picture of a strange shape, built around a letter I'd never seen before. Underneath it was a word: ██████████ Above it was written *Et Semen Masculinum*. It was the seal and the word for the third step.

"Can we keep this?" Lucas said.

Paul shrugged. "No, but you can borrow it. Why not? It isn't doing me any good. Lord knows I've tried."

"What did you try?" I asked.

"The usual things," Paul said. "When you've been doing magic as long as I have, you know when something's happening. Nothing happened."

He handed the photo to Lucas, who stuck it in his jacket pocket. Paul went to make us more tea.

"It was Haber," I said, as soon as Paul left the room.

"Probably," Lucas agreed.

"Are we doing the right thing?" I said. "Selling Haber the book?"

"Better than the General," Lucas said. "Imagine him in the White House."

"You think that was where he was headed?"

"Oh yeah," Lucas said. "That would make it all worthwhile for him."

Paul came back in with the tea and we all talked book world

gossip for a while: who'd sold what and for what price; valuable books found in unlikely places; the occasional scandal of a stolen book or a disputed ownership or possible forgery. The sun went down while we were talking.

"Well," Paul finally said, "if you're staying for the party, stay. We'd love to have you. If you want to leave, now's the time."

Lucas looked at me with a little anxiety. Paul noticed it and suggested we enjoy the library for a few minutes and meet him in the house when we were done.

I didn't know what I wanted Lucas and me to be to each other. Thinking about the future brought on a wave of constricting anxiety, and I was avoiding it at all costs. I didn't think Lucas knew what he wanted either. But I knew what I didn't want: limits, routines, possessiveness.

"Stay," I told Lucas.

He frowned. "You really don't mind?" he asked.

"I really, really don't," I said.

"OK," Lucas said. He looked confused. Maybe even hurt. "If you're sure."

"I want to be your friend," I said. "Not your parole officer."

"What will you do?" Lucas asked, still uncertain.

"Walk," I said. "Get some air. Then eat and sleep. Enjoy the hotel room."

"OK," he finally said. "But call me if you need me. And you don't mind if I…"

Suddenly Lucas was shy. Sometimes doing things was easier than talking about things. Doing revealed less; talking exposed more, including the parts that could get hurt.

"I want you to," I said.

Lucas seemed relieved but still a little anxious. I told him to thank Paul for me and be home by lunch tomorrow so we could get back to work. We kissed and I snuck out through the yard to a side door to the street.

The sun was long down and I wasn't quite sure where I was. I knew I could take out my phone and get a map or a ride if I needed one, but for now I just walked in what I thought was the direction of the hotel. New Orleans was a tough town, and the neighborhood was shabby, but I felt an inarticulate sense of safety. Somehow ordinary street crime wasn't a concern. I made my way back to the Quarter and found myself on a loud, dirty block filled with neon and tourists. I turned as fast as I could and wandered until I found a smaller, quieter strip on Royal Street. A small restaurant in a lush, tropical courtyard drew my eye, and I got a table for one.

For ninety-five dollars I got a tasting menu. The first course was four fat, perfect, briny oysters. Next was a small plate with upscale versions of boudin and andouille sausage and local cheese from the north shore. Then étouffée and blackened catfish served with mirliton and okra, each a mix of traditional seasonings and moneyed, geometric presentation. After that was a small plate of (more) local cheeses with local varietal honeys drizzled on top, then (decaf) coffee with chicory and a thin slice of chocolate pecan pie for dessert.

After dinner I walked back to the hotel. The lobby restaurant had turned into a bar at night, and it was busy. I passed by it and took the elevator up to our room. The room was big, with two queen beds with crisp white sheets and layers of light cotton blankets. I checked out the minibar scene and the toiletry situation, both excellent.

Lucas knew good hotels, which I was rapidly learning to appreciate. From the minibar I popped open a bottle of beer, and in the bathroom I ran a hot bath with jasmine bath salts. I took a bath, drank the beer, washed and conditioned my hair, and got into a thick white bathrobe before I blew my hair dry, styling it straight and sleek, which I rarely did. I was developing gray streaks at my temples. I liked the streaks. I messed around with my hair a little, pulling it back in different styles. I remembered when I was a teenager, in one of our battered trailers or efficiency apartments, fooling around with my hair in the mirror, hoping I was pretty enough to have a different kind of a life.

I changed from the robe to a clean T-shirt and pair of clean underwear and got into bed. At home, I was almost never truly alone. Awe and Abel were always both there and not there at the same time, a constant, annoying hum that was neither real company nor real silence. The quiet in the hotel room felt indulgent and luxurious. I ate a chocolate bar from the minibar and went to bed and slept better than I had in years. I woke up at dawn, briefly, when Lucas came in and stumbled into the other bed, and then slept soundly until close to nine.

I made coffee. Lucas woke up when he heard the coffeemaker hissing.

"Kiss me," he said, still in bed, eyes shining.

"Why?" I said. "I mean, I don't need a reason. But you sound like you have one."

"I might know who the Prince is," he said.

"That is a good reason," I said, and kissed him.

Out of all the names on Shyman's list, the Prince was the last name still entirely unknown to us. We'd identified the Fool, the General, the Accountant, and, we were pretty sure, the Whore. But the Prince had been a mystery—until now.

I ordered room service—two orders of overpriced, irresistible eggs Benedict and fancy coffee—and Lucas told me about his night. He didn't tell me what happened with the girl in the slip, if anything. Instead, he wanted to talk about the book.

"Paul and I got to talking again. I ran through the list of possible buyers and sellers with him, and he knew all of them. Like Singleton said, there's not a lot of people who deal in this stuff. As soon as I mentioned the Prince, Paul immediately had two guesses. One was Mikael Ashtar. Do you know who he is?"

I shook my head.

"You wouldn't," Lucas said. "He's a hedge fund person, and a very big collector. He's also originally from Russia, and claims some relation to the royal family. As far as I know, he isn't so much into the occult as he is into rare Medieval and Renaissance. He was charged last year with basically robbing the hedge fund blind, but he got off with, like, community service. The other option is Franz Oldenburg. Him, you might know."

"I don't," I said. "Oh, wait. The artist? That guy? I do. We've actually met."

Franz was a man who, by fate or by design, had been around for some odd and important moments in cultural history. He was a dilettante who dabbled in painting, music, and writing, excelling at none of them but sometimes producing interesting work nonetheless. He'd had a piece in an infamous art gallery show in New York's Alphabet City in 1981 that also included Keith Haring and Basquiat.

A few years later, he wrote a book about ritual magic with Genesis P-Orridge that got published by a highly influential but short-lived counterculture publisher out of San Francisco. In the 1990s, he had a bit part as a Romanian gangster in a Jim Jarmusch movie, and in the 2000s, he started a small music label with Kim Gordon. He also, on the side, bought and sold rare musical instruments, early tube radios, and rare books.

I knew that Franz was rumored to have a minor royal title and was an avid collector of books on magic. I'd met him once or twice, briefly, but he hadn't crossed my mind as a possible buyer or seller, because I hadn't realized he bought in the realm of books Lucas and I were hunting for—six figures and up.

"Wow," I said. "Great job."

"I know!" Lucas said, smiling. "I'm already tracking down email addresses for both of them."

Breakfast came, we ate, and then Lucas looked at me with a funny crooked smile.

"What?" I said.

He went over to his jacket from last night and pulled out the photo Paul had given us. The photo of the symbol.

"The third step," he said.

"Oh!" I said.

The male seed was not a challenge to produce. But I enjoyed drawing it out of Lucas, teasing him as he'd done to me, tricking him this way and that, and bringing it all to the expected conclusion in a new and interesting way. There was a whole universe of sensations I'd forgotten I liked giving and forgotten I liked getting. Every man tasted different but they all had the same base flavor of skin and sweat and salt. I hadn't liked going down on men before Abel. On the rare occasions I provided, it was at best begrudgingly, at worst with malice. But I loved Abel and I loved his nether regions, a source of such joy for both of us: he was well formed, symmetrical, dusky mauve streaked with blue veins, pleasantly large without being painfully big. Lucas was both the same, of course, and entirely different. He was paler and bigger. His skin was as thin and soft as silk, and nearly as sensitive. All touch had to be controlled and intentional—any rough or sudden moves were likely to result in a little yelp of discomfort. Getting to know Lucas was like reading a new book with a surprising little twist on every page.

After, we both rushed to the photo, dabbing it with fluid and saying the word. As soon as Lucas finished the word, a moment after I did, I felt a strange, swirling blackness come over me, somewhere in between an orgasm and a faint. I stumbled back to the bed and lay down. Lucas sat on the floor where he was. In my mind's eye I saw a series of images that could have been memory or imagination or something else: a crying man; a fire in a small house; an unusual, curling, vine growing over a mossy rock; a woman's sex, bright pink, surrounded by thick dark hair, opened like a heart.

And then in the end, a woman's face again—the same woman I'd seen when we accomplished the second step, with the strange pointed hat. She looked as curious of me as I was of her. She smiled a little, as if I amused her.

After two or three minutes, the fugue passed. I sat up. So did Lucas.

"Whoa," he said.

"I know," I said. I looked at Lucas. A strange moment of lucidity came over me.

"What are we doing?" I said. "I mean that—I didn't imagine that. Something is really happening."

Lucas smiled and wrapped me back up in his arms and began roaming his mouth over my body again.

"That was the point," he said.

"But..." I began. I wasn't sure what my *but* was. *But reality isn't supposed to be like this. But this isn't how physics works. But magic isn't real, right? But I should be back home with Abel, but none of this is real, but I can't be doing this and this cannot be happening.*

But all of those *but*s were overwhelmed by Lucas's mouth, and then his hands, and I pushed all my questions aside. Over the days and weeks to come, I avoided them at all costs.

After, we lay in bed, not tired enough to sleep, too dazed to get up.

"I think I always had some weird association with books and sex," Lucas said. "Like they were linked together somehow."

"Aren't they?" I said, although I'd never really thought about it before. "I mean, *Playboy*, dirty paperbacks—that was what we had, right?"

"Yeah," Lucas said. "But it's more than that. When I was a kid, I couldn't actually figure out what sex *was* for, like, way too long." We both laughed. "I mean," he went on, "I kind of got that it was, you know, genitals mashing together in some way. And then, eventually, I got that the one goes into the other. But I couldn't figure out what would happen once it was in."

"Me too!" I said. "I would read romance novels about people thrusting and I didn't really understand what was thrusting where. Then I did, and I couldn't understand why it would feel good."

"What was your first sexual fantasy?" Lucas asked.

"Oh, God," I said. "It was from one of those books. This woman was kidnapped and tied up and forced into, like, some very vague state of pleasure. I didn't understand it, but it made me, you know, feel things."

"I was lonely as a kid," Lucas said. "I didn't really connect with other kids. No one in my family was very warm at all. So I didn't have any of the normal...*Penthouse* in the woods, spin the bottle, birds-and-bees talks—I didn't do any of that. But my father had a copy of this utterly filthy book of Victorian erotica. Like so filthy, it was way too advanced for me. I liked it. I *loved* it. But I really didn't understand any of it. There was a lot of, like, anal stuff. And a lot of people tricking each other into fucking, which was...interesting. There was one story where this guy convinced his sister to sit on his lap, and then slowly, over hours, worked his hand into her skirts, then up her thighs, and then finally got one finger into her pussy. And I just couldn't figure out—what was the finger doing there? Why would either of them enjoy that? God, I just remembered, I stuck my finger in my mouth to see what it felt like. I thought it might feel the same. I got absolutely nothing out of it. It was all just this big frustrating mystery.

"Then," Lucas went on, with some amusement and a little drama, "I found *Wicked Wives*. A newsstand near my school had a whole rack of these dirty paperbacks, and I finally worked up the nerve to buy one."

"Oh!" I said. "That sounds exciting."

"It was terrible," Lucas said. "Truly an awful book. Two suburban families and the wives and daughters were, like, just fucking everyone. Just sex crazed. But there was this one scene…It was really gross, actually. It was this adult man deflowering his neighbor's daughter. She was eighteen but it was still…ugh. That's not— I mean, I don't—"

"I know you're not into teenagers," I said. "It was a scene in a book."

"Yeah," he said. "Yeah. I would never, ever…But the thing about this scene, in this book, is, before he fucked her—they were in the woods, oddly enough, it had started off as kind of a hike—he explained to her, step by step, exactly what he was going to do. The conceit was that she'd been in a Catholic school or something and had no idea what sex was and had never even seen a dick before. So he explained…like, he was stroking his cock and he explained that, and then got into some foreplay with her, and explained all that, and then when they got to the actual fucking, he went into, like, exhaustive detail. *Exhaustive.* And…it was actually kind of a funny moment. I was maybe eleven. And it all just fell into place. For the first time, I got it. And I jerked off, to full completion, for the first time. Like, immediately, while I was still reading."

We both laughed again.

"And then," he went on, "in the book, the girl had this, like, spectacular orgasm. She was screaming and she was begging him for more. He made her come two or three times. After he fucked her, she was entirely his. I think she used those words: *entirely yours.* It made an impression on me. Both that you could kind of…not control women, but have *some* control over them, have some power over them, if you were good at sex. Just for a minute, they could be entirely yours. And that books were kind of like, like where sex lives.

Even after we got cable a few years later and I saw *Red Shoe Diaries* and *Emmanuelle in Space* and all that, I still had this idea in my head that books are where all the real sex stuff is. All the secret wisdom no one will tell you. This whole current of underground, important, very precise information about sex lived in these hidden books on the back of people's bookshelves. The movies seemed very fake, and the books seemed very real."

"And so you became a librarian," I said.

Lucas laughed. "Of course," he said. "Who wouldn't? It wasn't just the prurience, the horniness, of it. It was this idea that books contained secrets. Important information that would be lost if someone didn't preserve it. And then I studied history and got really into that and I realized that was true not just about sex but lots of things. If someone doesn't care about books, shit gets lost. And *then* I became a librarian. And archivist."

I'd thought we were done for the afternoon but he rolled over and rolled on top of me again, very ready to re-engage.

"I want to make you entirely mine," he said. "Just for a minute."

"I'm yours," I said. "Entirely yours."

For now, we both knew was the unspoken coda. *For now.*

Sometime after two we got up and got dressed, planning on wandering around the city for the day while we plotted out our next step. But as soon as Lucas checked his email, we changed our plans. Someone had passed on his request to Franz Oldenburg, our possible Prince, and Franz had written back almost immediately.

"Holy fuck," Lucas said. "Oh my God."

"What?" I said. "What?"

"He has a copy of the book," Lucas said. "Listen: *Hello, Lucas. Of course I know you by name and I believe I've met Lily in person a few times. I prefer to keep it under wraps, but I do indeed have a copy of* The Book of the Most Precious Substance. *If you're going to be in Munich anytime soon, you're welcome to come by and take a look at it. In either case, give Lily my best.*"

The email had come in, of course, just as we were completing the third act.

18.

We flew business class from New Orleans to Amsterdam, and then again from Amsterdam to Munich. On the flight I felt as bubbly as the champagne we ordered, fizzy and extravagant. Like the other airports I'd been to in Europe, the airport in Munich was modern and clean and deeply confusing. The cab ride into the city was a blur. Lucas had booked us a last-minute room at one of the better hotels in the city, a stately Beaux-Arts-ish behemoth that took up a large city block and had a multitude of shops and restaurants, a bowling alley, and a small movie theater under its roof. I'd never been to Munich before and I didn't realize that it was a wealthy little city, a distinctive mix of high-end shops and spooky old churches and cobblestone alleys. The hotel felt grand and royal. A big Middle Eastern family with a colossal set of Vuitton luggage was checking out as we checked in. A sixty-ish woman in a full emerald-green evening gown stood with a glass of wine by the elevators, waiting for someone or something, annoyed and unhappy.

Once you had rent and food covered, all the money in the world couldn't bring you what mattered. But it sure as hell could make life without it easier.

After some further back-and-forth, Lucas had found out Franz was house-sitting for a friend and we were welcome to "pop on in for a drink" if we wanted to see the book.

"But did he actually say it was for sale?" I asked as we cleaned up and changed in our hotel room.

"People like him don't say things like that," Lucas said. "They say, 'Pop on in for a drink,' then you make an offer, then they pretend not to need the money, then you offer more and more and finally they pretend they're doing you a favor by accepting."

"So this happens to you a lot," I observed.

"Yes," Lucas said. "Strangely enough, it does. It's a pretty ordinary part of acquiring books. Rich people never want to admit they need money."

There was a paradox in there, but it wasn't worth trying to tease out. Instead, we talked about where Franz's copy of the book might have come from. It could be the copy the Whore stole from the General, if she'd sold it. It could be Johann Van Welt's copy, if the rumor mill was wrong about the book having been destroyed in the fire. Or maybe there was another copy, one no one knew about until now. It happened often enough with older books—a book might be found in an attic, or a bookstore, wrapped in the wrong binding on a shelf, even in a garbage dump.

In one of the many restaurants in our Munich hotel we got coffee and a plate of cheese, cured meat, pickles, and olives. This particular restaurant was a bright, sunny café with a few marble-topped tables, black and white tile floors, and layers of frothy, wedding-cake plaster trim around the top of the dusty white walls. I ate most of the snacks while we talked about Franz. I didn't know much about him. Was he a rich man who dabbled in the life of an artist, selling the things he collected as it amused him, or a poor man who had a title and knew rich people, wheeling and dealing in cultural artifacts to survive? Ordinarily, I wouldn't care. But if he had the book, we wanted it, and I didn't want to pay a penny more than necessary.

We had a few hours to kill, so we took a meandering walk around the center of Munich. There was a charming, highly Germanic open-air market in the center of town where people sold meat, flowers, fish, and honey. Less charming was a Starbucks, although I was happy to get another coffee. Wealth in Europe meant American trinkets, even if, like coffeehouses, they'd been imported from Europe, Americanized, and exported back. We walked around with our American coffees.

"Do you miss home?" I asked Lucas, Starbucks in hand. "Don't you need to get back?"

Lucas had an expression on his face I couldn't quite place—thoughtful, maybe a little sad.

"Not really," he said. "Which is kind of depressing." He laughed. "I wrote the library last night. I'm taking two more weeks off."

He thought for a moment, drank his drink, then said: "I don't know. I thought that was the life I wanted. Cool job, apartment in the city, Zabar's on Saturday, dim sum on Sundays. You know that life. That big New York life. You find your little corner of the city and put down roots. But now that we're here, I feel like...like that wasn't even real. Like for the past twenty years, I haven't even really been alive."

I knew what he meant. Every day, life was brighter and easier. It was like walking out of a dull, drab movie and into a technicolor reality. At the time, I chalked it up to excitement.

I don't now.

"I mean, I know I've been lucky," Lucas rushed to add, instantly sympathetic to the comparison of his somewhat charmed life to mine. "But it's like the past few years—fuck, maybe the last fifteen years—was this long, like, delusion. Get up, gym, work, date, cooking, home. I guess now I feel like: *Why?*"

"Why what?" I asked.

"Why any of it," he answered. "Why did I think living this unattached life in New York was some kind of fucking prize? Why did I take my job so seriously? Why did I never let anyone…It's like I was playing a game, and got lost in thinking it was real. But I don't want to play that game anymore."

We shivered in the German cold. Lucas put an arm around me and pulled me close.

Finally it was time to meet Franz. We walked about a mile out from the town square to an elegant townhouse across the street from a cemetery older than most cities in America, looked around for a doorbell, eventually finding one above Lucas's head next to the door, and rang. In a moment Franz answered with a surprisingly genuine smile. Franz wore black trousers, black motorcycle boots, and a clean white button-down shirt with faded paint stains in different shades of blue.

"Lucas, Lily," Franz said with a wide smile. He hugged me as if we really knew each other, even though we'd only met a few times, both years ago. Franz had a genuine, utterly natural way of connecting with people. It was quickly clear how he'd so often ended up in the right place at the right time. Not only was he charming, but as much as I was inclined to mock Franz's knack for minor celebrity, there was genuine heart in his work—a digging for emotion and truth that I couldn't help but respect, even if it didn't always work. I still remembered a video piece he'd made in the nineties in which he kissed one person after another—it wasn't sweet at all, but disturbing and a little scary. I thought it was brilliant.

Franz invited us in. We walked through a small courtyard into the townhouse beyond. The house was at least a hundred years old, maybe much more, but the interior had been renovated into a spare, modern space of concrete floors and blond wood. We walked into a large, bright parlor and kitchen on the ground floor that was clearly intended for guests. I figured we wouldn't be invited into the rest of the house, and we weren't. We sat in uncomfortable but beautiful Mies van der Rohe chairs upholstered in white leather around a low, strangely shaped table with a marble top. There, on the table, on a clean white cloth, was a book in familiar pale binding. But the title did not read *The Book of the Most Precious Substance*. Instead it read *Porcus Germaniae Historica*, which meant something like *The History of the Agricultural Pig*.

"May I?" I asked. Franz nodded and I opened the book. The frontispiece and the familiar illustrations made it clear no one was interested in farming pigs here. It was a re-bound copy of *The Most Precious Substance*. Rebinding a book like this—sex, heresy, other forbidden fruits—certainly wasn't unheard of. Then, as now, people both wanted and needed to keep their proclivities to themselves.

"So where did it come from?" I asked.

Franz leaned back and crossed his legs with an amused smile. He was slightly, pleasingly, effeminate in the way a lot of men in the art world are—confident enough in his sexuality, whichever direction it wandered in, to cross his legs at the thigh and gesture loosely with his hands, with no compulsion toward leg-spreading or fist-pumping.

"Well," Franz said, "in Europe, it isn't so uncommon to have an exalted title." He waved his hand in the air modestly, demeaning his pedigree. "So in my family, it was my uncle, my father's brother, who ended up with the title. Archduke of something no one cares about, and along with that comes a house with broken plumbing and some land. No money, sorry to say. Not anymore. At one point the house had some very valuable art and whatnot in it, but the grandparents and great-uncles sold that all a long time ago, mostly before the war. What was left, though, were a few of the books. All the obvious ones were long sold, of course, but they kept what they thought of as curiosities or family heirlooms. So last year, I'm at the house for a big wedding—not one of ours, we'd rented it out, and my uncle is a little old to deal with those people in the house, so I came to help. I was looking through what was left of the books, which of course I'd looked at before, when I pulled one off the shelf I'd never really noticed. You can see why. But for some reason I picked it up, took a look through—honestly, I thought there might be some nice illustrations of pigs and, well, here's something much nicer than pigs. As far as I knew, no one in my family was much interested in magic. But I guess someone in the family tree was a little more interesting than I thought."

"Do you believe in it?" I asked.

"Magic? Yes. This book? No," Franz said. "No. I did the first few acts with a friend. Nothing happened."

"So you'd be willing to part with it?" Lucas jumped in, always understanding an angle when he saw one.

Franz tilted his head to one side. *Maybe.*

"I prefer to keep my collection useful and beautiful," Franz said, and we all smiled in acknowledgment of his William Morris quote.

"Well, we have a very generous buyer," Lucas tossed out, with strategic nonchalance, as if none of us could ever actually need money, but as long as it was lying on the ground, we may as well pick it up. "So if you've ever considered it, now might be a good time."

Franz tilted his head again.

"And frankly, you'd be doing me a huge favor," I improvised, enjoying the excitement of the moment, the opportunity to persuade, to prove myself in a minor way. "If I can get this book for my buyer, it'll catapult my business to a whole other level. Which, honestly, I could use."

Franz smiled. We'd appealed to his ego, but I also sensed a genuine desire to be useful.

"And the offer would be...?" Franz asked.

"I think we can easily get you a half million dollars," Lucas said. "Very possibly more."

Franz moved his head from side to side again and then finally up and down, nodding assent. He asked Lucas more details about wire transfers and exactly when the payment might come and what currency it would be delivered in. I had no idea if the questions were important or not, never having handled so much money before, but

Lucas seemed to have anticipated them and had pleasing, convincing answers.

After the last question Franz was silent for a long moment, thinking about it or pretending to.

"Very well," he finally said, and smiled. "When you deliver the money, you have a deal."

Lucas and I looked at each other. We were both smiling. It was a clear, purely happy moment, so much so that for a moment everything else fell away: the still-to-come hassles of arranging the sale, my husband at home, what this would mean for me and Lucas, and the fact that I hadn't even really examined the book itself.

I hadn't examined the book. I'd glanced at it, but that wasn't enough.

I caught myself and looked back to Lucas, and then to Franz.

"May I examine the book?"

"Of course," he said. He gestured to it.

I stood up off my chair and sat down on the floor next to the table. I was so used to handling rare books that it was easy for me to get lost in it, and I didn't think about how ungainly I must have looked standing up and crouching down again, only to hunch over the book, touch it, and squint at it.

With each book being handwritten and hand-bound, and only a few copies to begin with, there were no specific points to look for, no telltale signs of it being real or fake. If I was looking at a first edition of *The Great Gatsby*, I would have looked for one of a number of specific typos (the most famous: "sick in tired" instead of "sick and tired" on page 205). You couldn't fake it, not well enough to pass a good inspection. But with *The Precious Substance*, each copy would be a little different. So authentication would be more intuitive and subjective.

So I wasn't looking for anything in particular. I was just looking. The front matter was like the other copy I'd seen, which was a good sign. I gently turned the first few pages. Nothing jumped out at me: the paper felt right, looked right, and smelled correct. The ink looked perfect.

All of it looked good. Now it was time for the specifics. I opened the book to the first page again. I couldn't read Latin *per se*, but I knew enough French and Spanish to muddle my way through the frontispiece and see that it basically said what it was supposed to say, which was the long version of the title.

Lucas's Latin was a little better than mine, so I called him over to the book.

"I'm going to turn the pages," I said. "We're both going to look, and you're going to read."

Lucas nodded.

"The whole book?" Franz asked.

"He's just going to skim," I said.

I was turning from page four to five when Lucas told me to stop. "What?" I said.

He looked at me and shook his head.

"I'm sorry," Lucas said to Franz. "I'm sure you didn't know this, but this book isn't *The Book of the Most Precious Substance*. It's a beautiful book, and it's probably nearly as old as that. But it isn't the book."

Franz frowned.

"The word for the second step," Lucas said, respectfully. "It's wrong."

I hadn't noticed, but now that Lucas said it, I saw that he was correct. I couldn't have told you exactly what the correct word was, but this wasn't it. This one had a *p* in it, which I was almost sure the real word didn't have. And it was short—the real word, whatever it was, was much longer.

"How do you know?" Franz said.

"We know," Lucas said.

Franz gave us a funny look—a little amused and a little angry and a little knowing and a little something I couldn't place. A little something that made me worried that someday, somehow, this would come back to bite me in the ass.

"I see," Franz said, nodding his head graciously. The funny look was gone, as if it had never been there, replaced by a friendly half-smile. "Are you sure your client wouldn't be just as happy?"

"He's pretty knowledgeable about the book," I said. "I don't think that would work."

"But thanks for letting us look at it," Lucas said. "We know how busy you are."

Later, when we compared notes, we realized that for some reason Lucas and I both felt a little scared in that moment. It wasn't so much that we thought Franz would actually hurt us. But for that quick second, anything seemed possible. We both realized we were in the house of a strange man trying to sell us a fake book for a substantial piece of money.

But the moment passed, and Franz straightened out his smile and stood up. We did the same. Franz extended a hand and we all shook.

"I'm not sure you're correct," Franz said. "But all for the best. Perhaps I'll keep it after all."

"It's a beautiful book," I said. "You really should."

"Indeed," said Lucas. We all smiled again and said cheerful good-byes and Lucas and I left. We had the rest of the day free in Munich, so we did what we'd discovered we both like to do in foreign cities: walk nowhere in particular.

"Wow," I said, as soon as we were safely a few blocks away.

"Whoa," said Lucas. "Do you think he knew?"

"I don't know," I said. "What do you think?"

"I think he knew," Lucas said, "and he was hoping we wouldn't know. I sure as shit don't think it was a family heirloom. What a fucking scene." He took a deep breath and then said: "I want to eat something very, very German for dinner."

But it was too early for dinner, and after walking a few miles we found ourselves in a park with a magical, improbable outdoor beer garden with a Chinese theme, under the shadow of a three-story wooden pagoda. It was cold out, but the offer of German beer and hot, fresh pretzels was too generous to pass up. The beer was served in colossal mugs. We each went through one and then another, leaving us a little drunk. We sat next to each other on a bench at a picnic-style table and kissed in between sips of beer and bites of pretzel. In between kisses and bites and sips, Lucas pulled back and looked at me appraisingly.

"You look different," he said.

I did. Earlier that day I'd finally bought some new clothes at a cheap chain shop near the hotel: a few tops that weren't T-shirts, a bright green sweater, a pair of jeans that fit, a leather jacket, on sale, and a new pair of boots. It wasn't much, but altogether it was more than I'd spent on clothes in the past year. And my body felt lighter and less rigid. I could see it and I could feel it. My face felt open and closer to a smile than the scowl I'd had for the past few years.

"I think I'm good for you," Lucas said teasingly.

I smiled but I didn't say anything. He was at least a little bit right. I liked Lucas, and I liked everything we were doing together—traveling, looking for the book, walking, eating, having sex. And, maybe most of all, talking. Talking, laughing, cheering each other on. I'd been so alone that I'd thought it was just the feeling of life when it went on too long.

Lucas was turning out to have more to him than I'd imagined. He was thoughtful in a way that I'd first assumed was manipulative, but now I knew was a genuine, simple desire to make life fun by making the people around him happy. He was always ready to detour down an interesting-looking street or into a new restaurant or to try a new plan. He wasn't stupid, but he was optimistic and effective and confident that he could get done whatever needed to be done, which made him fun to do things with.

But I still wasn't sure I trusted him. I knew Lucas cared for me, and I was starting to believe him when he said he'd liked me long before the book came along. I had been in a kind of hallucinogenic depression, I now saw, where my heart had been so broken that I couldn't see any possible good in life.

And I didn't think Lucas was a bad person. I just wasn't convinced he was a good person, either. I suspected that if he had to choose between me and a stack of money, he'd choose the money. His life was dominated by, and determined by, his desires and comforts. He wanted a certain lifestyle more than he wanted any specific achievement or particular person.

Or maybe that was another protective lie. I looked at Lucas. He looked different too. His eyes were brighter, his shoulders more relaxed. At the time, I stupidly thought the changes in us were good. A mark of health.

Now I know better.

"I think it's the food," I finally lobbed back in the Chinese-German beer garden, with a smirk that made me look more confident than I was. "I needed to fatten up a little."

Lucas, always quickly intuitive, changed the topic.

Life for the past few weeks had been a bubble, suspended high above the everyday—but at some point, that bubble would burst and I'd come back down to earth. Maybe I would crash down with less than I started with. Maybe I'd float down with half a million dollars in the bank and a relationship with Lucas that pleased without confining—or imposing. Either way, it was going to end.

I felt a familiar anxiety start to rise. I pushed it away. Today we were in Munich. The future would come whether I worried about it or not. After more kissing and beer we decided on room service for dinner, and made our way back to the hotel.

19.

We flew to Paris three days later. I'd been in so many time zones over the past week, time itself had stopped making sense. Was it a.m.? p.m.? Tuesday? Thursday? What, exactly, had happened to Wednesday? The result was a happy mild delirium, as if Lucas and I were above clocks and calendars, rock stars on a spontaneous European tour.

In Paris we slogged through the airport and into a cab. I didn't quite grasp that we were in Paris until we drove into the city. It was early morning, and the sun came up as we reached the hotel in the Latin Quarter.

The hotel Lucas had picked was European-old and Parisian-elegant. The room had a large bed, a small closet, and just enough room for both of us to stand up at the same time. After bumping into each other for fifteen minutes we resolved to take turns getting dressed: I sat on the bed while Lucas showered and changed, then he waited in the lobby while I did the same.

I'd been trying to get in touch with the Whore Lady Imogen Southworth ever since the General gave us her information. According to the deceased General, she had his copy of the book, which as far as we now knew was the only complete copy. Lucas and I both agreed I was the better ambassador, and I'd emailed twice and called once with no response. Seeming too aggressive might shut the door once and for all. But she was the only lead we had, so after a few days in Munich, we decided to fly to Paris, where she lived, and hope for the best.

We went for a short, disorienting walk for coffee and a croissant. When we came back, we both sat on the bed and I called Imogen's number again. We'd both made a few calls and done some internet searching to find out what we could about her. Lady Imogen Southworth had first been in the tabloids at twenty-one, as the wife of an older, wealthy rock musician who was rumored to dabble in the occult. When he died from an overdose, Imogen was questioned by the police, though ultimately released. There were rumors that she'd killed him for his money. She did profit handsomely from his will, which doubled her already-generous inheritance. Imogen next showed up in the public eye when, at thirty, she bought a well-known occult bookstore not far from our hotel. She also started a small publishing arm to reprint famous occult works: John Dee, Austin Osman Spare, Marjorie Cameron, and of course Crowley. According to the internet, she was now in a magical triad relationship with the painter and channeler Frieda Heinz and artist Arjun Banks. I'd never heard of either of them.

As far as we knew, there was only one copy of the book left, and she had it.

This time, Imogen answered her phone on the first ring.

"Hello," I said. "Hi. My name is Lily Albrecht, and—"

"Lily Albrecht!" said a bright, loud voice with a British accent. "I've been meaning to call you back. So sorry to make you wait. I love your book. And we know thousands of people in common. Including your husband. I knew him back in San Francisco."

"Oh, wow," I said. I hadn't been expecting that. For a moment I felt jarred out of my European dream and back in my dreary everyday life, with Abel's ugly illness blocking out any possible sun. But as soon as Imogen, with her crisp accent, talked again, it passed.

"Jesus, I miss him," she said. "But that's not why you called."

"No," I said. "I'm also a book dealer, and—"

"So I've heard!" she said. "I hoped it wasn't true. I want you to write another novel. Stop with this bookselling bullshit and get back to work!"

Another time this might have made me furious. *Doesn't she know how hard my life is? Does she think I want this?* But she clearly meant well. I'd written something, years ago, and it was still out in the world, meeting people. Maybe a little like *The Precious Substance*.

"Well," I said, "I, I mean, Abel...Maybe someday."

"Look at me, being a cunt again," Imogen said, sensing my discomfort. "I just do love your work. Why are you calling? What can I do for you?"

"It's about a book," I said. *"The Book of the Most Precious Substance."*

"Oh, right," Imogen said. "You said that in your email. What do you want to know?"

"Everything," I said.

"Are you in Paris?" she asked. "Come over tonight. No, not

tonight. Not tomorrow. Not the next day. No, Friday. Friday is actually perfect. Actually, what?"

I heard muttering in the background.

"Tonight!" Imogen said again. "Is that OK? Around seven or eight."

"It's perfect," I said. "Thanks. I'll see you then."

"Bye," Imogen said, after giving me the address. "Oh no—wait. Wait."

I heard muttering in the background again, and a few loud voices.

"Frieda says the spirits have something for you," Imogen went on. "Frieda says the spirits say—what's that? What? Oh, OK. The spirits say: Don't be late, you don't want to miss the champagne."

Success. Lucas and I celebrated with a quick roll around in bed before we started to get ready for dinner. Lucas got great joy out of bringing other people pleasure. At first I'd assumed that for every act of satisfaction he'd expect reciprocation. And of course, there were times I was as eager to please as he was, and he certainly never stopped me. But reciprocation was never the goal. And Lucas had a deep knowledge of, and fascination with, the strange, broad, and varied ways women's bodies could experience pleasure. I'd met men like him before—it was almost a synesthesia or psychic empathy with the object of their efforts. It was also a way of exerting power over whoever he was in bed with, directing and fine-tuning their experience, pushing his partner up to and past their boundaries, controlling exactly what they would feel and when.

But we still hadn't generated the Precious Substance. I'd never made it before and I wasn't sure if I could.

After, I took a long bath. When I got out, Lucas was still naked, sleeping in bed. I told him it was time to get ready and he made a sound in between a moan and a grunt. Excitement and jet lag and sleeplessness were all catching up with him.

"I'm getting up," he said. "Just one more minute."

I kissed his cheek.

"Stay," I said. "Sleep. I'll be fine alone."

"You sure?" he said. "You won't feel weird?"

"Going to the house of a famous, vaguely titled sex magician to beg for a million-dollar book?" I answered. "I mean, I wouldn't feel particularly less weird if you were with me."

We both suspected that Imogen would be more willing to sell to me than Lucas, anyway—we had much in common; she and Lucas, nothing. But Lucas was anxious about me making a deal without him, for good reason: I'd never bought a book for more than maybe two thousand dollars before. We both agreed that I'd hold off until tomorrow for an offer if the book looked good. But just in case I was put on the spot, Lucas gave me a short lecture on negotiating: be respectful; offer fifty percent less to start; don't nickel-and-dime; remember that compliments are highly persuasive; don't hesitate to say you need to think about it.

"Got it," I assured him.

"And call me," he said. "Just put me on speakerphone and it'll be like I'm right there."

"I will," I promised.

Lucas promptly fell back asleep. I finished my makeup. I hadn't done a full face in a few years, but a little lipstick and blush and eyeshadow wouldn't hurt. I looked in the mirror. Not so bad. I left my hair alone and dug around in my suitcase for something to wear.

I found a black slip dress I hadn't worn in years. Wrinkled, but it would do. I wore it with tights, my new leather jacket, and a pair of ankle boots.

Lucas gave me a deep, long kiss and firmly grabbed my ass before I left.

"Something to remember me by," he said.

"You weren't at risk of being forgotten," I said.

Imogen lived in an apartment in the Marais neighborhood. I took a taxi. Driving through Paris in the evening was beautiful and surreal. Like nearly every building in the city, Imogen's was simultaneously older and shabbier than anything in America and far more elegant. I was buzzed in and walked up three flights of wide art nouveau stairs to Imogen's apartment. The door was closed. I knocked for half a minute or so before someone answered.

The person who answered was a man in his late thirties. He was British, of Indian descent, and spoke with a clipped London accent. He wore a three-piece suit with a wrinkled shirt and no shoes. His hair was thick and wild and black with streaks of gray.

"Hello. You must be Imogen's friend."

"I think," I said.

"Come in," the man said. "I'm Arjun."

I followed Arjun into the vast, messy apartment. The ceilings were fifteen feet or higher. Full-to-the-brim bookshelves lined the walls, with stacks of more books in front of them, paperbacks mixed with first editions mixed with rare art books I recognized from across the room and even rarer occult texts I didn't know but smelled like money. The furniture was from every era: a Victorian velvet sofa in emerald green, a modern Lucite coffee table, a white seventies egg chair hanging from the ceiling. In the middle of the giant room was a dinner table set for four with candles; lighting them was a Black woman about the same age—maybe thirty-five—wearing a long white dress. The woman looked at us and smiled. Her hair was expansively curly and she had an appealing gap between her front two teeth and big bright brown eyes.

"That's Frieda," Arjun said, as he walked into the kitchen. "Drinks?"

"Sure," I said.

"Hello," Frieda said. "I'm glad you're here. The spirits said it's going to be an interesting night."

Just then Imogen appeared from another room. "I try to make every night interesting," she said. "But I think Frieda is right. Tonight will be special."

Imogen wore slim black pants, a black jacket, and a funny little hat, like a tiny top hat, that was maybe the most British thing I'd ever seen. She had on red lipstick and her black hair was wavy and loose around her face. There was an electric energy around her. She had a huge smile that seemed not just genuine but inspired. She was at least fifty. Her teeth were crooked and she had crow's-feet wrinkles around her eyes, but she brought the same feeling with her that a rambunctious child would: slightly overwhelming, but full of possibilities and full of life.

She came over and hugged me. "Lily Albrecht. What a treat to have you here. Did someone get you a drink? Arjun, get her a drink."

Arjun came over with our drinks, champagne cocktail in flute glasses. Arjun's hand brushed mine when I took the glass, and he watched me as I took a sip. I tried to identify the taste. Sweet, but also a tiny hint of something bitter. Earthy.

"Berries?" I guessed.

"Brilliant," Arjun said. I never knew what British people meant by that.

"And…I don't know," I said. "Not to be rude. But it tastes like dirt."

Everyone laughed.

"You're perceptive," Frieda said. "Mushroom tea. Just a drop in each glass."

Of course, I knew what kind of mushrooms she meant. Frieda, Imogen, and Arjun laughed. I drank it.

Arjun came and took my glass.

"Refill?" he said.

"Why not?"

We sat down to dinner. Arjun served. I wondered who in this strange, merry family might cook: The answer was no one. Dinner was an assemblage of store-bought snacks: pâté, olives, a plate of cheese, smoked fish, tiny champagne grapes, compact piles of vegetables, little salads made of herbs and flowers. Bread, honey, and butter. The food was expensive and delicious.

"Lily," Imogen said to Arjun and Frieda, "is here about *The Book of the Most Precious Substance*."

They both raised their eyebrows.

"Admiral Masters," I said. "He said you have the copy that used to be his?"

All three of them laughed. Apparently they knew the story.

"Did he say I stole it?" Imogen asked, still laughing.

"He implied it," I said.

"Such utter horseshit," Imogen said. "Here's what really happened. We were in a group together. A study group. Well, a little bit of a practice group, too. Mostly we traded scans of books like *The Precious Substance*. Although not that actual book—it seems to resist being copied."

"So I've heard," I said.

"You can try when you get it," Imogen went on. "*If* you get it. First we tried to scan it, and the impression never came out clear. Then Frieda tried to photograph it—well, we burned out a few digital cameras on that."

"Then I tried film," Arjun said. "Didn't come out. Overexposed."

"Sometimes," Imogen said, "you just need to accept what a magical object is telling you, and this one was saying: *Do not reproduce*. So we gave up.

"Anyway, our little group. The heart of it was a private internet forum run by a witch named Stacy in Los Angeles. Very rarely, a few of us did rituals together. Admiral Masters was in the group. I didn't know he was a real admiral. I never would have shared my books with him! Now I know all he cares about is power. Worse, *political* power—the most boring thing on earth. He just hexed his way up the ladder and now he thinks he's a big shot. Anyway, we'd never met. He came to Paris for some war convention and he very much wanted to see me. We'd had some correspondence about *The Precious Substance* and sex magic in general. I suppose he thought I was going to be available to him, at his convenience. He came over, these two weren't around, and immediately he thought we were going to perform the acts. Not fucking likely! I had no interest in fucking him or performing magic with him. He kept trying one or the other. He was obsessed with the book. Finally I told him he could borrow it, but only for a day or two, and only for use at his hotel. The book is worth a small fortune. And of course, I wasn't terribly interested in encouraging whatever that half-wit had planned for it.

"So he took the book to his hotel room, but he didn't return it. Four days went by, then five. First he made excuses, then he started avoiding my calls. So I get a few friends together, we find out where he's staying, and we go get my book back. We get to his hotel room and he's in there with two escorts, lovely girls, trying to get them to produce the Precious Substance with each other. No one has any idea what they're doing, he's got his come all over my book, and he's barking orders at these women: 'Find the G-spot! Find the G-spot and apply pressure!'"

We all laughed. Imogen was a fantastic storyteller. Arjun brushed against me as he reached across the table. He smiled at me by way of quick apology. I smiled back.

"Obviously, fuck all of that. We took my book and left. And now he runs around calling me the Whore and saying I stole his book. Which I rather like, honestly."

Everyone laughed more, including me. Then I remembered he'd been murdered. I told Imogen and everyone was sober and respectful for a moment. Then we went on with our evening. No one here would miss him.

"So what's your interest in *The Precious Substance?*" Imogen said. "Tell us all."

Frieda said, "I assume you've done the Banishing Ritual of the Lower Pentagram? Care and Comfort of Your Guardian Angel? You don't want to jump into the Precious Substance!"

"Ah, no," I said. "I'm a book dealer. Not a magician."

Frieda raised an eyebrow. "OK," she said, with no small amount of sarcasm.

"What?" I asked her. She looked up and to her left, as if she were listening to someone there. I'd noticed she did that often.

"The spirits don't agree," she said.

We ate. The food was rich and decadent and wonderful. I finished my second glass of mushroom-blackberry champagne. Arjun got me a refill. I was starting to feel relaxed and the slightest bit unbalanced, in a good way. Arjun checked in a few times to make sure I was OK. I actually felt wonderful, and I told him.

"Imogen says you're a writer," Frieda said. "A good one."

I shrugged. "I haven't done that in years. I'm a book dealer now."

Imogen frowned. "You can't be," she said. "You've got to write another book."

"Someday," I said, through a tight smile.

"I knew your husband," Imogen said. "Abel. He was a wonderful man. We had friends in common in San Francisco, long ago. Rodriguez Santos. Jackie Hill."

Usually people avoided mentioning Abel's name, as if he'd done something unforgivable. Which I guess he had: He reminded people of the cruel unfairness of life, and the closeness of death. I remembered Rodriguez and Jackie. Abel had been in a noise band with Rodriguez. Jackie was another writer. Abel had helped get her first book published. Like most of his friends, they became very, very busy as he fell apart. They *wanted* to come over and visit, wanted to very badly, in fact, but could never find the time.

"I heard about what happened," Imogen said, as if reading my mind—although it was more likely just common sense. "That they just left you. They were shitty. They should have been there for you. I mean, first of all, they should have given you money, brought over meals, all that. But they also should have been there emotionally. They didn't even know Abel had moved to New York. I tried to get in touch with him but it was too late, and I didn't want to bother you, being strangers. I gave them a good talking-to, if it makes you feel any better."

I nodded. It did make me feel a little better. Funny to know someone had stood up for us, after all. Arjun put a hand on my shoulder.

"Thank you," I said.

"But I'm sure everyone wasn't like that," Imogen said.

I didn't say anything. Suddenly the table got quiet. Imogen frowned down at her food.

"Family?" she said. I shook my head.

"Well, that's some bad luck," Arjun finally said.

"It was a long time ago," I said, suddenly feeling stiff and uncomfortable.

"Not really," Frieda said. "People sure can be shit, can't they?"

"Jesus," Imogen said. "I hate selfish people. They make the world boring. People think they're on some, I don't know, some fucking spiritual path, or some big creative adventure. But then they can't be bothered to help out their neighbor or be there for a friend. Bring over some fucking biscuits. Half the people I know who think they're enlightened didn't pick up the fucking phone and call me when Johnny died."

It took me a moment to realize Imogen meant her late husband. A look crossed her face: I hadn't realized how much she loved him. I could see she still missed him. But here she was, going on without him. Imogen shook it off.

"The trick isn't to protect yourself," Imogen went on. "It's to accept life. Not push it away when it gets messy."

"Oh, so *that's* the trick," Arjun said teasingly.

"Well, you know me," Imogen said. "I don't believe in answers. I don't believe in big sweeping philosophies. All the great men of history tried to make these absolute laws, answer all the big questions, and they were always wrong. There's no big answers out there, not that we can understand. I think the thing is just to somehow accept that life doesn't always make sense. Terrible things can happen. It's ridiculous to try to spin it. I mean, maybe in the grand sense, you know, when we all come out to take our bows at the end, it'll all seem logical and wonderful. But in the meantime, life can fucking hurt. We need to be there for each other. That's the real magical act—making someone a sandwich, cleaning the flat."

"But isn't magic selfish?" I asked. "I mean, you're obviously not selfish people. But all these rituals and sacrifices to get what you want—it just seems self-serving."

Imogen, Arjun, and Frieda all seemed to consider the question. I liked all three of them, although I also felt something I couldn't place until about halfway through the meal. Then I finally realized: I was jealous. Strange dinner, strange mushrooms, the great sex I imagined they had, interesting guests—this was the life I thought I would have. The life I thought was in my future before Abel got sick. I still couldn't believe how different life had turned out.

When I thought of my life—my real life, not this fleeting escapade with Lucas—I felt a lump in my stomach. Suddenly the spell the last few weeks had woven around me dropped away, and here was my real life again. It was all drudgery—Abel, the books, the house.

I couldn't go back without the book. I couldn't.

"It isn't magic that's selfish," Frieda said, bringing me back to real-ity—or whatever this was. "It's people. People do spells to get money, to get love, all the usual horseshit. I do too, sometimes. But it doesn't have to be that way. There's a bunch of us who do regular rituals for the earth. I know a coven who does political work. Binding spells on fascists and racists."

"Magic is like money, or fame, or any other form of power," Arjun said. "It works. It's real. You can get what you want. Whatever you think will make you happy. But the problem seems to be that most people are wrong about what will make them happy. Most lottery winners are miserable again within two or three years. Most celebri-ties are on medication to get through the day. Lord knows we know enough of them."

I knew that about lottery winners and celebrities. But I also knew: I wasn't like those people. Most of those people weren't where I was, or had been a few weeks ago—broke, alone, loveless, and sex-less. And most of them, I guessed, had vague dreams about money and fame: they'd be prettier, more alluring, smarter. I had no delu-sions. I knew exactly what I wanted from the book.

And I knew, if the book could deliver, it would make me happy again.

"So you all tried the book?" I asked. "Or two of you? Some of you?"

All three laughed and I did too. I felt the lightness of the mush-rooms spread through my face and then the rest of me.

"We did," Arjun said, looking at Imogen, who nodded. "It really is a working for two."

"And it isn't my thing," Frieda said. "I like to keep clean."

"Clean?" I asked.

"The spirits," Arjun explained. "They demand purity."

"No judgments!" Frieda said, laughing. "I mean from me. The spirits judge everyone."

"So what happened?" I asked Imogen and Arjun. "Did you do the acts?"

Arjun and Imogen exchanged amused, inscrutable glances. Arjun turned a little pink.

"Well," Imogen said. "We went up to the fourth act. Just for fun. And it started to get…"

"Weird," Arjun said.

"And not in a good way," Imogen clarified.

"Weird not in a good way how?" I asked.

"Strange energies were stirred up," Imogen said. "A pipe burst. We had some money stolen—"

"And some art," Frieda added.

"And I got mugged," Arjun said. "And roughed up a bit."

"We all had nightmares," Imogen said. "We decided to call it quits and sell the book."

They didn't have the book. A sense of relief passed through me, a wordless thought something like *Thank God we aren't done.* That meant I didn't have to go home.

"The book," Imogen went on. "It isn't good. There's no big history of success stories behind it. Of course, we would never have done the fifth step, not literally, but we were thinking of working up some kind of art project around it, some metaphor. Like making a sculpture and plunging a knife into it at the right moment. Or…What was the other one?"

"Something to do with plants," Arjun said. "I think we were going to kill a rosebush? Or something?"

I could tell Imogen liked to lecture and illuminate. She'd probably spent half her life reading, a quarter fucking, and the last quarter telling everyone what she'd learned. Which didn't sound bad.

"Did you have any trouble with…" Everyone looked at me, eager to help. "The fourth step?" I ventured. "The Precious Substance?"

They all laughed.

"I'm with you," Frieda said. "My body just doesn't seem to make it."

"Nonsense," Imogen said. They'd had this debate before. "Everyone with a cunt can do it."

Frieda lovingly rolled her eyes and they all laughed again.

"Well, I suppose I just don't have the patience these two have," Frieda said. "They'll spend hours on it. *Hours.*"

"How's your partner?" Arjun asked. "Does he understand the territory?"

"Oh, yes," I said, and everyone laughed again. Arjun poured us each another glass of mushroom-blackberry champagne cocktail. "He's accomplished it before, with other women."

"Oh!" Imogen and Frieda both said, nodding approvingly.

"The thing is," Imogen said—I got the impression she said that a lot—"you have to be able to accept that the extraordinary is possible. That pleasure doesn't end where you always thought it ended. It's a little scary, especially the first few times. A step into unmapped woods."

"So who has it now?" I asked. "The book, I mean."

"I sold it to someone you must know," Imogen said. "Madame M."

Frieda smiled serenely at the name.

"No," I said. "I don't know her."

"She'll love you," Frieda said. She turned to Imogen. "We should call her. Can we call her?"

"Who is she?" I asked.

"She's a dominatrix," Arjun said. "And a witch. And a countess."

"A duchess," Imogen said.

"That makes her sound scary," Frieda protested.

"She *is* scary," Arjun insisted. Frieda and Imogen laughed.

"She changed my life," Frieda said.

"She's a dear friend," Imogen said. "I'll call her. I don't know if she'll sell you the book, but I'm sure she'll let you take a look at it."

"I'd at least like to make an offer," I said. "My client is very generous."

"And she's very rich," Imogen said. "But she'll see you. Or at least, I'll do my best."

Dinner was winding down. We moved into the living room and Imogen served tea and coffee. Suddenly Frieda perked up and tilted her head, as if she'd heard something. We all looked at her expectantly. She held up one finger: *Wait.* Then—

"They're here," she said. "And they have something to say."

A hush came over the room, a strange energy like ozone before a storm.

She turned and looked at me. Maybe it was the light, but for a moment, she looked like a different person—her cheekbones looked higher, her eyes farther apart, her forehead wider. She tilted her head again.

"Be careful," Frieda said. "You think you're looking for an answer. But you're going to find a question. The answer will tell you who you are. Don't fuck it up."

I had no idea what it meant. Then Frieda blinked, and laughed, and it was over. She looked like herself again, and it was as if the moment had never happened.

Dinner was over, and I stood up to leave and began thanking everyone for their time.

"Don't go yet," Imogen said. "No one's going to sleep for a good long time yet. Arjun, get her more of your potion."

Arjun got me another glass of champagne cocktail and sat next to me on the emerald-green sofa. He hadn't made a secret of finding me attractive. It felt silly—we were middle-aged people, or at least I was, and I felt like we were waiting to make a move on each other like high school or college kids. But Arjun's smile was knowing, and no one was pretending this was anything other than what it was.

"Actually, I *am* going to bed," Frieda said. She looked at me kindly. "They exhaust me." She meant the spirits. Maybe also her partners. "Lily, what a treat to meet you. I hope I see you again." She noticed Arjun sitting close to me on the sofa. "Imogen," Frieda continued. "Come tuck me in."

Imogen agreed and came over to say good night.

"Lily, I'm so glad we met," she said. "I feel like we're friends."

"Me too," I said. I stood up. She took my hands and I squeezed them back. I liked her. "Can I ask you a question?"

"Anything," Imogen said.

"Did you sleep with Abel?" I asked.

Imogen smiled. "Of course I did," she said. "Before you were married. It was wonderful. He was so good at it. He was brilliant, your husband."

I hugged her, and she hugged me back. Imogen looked into my eyes.

"You need joy in your life again," she said. "Lightness. Fun. Sex. Beauty. This book…it won't bring you any of that."

"I know," I said. "But I'm hoping it'll bring me something better."

Imogen shrugged, gave me a long kiss on the lips, and went off to bed with Frieda. I sat back down next to Arjun.

"So," he said, eyes shining. "Out of the noble, generous goodness of my heart, I might be able to help you with your struggles to reach the fourth step."

I laughed. This was fun.

"I don't know," I reasoned. "I'm not sure it's possible."

Arjun leaned toward me, as if he were going to kiss me on the lips. But then he stopped and brought his head down to my chest and instead kissed the top of my breasts. His lips were hot and soft and asked for nothing. I felt myself relax into the sofa behind me.

"Well, we'll just have to investigate," he said, in between kisses. He moved up to my throat.

We did investigate. We tried, and had a very good couple of hours. But despite some very valiant efforts, we didn't reach the fourth step.

20.

I got back to the hotel around three a.m., after a dark and glittering drive through Paris. Lucas was gone when I got to the room. He'd left me a note:

Can't sleep
Going for a walk
Call me if you need me
XOXO

I slept for hours and woke up around eight with the deep relaxation and contentment that comes from extraordinary sex. Sex with Lucas was good. Very good. But Arjun had made a study out of pleasure, and I felt relaxed and content. It was as if I'd been obliterated and replaced with raw sensation—like a vacation from myself. I still felt it this morning. I'd forgotten that sex itself could be a drug, that it could lead to altered states of consciousness. It certainly made the prospect of sex magic seem more real.

Every day, what was left of my skepticism was getting chipped away. The strange part, looking back, was how little I thought about it all. Of course Frieda talks to spirits. Of course sex nips away at the fabric of reality. Of course I should devote my days to threading the needle of getting this rare book that may or may not exist, may or may not work, may or may not bring me what I want and need.

I took a bath and got dressed and went outside. I was still high from my sexual buzz, the sun was shining, we were close to the book, I was in Paris. The last time I'd been here was years ago, with Abel. The years in between felt, on this sunny morning, like a bad nightmare I was finally shaking off.

I stopped into a Turkish café for breakfast. First I texted Lucas everything about last night—everything about the book, at least. I'd tell him about the rest of the night when I saw him. There was no reason to think he'd be jealous or otherwise unhappy with my sexual escapade, but a text seemed unkind.

In the café I got a plate of eggs cooked with tomatoes and a salad of green herbs with a sweet-tart pomegranate dressing. With it was a basket of hot bread just out of the oven. The woman running the place was about my age and kept refilling my tiny glass of hot black tea with mint and sugar in it. When she brought my food she looked old and hard, but when she wasn't working, she sat at a table by the register and texted with someone who made her laugh and blush. Each text made her younger and softer.

In my mind I started to do what I usually did during a free moment, which was go over my never-ending list of errands to run, prescriptions to fill, books to mail, emails to answer, bills to pay, and on and on. For years this list had been a dreary soundtrack to my days and nights. But Awe was taking care of all the prescriptions and errands. If he needed help, he could call someone in for the day. He'd been texting me once or twice a day just to let me know all was well. My bills were paid and everything was fine with my book sales. For the first time in years, there was nothing on the list. It felt like my mind had been locked tight around this list for years, blocking out everything else. Now, life could come in.

When I was done eating I got a text from Lucas. He'd been wandering around Paris since midnight, too jet-lagged to sleep. We made plans to meet back at the hotel in an hour or two. Roaming down a side street on the way, I stopped in front of a *patisserie* to see that Imogen had emailed:

> *Lily,*
> *We were all so happy to have you over last night. Can we come visit you in New York in the summer? I'd love to see Abel again, in any condition. Do call anytime.*
> *Madame M. will happily see you about the book. She's expecting you later today. 12 pm train. Directions attached.*
> *Keep in touch,*
> *Imogen*

I looked at the attachment: it was a document with an elaborate set of instructions involving a train and coordinates for Madame M.'s house, a few hours south of Paris, which had no street address.

By now, there was no fretting over details, no worry over Abel or Awe or scheduling or travel arrangements. Inarticulately, I knew that if I needed to get to the south of France to meet Madame M., I would.

We were on a ship and the book was our captain, leading us through treacherous straits and past all sirens, taking us to the exact shore where we needed to be.

21.

I met Lucas in our hotel room. He was lying on the bed reading a biography of Virginia Woolf. I sat down next to him and he wrapped me up and kissed me. He was starting to feel familiar to me: his arms, his smell (different now, with French hotel soap, but still pleasing), his ever-present cup of coffee, his quick smile.

"Tell me everything," he said.

I told him everything, lightly skimming over sex with Arjun. We both agreed that since the invitation to Madame M.'s had only been for me, I ought to go alone. I changed clothes and packed a small bag, kissed Lucas goodbye, and rushed to the train station.

The train from Paris to the countryside was beautiful and, being France, delicious. The ride was about two hours. A little ham sandwich and a hot chocolate from the train station café ranked with the best meal in the upstate town where I lived. Once we flew past the suburbs, the countryside was green, lush, and damp, farms and wetlands interspersed with thick woods.

I got off the train in the small, dense city, and hailed a taxi. In fumbling French I tried and failed to communicate my destination to the driver. Finally I just showed him the non-address on my phone, and his old Gallic face lit up with recognition.

"Oui!" he said. *"Le château!"*

We drove through the cobblestone-streeted town, through a ring of placid suburbs, and out to the countryside. There were fields of corn and apple orchards and pig farms, dotted with the occasional bigger, wealthier home. After a thirty-minute drive and a thousand roundabouts, the driver turned down a smaller, unpaved two-lane road into a wooded area. Then another, even narrower road, and then onto a long gravel driveway, where we drove up to an iron gate. At the gate he buzzed an intercom, exchanged a few words in French about *"une femme américaine…Non, je ne sais,"* and the gate swung open. We drove down the driveway for at least another five minutes, woods on either side, until we came to a mile-wide clearing of bright green grass with an ancient house in the middle of it, easily from the 1600s. It was not huge and was made out of rough stone that made it look more like a church than a home. On all sides of the lawn were woods that looked older than the house. To one side was an elaborate garden, to another a gazebo, and later I'd see that behind the house were stables, sheds, and a few other outbuildings.

I hardly knew old money came quite so old. The car stopped about ten feet from the entryway to the house. As I got out, I saw a small, open horse-drawn carriage pull up from a path in the woods and approach the house. Inside the ornate black carriage were three women. I could hear them laughing as I walked up to the house.

One of the women had white-blond hair and wore a black bustier and a long, full black skirt. She had red lipstick on her lips and big, round, dark glasses over her eyes. Soon I would learn she was Kat, French-Chinese, somewhere between forty and seventy. A second woman, much younger, had long wavy blond hair that cascaded down her back and wore jeans and a lace-trimmed camisole top. She had no makeup on her face and beat-up sneakers on her feet. That was Carrie-Ann. The third woman, Maude, about my own age, had steel-gray hair swept into an updo and wore a black suit with a thin, transparent white T-shirt underneath, revealing her taut waist and high, small breasts.

I stopped walking and watched them. Now I saw the carriage wasn't drawn by horses. It was drawn by two people with large, elaborate horse masks over their faces and black leather or synthetic costumes covering their bodies.

Still laughing, the woman in the black suit—Maude—pulled the reins on the horse-people, telling them to stop a few yards from the house. Kat, the woman in the bustier, stood up. She had a long leather whip in her hand. Expertly, she lashed the whip; it made a loud cracking sound and caught both horse-people across their backs. One stood perfectly, rigidly still. The other shivered a little when the whip touched his back.

"Why, hello!" Kat called out to me. "You must be the American. Come in. We're having a late lunch and you must join us."

I met the three women at the door, they introduced themselves, each shook my hand warmly, and we all walked into the house together.

Inside, the house was grand and crumbling and beautiful. The floors and the walls were stone, with a staircase leading up to a second floor. It was hard to believe it was real.

"We're back," Kat called out to no one I could see. She turned to me. "You will stay the night?"

"Actually," I said, "I'm just here for—"

"Of course she will," I heard. We all looked up. Coming down the grand staircase, slowly, one deliberate step at a time, was Madame M. She was small, maybe five two, and razor-thin. Her hair was white with a few streaks of black and she wore a set of black silk men's pajamas.

She came down the stairs, walked over to me, and clasped my hands.

"Lily," she said. Her voice was rich and smoky. "We're very pleased to have you join us. But you're going to be disappointed. I don't have *The Book of the Most Precious Substance*. It's a dark thing, and I don't need it. I sold it a few months ago."

My heart fell a little. This was our last lead to the last copy of the book. But I was nowhere near giving up. I would follow it to the next person, and the next if I had to. I wasn't going home without it.

"To who?" I asked.

Madame M. smiled a smile that said she wasn't going to tell me.

"Then why am I here?" I asked.

"Because," she said, "I hope to convince you not to look for it. It's evil, you know."

"I'm just a book dealer," I said. "Not a magician."

Madame M. looked me up and down with a sharp eye. Then she laughed.

"Just a book dealer!" she said mockingly, although I wasn't sure what she meant by it. "Come, let's eat."

Kat and the other women led me into the dining room, where a long formal table was set for us. Standing by, ready to serve, were three women wearing only tiny black silk underwear and black high heels with bright red soles. No one acknowledged them as we sat down. Immediately one of the women snapped to work and served champagne. As she leaned over me I saw that she had a knotty scar over her ribs on her right side, probably from a brand: *MM.*

Madame, me, and all three women from the carriage—Kat, Carrie-Ann, and Maude—sat at the table. Madame sat at the head. Someone put on a record of a classical waltz, volume low. I sipped my champagne.

I felt no need to hide my amazement or act like I understood. The chateau was entirely unlike life as I'd known it thus far. Madame looked at me again from her place at the head of the table. Her eyes were dark and strangely direct. Food and wine were served. Finally Madame addressed me.

"Lily," she said. "I knew your husband's work. I read all his books. He was a genius. Very tragic, what happened to him. Tragic for both of you. But I have to admit, I don't read many novels, so I didn't know who you were. I think they're ridiculous, usually. Some middle-aged person's fantasy of what life ought to be like. But I read a bit of your book last night after Imogen wrote. Very good. Shrewd. How come you stopped writing?"

Everyone looked at me. I didn't try to feel OK with it, or brush the question off.

"I gave up," I said.

She continued to look at me with those strange eyes.

"Why?" she said.

"Because," I said, "I missed Abel so much, I couldn't live. And he needed me, so I couldn't die."

I'd never said that out loud before. But the women all nodded, as if it were a normal thing to say. In the strange world of the chateau, apparently, it was perfectly ordinary to want to die, and an everyday matter to lose the people you loved.

"So what do you think the book will change?" Madame asked.

"Money," I said. "I don't care about being rich. But taking care of Abel is very, very expensive."

"But I don't think that's the whole reason," Madame said. "I want you to know, the book is very dangerous. Magic is a tool, like fire, or money. If you know what you're doing, it can be wonderful. If not, people get hurt. They die."

I knew there was no point in lying to her about having done the first few steps. I accepted by now that somehow, people could tell.

"I promise you," I said, "that's secondary to the sale."

"Secondary to *you*," Madame said. "Life has its own ideas." She gave me another long look. "Let me try to convince you to give this up," she said. "Stay the night. Play a little game with us. If I can't convince you to let it go, then tomorrow, I'll tell you who now owns it. *Oui?*"

I had no idea what she meant by "a little game." I wanted to find out.

"Maybe," I said.

The women all met eyes. Carrie-Ann raised her eyebrows. Kat smiled.

"So you practice magic?" I asked, looking around the table. "All of you?"

"*Oui,*" Kat said. "But I think all of us, maybe like you, had to learn exactly how to use it. Like Madame says—it's like fire. It can warm you, or—poof!"

She made a gesture: *up in smoke.*

Madame nodded at Kat. Kat reached to the large gold necklace around her neck, which I now saw was a locket. She opened it up.

"When I was twenty-five my daughter was born," Kat said. "She was perfect. The most perfect baby you ever saw. Look—"

Inside were two pictures, one of an infant, the other of a girl of about twelve. The baby was, as she said, perfect. The twelve-year-old, though, was thin and listless, her eyes vacant. The photo was cropped under her shoulders, but it looked like she was lying in a hospital bed. Her eyes and hair were a dull, lifeless brown.

"She was perfect," I agreed. "She got sick?"

"Cancer," Kat said. "In her brain, in her blood, everywhere. Even her bones. You can't imagine what it's like to hear your own child scream like that. You'll do anything to relieve the pain."

The other women at the table nodded knowingly. Each had a slightly different look on her face: Madame M., serene but strangely firm; Carrie-Ann, sad and a little angry; Maude, a strange blank expression. I could see they each had some understanding of what Kat and I knew: a loss so dark it changed who you were, changed the planet you lived on, changed what words meant.

"Soon, we lived at the hospital," Kat went on. "Her father left. He couldn't bear it. All our friends…they just melted away. Just slid out of our lives. I had only my mother. But then I lost her, too. Heart attack.

My daughter died less than a year later. My mother and my daughter were my heart, my life. I didn't want to live without them."

"But you're alive," I said. Kat had been through much worse than I had, but seemed to have found some kind of peace.

Kat smiled. "Madame," she said, glancing at her savior. "She saved my life. It's a long story."

"We have time," Madame said, gently but firmly.

Kat resumed: "After they were gone, I became obsessed with trying to reach them again. My daughter and my mother. I was furious at them for leaving me here alone. So jealous that they were together. I couldn't forgive them. I wanted to join them. So I began to visit psychics to try to connect with them again. I went to some real con artists, of course. But also some people who seemed very genuine. But we could never reach them, not Marie, my mother, or Michelle, my daughter.

"My grief turned into rage. I couldn't forgive God for taking my mother and daughter away from me. Everything was gone and I was left alone, in this fucking wasteland. That was how I saw it. Death couldn't come soon enough. The only reason I didn't kill myself was I was scared I wouldn't see my daughter again. I became obsessed with Michelle's father for leaving us, friends who abandoned us, the doctors who had let my mother and daughter die. I had always been religious; it was just a small step to black magic. I stayed up night after night, going to graveyards for dirt, picking herbs, lighting candles, all to curse the people who'd stolen my life from me. I became an expert on hexes and curses. It had been ten years since I lost my mother and child. I had become something ugly. Something unforgiving and unforgivable."

"Did they work?" I asked. "All your curses?"

"Mais oui," Kat said. "But it never made me happy. And then I met Madame." Now her face was clear and bright again. "I had heard she was a great magician. I was trying to enact a very complicated working to kill Michelle's father, and it kept failing. He got sicker, and sicker, but he just wouldn't die. So, through mutual friends, I sought a meeting with Madame. She said, 'Of course I can tell you how to kill him. And maybe he deserves it. But I think that you, Kat, deserve better than to become a murderer.' And she showed me what there is to live for after all."

"What is there?" I asked.

"Spirit," she answered immediately. "Pleasure. Love. Curiosity. Other people. Beauty. I was only interested in what I lost. I had no interest at all in what was still here, just waiting for me. I thought nothing could replace the love of my family. Of course, I was right. Nothing will ever be like that again. But the world is still a very full place, and we're fortunate to be able to live it, taste it, smell it. *Non?*"

I shrugged. I still wasn't sure. Certainly the past few days had been spectacularly fun. But they didn't cancel out years of life in a state of dull despair like the one Kat had described. I didn't practice black magic, not literally. But I had a lot of dark thoughts about doctors, old friends, other writers.

If I didn't find the book, I'd have to go back to that life. Lucas, no matter how affectionate he'd become, certainly wasn't going to stick around for the Ensure feedings and thrice-daily changings. In a few weeks, maybe less, it'd be back to cold nights alone, to—

I realized I'd become lost in my own anxiety again. I looked up. Madame was looking at me, eyes bright.

"Maybe," Madame said, "we will convince you."

I looked around the table. The women all looked at me with different expressions—curious, seemingly teasing, pleased.

I had no idea what she was talking about. But it wasn't hard to admit: I wanted to stay. I'd never been anywhere like this in my life, and I was in no hurry to leave. And she was my last lead on the book. As far as I knew, she was the only person who knew who had it.

"I'll stay," I said.

22.

After our late lunch, Madame and Maude went alone to another wing of the vast house to work—whatever that meant—and Kat and Carrie-Ann took me on a tour of the home and property. We started outside. Behind the house there was a large swimming pool, tiled in blue, with a small herb garden on either side. I saw basil and thyme but also henbane and Datura, herbs I'd read about in witchcraft books. Past that, closer to the woods, was a vegetable garden and a few rows of espaliered fruit trees. Carrie-Ann spoke French, and Kat translated for me when necessary. After the gardens we went around to the side.

"Come," Kat said. "We'll give the horses a treat." She picked a handful of grass and we walked into the stables. There were six stalls; two had horses, two were empty, and two held people, the same two people in tight leather, faces obscured, I'd seen pulling the carriage before. One was lying in a stall reading a book, the other was scrubbing their stall clean with a brush and a bucket of water.

Carrie-Ann approached the reading horse-person and shouted at them in French. The horse-person jumped and stood in a submissive posture, head down, while Carrie-Ann yelled some more. Carrie-Ann pulled a riding crop off the wall; the horse-person got on all fours and Carrie-Ann gave them a few good whacks. While all this was going on, Kat was feeding her handful of grass to one of the horses that was actually a horse. I went up to a real horse and petted it. It was a dark bay with black mane and tail. When I leaned in to pet him his big brown eyes met mine and he pushed his snout toward me: *Rub me here.*

Carrie-Ann left the horse-person and came over to the horse I was petting. She spoke to Kat in French and Kat translated.

"She wants to know if you ride?" Kat asked.

"I used to," I said. My mother rode horses and I used to ride with her sometimes. We had less than nothing—whenever we got a little something, my father, an alcoholic with big schemes and grand plans, would leverage it for more, and we'd end up in more debt than we'd started. But my mother wouldn't go without her horses, and she worked at a stable nearly every Sunday, everywhere we lived, to earn the privilege to ride there once in a while, and sometimes take me with her.

"*D'accord,*" Kat said, smiling. "Then we will ride."

Carrie-Ann yelled in French again and the two horse-people came to saddle up the real horses for us and boost us into place. I got on the dark bay I'd been petting. I hadn't been on a horse in years and I forgot the strange, exciting feeling of being at the mercy of an animal a couple of thousand pounds your superior, with a mind of its own.

Kat and Carrie-Ann both got on the other horse; they were not much more than a hundred pounds each and the big palmetto could easily take them. Muscle memory took over and I somehow still knew how to work the reins and nudge the horse with my heels. The horse smelled like childhood. Like my mother. I couldn't help but think of her: Her life had been small and confined, constrained by the boundaries of her own lack of confidence and my father's fuck-ups—and, of course, her love for me. She was a good mother. She wanted me to have a big and exciting life. She didn't want me to miss everything she had missed—not just the parts of life that come with money, like travel and fancy cars, but the parts that are free: She wanted me to be with people who loved me, to pursue my whims, to see with eyes clear from resentment and bitterness. And I had, for a while.

Kat led us into the woods. The sun was leaning from the west and it was close to sixty degrees. A hawk circled overhead and mockingbirds called from the trees. The horses were well trained and knew their way around the small network of trails and paths.

Carrie-Ann and Kat spoke for a bit in French before Kat began to translate.

"Carrie-Ann thinks you're probably wondering how she came to live here," Kat said.

"That's true," I admitted.

She and Carrie-Ann spoke a few more words in French. Kat translated as we rode through the woods.

"I lost my wife," Carrie-Ann said, and Kat translated. "She was murdered. The details aren't interesting. Just a terrible man. Like many stories, *oui?*

"Like you, maybe, I lost hope in life. I drank, took drugs. I went to psychiatrists, got prescription after prescription. Everything that was supposed to make me better made me worse. I felt like I was living in a *Twilight Zone* episode, where no one would admit the fundamental unfairness of what had happened to me. Instead, it was like I had a disease, but one that was my own fault. Everyone kept telling me I should be happy again, but no one told me how. 'You'll meet someone else'—what an utterly revolting thing to say to a widow."

We rode down a path that took us under low oak trees that were probably as old as the house. We each bent down to avoid the sweeping branches. Our horses knew the territory well and slowed down as we approached, all as perfectly timed as a ballet.

"Finally," Carrie-Ann and Kat went on, "I ended up in a hospital, and then rehabilitation. I got completely sober—well, I'm French, of course I have a glass of wine now and then, but *mostly* sober. And then the full weight of how I'd abandoned myself hit me. Jillian, my wife, had loved me so much, and now everything she'd loved was gone.

"I went to retreats, to gurus, to spiritual teachers. But no one ever really spoke to me about Jillian. About missing her. All of them were completely in denial about the size of my loss, utterly trite, lacking in any depth at all. 'Let go,' they said. 'Move on.' No one had any real answers for me. How do you go on? How do you live in a world so fucking unfair? 'You'll find someone.' Fuck you. I met someone already. She's dead."

I laughed out loud. Kat and Carrie-Ann laughed with me. We were a strange little club.

"Then I met Madame. It was a small party in Paris. We had

a mutual friend. And she came right up to me and said, 'I heard about what happened to your wife. It's absolutely terrible. How are you getting by?' Just like that. That's true magic, Lily: to say the words no one else will say. All magic lives in words. She said the thing that no one would say out loud. And then she asked questions—was the man who killed her in prison, how was I feeling, how was her family dealing with it. We started talking, and we kept talking—and talking, and talking, and talking. And I started to work with the rituals she does here. *We* do here. Then, finally, I could start to move on. Without leaving my wife behind."

"How?" I asked.

"Ah," Carrie-Ann said. Kat translated: "The answer is different for everyone. But you need to somehow begin again. The old you, the old life—it's over. Gone forever. And it's very sad, because you lose the person who your wife—your husband—loved. It's another loss. After I met Madame, I found out who I was *now*. Who is this new person, this person who has lost so much, been so scarred? I realized that for me, I could only find meaning in life through helping others now. It was—how do you say—it corrected the course. Before losing her I'd worked in finance—money money money, boring and selfish. Other than Jillian, I was never truly happy. Now, Madame and me, we created a little fund, a little nonprofit, for women who love women, women whose families won't accept them. And, ironically, Jillian's family, who didn't accept me at all, are now our biggest supporters. Everything they didn't do for Jillian—love her, accept her— I now see them do every day for other young women. They don't want anyone to go through what we went through. They've changed, truly changed, in their hearts."

"But you can't say that makes it all worth it," I said. "The good they do now doesn't negate how awful they were. The new life doesn't make up for losing the old."

Kat translated back and forth.

"Of course not," Carrie-Ann said. "You're missing the point. The past is over and done. You have no choice but to live with it. There's no getting over, no making up for. But there's a chance to see and create something new. That's the only chance—*your* only chance."

Carrie-Ann turned to me with a strange smile: strong, but at the same time, pleading.

"Loss changes us," she said, through Kat. "But I want you to know, you can be happy again. Happy in a different way, certainly. A strange way. Others can't understand it. You'll always feel the pain. You have to begin again, while somehow keeping the past with you. But truly happy, nonetheless."

Here in the sun-dappled woods, I almost believed her.

We'd arrived back at the stables. The horse-people came over to help us off the animals and brush them and put them away. My legs were pleasantly sore. The three of us walked back to the house. It was growing cold in the shade, and even in the sun the air was growing cooler. Carrie-Ann stripped off her clothes, leaving them in a pile on the lawn, and dove into the swimming pool. Kat and I went back into the house through the kitchen door.

"Now," Kat said, "the house tour. Here you see the kitchen is original to the home, when Madame's ancestors built it in fifteen-something-or-other. The home has been occupied by her family ever since."

We went through the kitchen to the dining room, which I had

seen, the ballroom, which I had not, and the library, where I spent half an hour admiring her collection of family heirloom editions and modern erotic art books. Then Kat showed me to the guest room I'd be staying in upstairs. On the way, still on the first floor, we passed a large empty room with strange black wallpaper, a pattern of black vines and roses printed on it in a velvet-like texture.

"What's that room for?" I asked.

Kat laughed, eyes bright, as she led me up the stairs.

"You'll find out," she said.

My room was pleasant, simple, and clean, with white plaster walls, a desk, a large bed on a brass frame, and two ancient, comfortable-looking quilts on top. On the desk was an unmarked bottle of wine, a glass, and a plate of cheese and tiny wild strawberries.

On the bed was a large cardboard box, the kind expensive gifts come in.

"You'll find your outfit for the evening in there," Kat said, nodding toward the box. I opened it. Inside was a layer of tissue; under that, a set of very expensive lingerie. I raised my eyebrows and didn't say anything.

"Rest," Kat said. "Take a bath, get ready, and I'll be back in two or three hours for the ritual."

I called Lucas.

"I'm at a dominatrix witch's house in the south of France," I said.

Lucas laughed. I told him the bad news about the book (Madame didn't have it) and the good news (I was hoping I could persuade her to tell me who did).

"Are you having fun?" he asked.

I thought about it before I answered.

"Yes," I said. "Not jump-up-and-down kind of fun. But I'm glad I'm here."

"I wish I was with you," Lucas said. "Take your time. You deserve a ritual, whatever the fuck that is. Don't hurry. I'm making calls."

We got off the phone.

Surprisingly, I did rest. Between the strangeness of the day, the travel, and the horseback riding, I was wiped out. I poured myself a glass of the wine—a red that I guessed was made on the property or nearby—and ate a few strawberries and bites of cheese and found the bathroom, where there was a big claw-foot tub. I drew a hot bath, had another glass of wine while it was filling, and got in the bath and almost immediately fell asleep.

When I woke up it was dark and the water was lukewarm. I got out and dried off. It was after ten, more than two hours since Kat had left me.

I opened the box on the bed. There was a black over-bust corset with garters attached, stockings, a tiny pair of black underwear, and a satin wrap to wear over it. Under the clothes was a pair of black high heels with red soles like the ones the servant women wore.

I had just got on the stockings and the underwear and the wrap when there was a knock at the door. Without waiting for an answer, Kat entered, holding a glass of champagne for me.

I tightened the wrap around myself, self-conscious. Kat smiled, as if this was all very everyday. Which to her, of course, it was.

"I'm here to help you," she said. "Madame likes her corsets tight and her stockings straight. Turn around."

I turned so I was facing the bed. Kat gently lifted the wrap off my shoulders, leaving me naked except for the underwear and stockings.

She put her cold hands on my waist first, as if smoothing out my flesh, and then wrapped the corset around me.

"Hold on," she said, fixing the corset. I'd seen enough old movies to know how this worked. But when Kat pulled tight on the laces, tightening the restraint around my waist, I hadn't anticipated how it would feel: confining, a little scary, and highly erotic. The tightness seemed to hit some new muscle, deep inside my abdomen, that I hadn't felt before.

"Ah," Kat said in her lilting French accent after she tied it up. Every breath pushed that strange new muscle. "Madame would prefer the panties *over* the garter. So we will adjust—"

She slid the garters under the underwear, pulling them tightly against me as she did so, causing a flood of sensation. Then she ran her hands up and down my leg to straighten the stocking, then did the same on the other side. She pulled the little black underwear up tightly, applying a pleasing pressure, and fixed the garters. With nothing on over the corset, and a long, exposed gap of thigh between the bottom of the panties and the top of the stockings, I felt a combination of confined, covered, and exposed.

I tried on the shoes and then immediately stepped out of them. They were way too high for me.

Kat shrugged, turned me around, and looked at me. She smiled.

"Very good," she said. I reached for the wrap, but she frowned.

"Oh, no," she said. "Madame wouldn't like that at all."

Kat reached into her pocket and took out a small silver pill box. She opened it. Inside was one white pill. She held the box out to me.

"What is it?" I asked.

"Madame's special blend," Kat asked. "We have a pharmacist

friend who makes them up for us. A little something for joy, a little something for relaxation, a little something for insight. Just a touch. Good with champagne."

Kat took the pill out. I hesitated.

"You don't have to," she said. "But if this is going to work at all, you need to trust us."

"If *what's* going to work?" I asked.

"All of it," Kat said, avoiding my question.

She held the pill out again. I stuck out my tongue.

I didn't know if I trusted any of these women. But all my travels of the last few weeks had led here, and it would be a fucking shame to give up now.

Kat laughed as she put the pill on my tongue, and I took a drink and swallowed. I was already a little tipsy. The pill was bitter.

"Come," Kat said. "Everything is ready."

We left my bright little room. I wasn't sure if the unnamed pill was starting to kick in or if it was the situation I'd put myself in, but the house was different now, disorienting and eerie. The hallways were dark and there was a low rumbling sound I couldn't place coming from somewhere.

As I'd feared, and maybe also hoped, Kat led me to the room with the black rose wallpaper. We entered the room. On the floor a strange symbol, a few feet across, was drawn with a fine white powder with what looked like herbs and minerals mixed in. It wasn't entirely unlike the symbols from the book, but legible. A series of similar symbols, none of them familiar to me, was written across the wallpapered wall in white chalk. I recognized the symbol for Mercury; others for the sun and the moon.

Against one wall stood the maids from that afternoon, but now there were four of them. Each looked at the floor, perfectly still in their silk underthings and red-soled shoes. Standing closer to the center of the room were Madame, Carrie-Ann, and Maude, all in black dresses of varying lengths and styles. The room was lit by candles, and strong, churchlike incense was burning. After a moment I placed the low rumbling sound: Madame and the other women were chanting in what I thought was Latin.

In the middle of the room was an ordinary chair, black wood with a high back, with a small, flat, red leather cushion on the seat. Kat led me to the chair and gently pushed me in. No one spoke to me. Kat and Carrie-Ann looked at me with gentle, encouraging smiles. Maude ignored me. Madame M. looked at me with an expression on her face I didn't understand—maybe curiosity, maybe something else. Of course, I'd known this would be a sexual encounter in some way. Beyond that I had no idea what was going to happen.

The leather of the seat of the chair was cold against my legs. Kat tied a tight black blindfold in a silky material over my eyes. I felt my heart rate rise. I was quickly falling into some kind of intoxication. I felt the erotic pull of helplessness; the deep satisfaction of freedom from all responsibility, even responsibility for my own pleasure.

"You're mine now," I heard Madame say. I felt her face come close to mine, her breath warm and sweet. "You have no say in what happens, not until I'm done with you."

The chant became louder and I realized someone must have put a recording on, although occasionally one of the women would chime in. In blackness, someone held my hands behind my back and tied my arms together at the elbow with the same silky material.

Next my ankles were grabbed, roughly, and tied to the chair so my legs were slightly parted. I couldn't see and I could barely move. I felt myself growing tense.

"Breathe deeply," Madame said.

I took a few deep breaths. Whatever was in the pill started to kick in, spreading a warm relaxation and a heightened sensitivity. There was a touch on my shoulder—not skin, but something light and tickling. Whatever the touch was, someone ran it across my shoulders, my chest, and over the top of my breasts. My initial wave of anxiety had passed. I was nearly sure now that the bitter pill had been ecstasy, and I settled in to the intense pleasure I was starting to feel.

And then I felt a quick burning pain. I yelped. It was a moment before I realized someone had slapped me across the face.

"Life isn't always so fair, is it?" someone said.

Now four firm hands, two on each side, massaged my shoulders, my back, my arms, and my hands. I recovered from the slap and relaxed into easy pleasure again.

Then I felt a horrible sharp sting in my hip. Someone had stuck me with something—a thorn, a needle. I was starting to get anxious. I hoped to God it wasn't a syringe.

"Ow," I said. "Stop. I don't want—"

I felt hot breath on my ear, then heard Kat's voice: "If you really want us to stop, Lily, all you have to do is say so, three times. Now you've said it once. Two more times and we'll leave you alone. But I don't recommend stopping in the middle. You didn't come all the way here just to give up, did you?"

No, I hadn't—but I also hadn't traveled here for *this*, whatever this was.

There was another sting in the other hip. The thought crossed my mind that they were stinging me with bees. Later I would find out that they were acupuncture needles, as thin as a hair.

"Ow!"

Someone caressed my breasts under the corset, then wrapped a hand around my throat—and then hit me again, this time harder. It stung physically but also mentally; there was something degrading about it that was both uncomfortable and erotic. This was followed by more caresses and more teasing.

"Don't struggle," someone said. "Give in to this moment entirely."

But instead, the opposite happened: I felt a little snake of panic rise. Just then a hand slipped between my legs and I gasped. That made it easier to relax. There was a gentle, teasing touch. The touch went on, and I got closer, and closer—and then the gentle caress was suddenly replaced with a sharp, painful pinch.

There was another slap on my face, this one a little harder. Then again.

I was a little scared. This was much more visceral than I'd imagined. I'd imagined some slightly rough sex games. Not actual pain.

"Happiness is for other people," Madame M. said. It was the cruelest thing I could imagine, because I was nearly certain it was true. This was ugly and real.

"And you thought you were better!" another woman said. "You were so special, weren't you? The great writer. I bet you were a great beauty, weren't you? So pretty and young. Look at you now."

"Stop," I said.

Another slap, this one across my breasts, and then another across my face, hard. Now someone rained little smacks all over my face, shoulders, a slap across the ear.

Some roughness while aroused felt like sugar in coffee. This was not that. This was just pain. Just salt in my wounds.

"Stop," I said again. "I don't want this anymore."

It was the third time I'd said it. But no one stopped. Instead, someone stuck a square of fabric in my mouth. I tried to scream, but it came out as more a strangled moan.

"No one cares," Madame M. said. "It's too late."

"You have nothing," another voice said. "And life has nothing for you anymore. Maybe we should end it now."

Someone put a hand over my nose and mouth and now I couldn't breathe at all. I tried to scream but I couldn't. I moaned. The hand didn't let go.

The hand came off my mouth for a long moment. I wheezed and coughed and sucked in breath.

"Help," I said, voice damaged and scratchy, to no one in particular.

"No," Madame said. I gasped in air, my lungs burning. The tight corset made the feeling of suffocation all the stronger.

They're going to kill me, I thought. *I'm going to die here.*

"I don't want to do this anymore," I said. I started to sob. "Please let me go."

"What don't you want anymore? Life?" Madame said. "We can arrange that."

She clamped her hand back over my mouth.

"I thought this was what you wanted," Madame said. "You don't value your life. You don't value yourself or anyone else. You have no interest in pleasure, in joy. You want to die. You told me yourself. So let us kill you. This is your chance."

She lifted up her hand for a quick second, letting me inhale one painful, sandpapery breath before she brought her hand back.

"You told me you wanted to die, but were too worried about your poor dear husband," Madame said. "I have no such inhibitions about your life.

"Stop me," she said. "If you want to live, you'll have to stop me. No one here cares what happens to you. Maybe no one anywhere. Why should they? It's your life, Lily, no one else's. If you want it, you have to fight for it. You have to want it and you have to fight."

I was beyond words, beyond thought, dizzy from lack of oxygen, drowning in fear. I strained against the fabric tying me tight, tried to grab at anything with my hands, but only found air. I'd been struggling against the arm restraints and loosened them up a bit—enough so that if I squeezed my arms together, I could start to work the restraints down my arms. When they were down to my wrists, I'd be able to pull them off.

But I wasn't at my wrists yet, and I was starting to feel light-headed. It felt like a vise was strapped around my chest as my lungs screamed for air. I didn't know if I was going to make it.

Behind the blindfold, my vision was starting to go red, and then white around the edges, as I got the cloth down to my forearms and then down to my wrists.

With the last of my strength I ripped it off. I tried to pull Madame's hand off my face. I was furious. She fought me, but using both hands I fought her off, freed my nose and mouth, and took a wheezing, horrible, painful breath as I tore off my blindfold. As my eyes adjusted to the light I could see that the room was dark. I could just barely make out the four women standing around me. On the back of the wall was a rack of strange wooden tools that I couldn't imagine any sexual use for.

Still shaky, I stood up and loosened the top of my corset so I could breathe. I realized I was crying, and now I heard myself sob.

Fuck these women and their games. I hated them.

But maybe I didn't want them to kill me, either. Maybe I wanted to live.

I stumbled out of the room and to the hall, where, overwhelmed by drugs and emotion, I fell down. I felt myself losing balance and consciousness as it was happening, and was able to steer myself down to my knees and then to the floor, on a thick rug older than America.

I heard women's voices speaking in French. And before my eyes, I saw that same strange woman with the pointed hat, looking at me with curiosity, just before it all went black.

23.

I was standing in the hallway. No, I was walking. But hadn't I been walking for far too long? Of course I had. It was time to stop now.

I opened a door. There, behind it, was Abel. But he was, if not healed, at least able to stand and speak.

"You aren't supposed to be here," he said, and shut the door on me.

I was back in the hallway again. I opened another door. Behind it was my mother. Seeing her again made me sad. I missed her and I wished I'd been able to do more for her. I wanted to tell her I loved her and missed her. But she closed the door on me.

"This is not for you," she said.

I was back in the hallway. There was only one more door.

I knew what was in the room. But I couldn't bring myself to open it.

Beauty. For years now, I saw, I'd been angry at my book and even angrier at that earlier version of me, the young, hungry, hopeful woman who'd written it. The book and the young woman had both tricked me. They had fooled me into thinking life would be an endlessly fascinating adventure. I'd look at other people's lives—at their boredom, their drudgery, their pain—and imagine that my book had given me the key to escape from all of that.

I wasn't just wrong. I was wrong in such a vast and specific way that I felt like the punch line of a cruel joke. In a few years I went from being a minor celebrity with a life full of glamour, travel, and praise, to living alone in the farmhouse with Abel, cleaning his shit, wiping his drool, counting change to buy our groceries on bad days, and fighting with insurance companies and doctors on the best.

I opened the door, expecting to see a copy of my book, ready to mock me and the idiot I'd been, and still was.

Instead, though, the door led outside. The sun had come up and the sky was bright and sunny, brilliant in technicolor pink and purple. On the great green lawn was a huge book, an elephant folio, open to about the middle. The pages fluttered in the breeze. Something was written on them, but I couldn't see what. I stepped closer...

"*Chère*. Wake up, *chère*."

"Come along, my dear. Don't worry us."

Slowly, I opened my eyes. I had no idea how much time had passed. Someone had carried me back into the room with the black rose wallpaper. The room had been cleaned up and the maids were gone. Kat was sitting above me, gently waking me up. The other witches were sitting on the settee along the wall. They all looked at me when I sat up.

Madame came over and hugged me warmly. I hugged her back.

"Here she is," she said. "Our beloved."

She poured me a glass of champagne and gestured for everyone to stand up. They did. Madame held up her glass in a toast and we all joined in.

"Sometimes in life," she said, "we need to be born again, as you were tonight. We welcome you to your new life. All things are possible—pleasure, love. And some are guaranteed—sadness, heartbreak, and disappointment. Life is always a risk. I hope going forward, you find the risk worth taking. But you have to want it. You have to want to live."

"The first half of your life is written," Kat said. "But, I remind you, the pages of the second half are blank. They wait for you to write them."

Another wave of pleasure from the pill, whatever it had been, overcame me. I started to feel the slightly mechanical, highly pleasurable feeling of a flood of serotonin.

I looked at the women. Somehow, something had changed. It was grueling and painful and somehow a little humiliating to see, but Madame was right. I wanted to live.

Madame gestured to Kat, who came to my side and began to untie my corset. Carrie-Ann slid the little silk wisp of my underwear down to my ankles. As she did she brushed her hands between my legs. Feeling an encouraging wetness, she brushed again.

"Kneel," Madame said. I did. I saw they'd put a rug on the floor, thick and plush under my knees and shins. I kneeled, sitting back on my feet. Kat took a big silk kimono in pale lavender off the settee and wrapped me up in it, warm and comfortable.

Maude must have left the room and come back, because she now sat in front of me with a tray of fruit and cheese and dark chocolates.

I reached for them. Maude gently pushed my hand back, picked up a fat, ripe pear, took a bite to break the skin, and held it up to my mouth. I bit in; it was sweet and delicious. I realized I was ravenous and ate the rest of it. Next she held up a dark bitter square of chocolate to my lips, then another; I ate three, the tart chocolate meeting the sweetness of the pear.

As Maude was feeding me, Kat gently tied my hands behind my back with a soft, silky fabric.

Madame left the room with purpose. Maude held up an apple to my mouth, I shook my head no. She put the apple down and put her hands on my breasts and leaned in and kissed me on my lips. I moaned. Her lips were soft and full of affection, and when she brought them to my lips it felt like sweetness, like a kiss from a nectar-heavy flower. Excruciatingly, she pulled her lips from mine, leaving me cold and wanting, and then brought her mouth down to my breasts, which was sweeter still. It wasn't long before I was breathless and nearly writhing. My eyes were closed and I was falling into a fog when I heard Madame's voice.

I opened my eyes. She was crouched down next to me, holding a small silver tray. On the tray was a long sewing needle, a little glass jar of black ink, and a bowl of clear liquid with a cotton ball floating in it. After a moment the smell reached me and I realized the clear liquid was rubbing alcohol.

"Do you trust me?" Madame said.

I shivered and thought about the past day.

"Yes," I said. "I trust you."

Madame smiled. *"Bien,"* she said. She nudged me to shift my position so I was sitting on the floor, legs bent in front of me, feet apart. I felt raw and inspected, utterly vulnerable. Maude moved behind me and Madame in front of me, sitting in between my open legs with her silver tray between us. Kat and Carrie-Ann had made their way back to the settee, where they were languidly kissing and fondling each other with familiar comfort, long-term lovers who still thrilled each other. Carrie-Ann pinched Kat's nipple, hard, and Kat leaned back and shivered.

Maude roamed her hands over my body, finding all the most sensitive parts, while Madame prepared her needle and ink. She took the cotton out of the alcohol and swabbed clean a small spot high on my inner right thigh.

"Relax," Madame said. "It won't hurt much."

Maude gently pulled me back until I was leaning against her. She brought her hands down between my legs and carefully began to push, stroke, tap, and tease. I closed my eyes and leaned against her and moaned. She was extremely skilled. I was breathing hard and had nearly forgotten about Madame and her needle when the first poke came. It stung like a bee, but felt almost unbearably good at the same time. As soon as the sting was over, I desperately wanted it again. The two women both continued, each on their own schedule, Maude caressing, Madame pricking. Together the two sensations brought me to a place I hadn't known existed. I hadn't slept in over a day, which added to the strange floating sensation. I felt like I was off the earth, suspended in a realm of pure sensation, where pleasure and pain were no longer distinguishable. Dimly, through my sex-addled brain, I saw that this was a gift Madame had given me—the knowledge that plea-sure and pain were both sensations, nothing more and nothing less. A sensation could be borne, felt, and lived through.

Madame continued to poke. Periodically she wiped away blood and ink with the cold alcohol-soaked cotton. Maude put one and then two and then three fingers inside me, in and out in a strange, unpredictable rhythm. She found a spot that she seemed to know well enough to look for. She pushed against the spot, varying her rhythm and pace, gentle but precise and firm.

At first I didn't know what it was. I felt pressure, somewhat like having to pee but not like that at all. I was beyond words, nearly beyond thought, but I realized: this was it. This was the Precious Substance.

She kept gently, rhythmically, pushing on the spot. I felt it gathering like a tidal wave. An unnamed, internal part of my body grew as tense and insistent. I barely felt Madame's stinging needle and the wave grew stronger and stronger.

"I'm—" I managed to get out. "I—"

But before I could say anything, fluid rushed out of me and I was overwhelmed with the tidal wave, dropped into the voluptuous blackness of pure empty space, all thoughts obliterated by pleasure that almost hurt, falling through a void. The wave was like an orgasm but not exactly one; the strain didn't so much break as dissolve into a dark, ecstatic nothingness. Just as it was ebbing, I began to build to an intense orgasm, every muscle reaching an exquisite tension before overflowing into a seemingly impossible, nearly painful release, bringing me again to blissful blackness, peaceful and pleasurable beyond all thought.

I spun up into blackness, and then back down to the ground. Slowly, I became aware of my ordinary physical body again—the feel of the rug on my legs, the awkward angle of my arms. I took a few deep breaths.

I was physically wet but just as strongly some spiritual dam inside me had fallen down, a wall I'd built around something too broken to trust the world with it. But that wall had never kept me safe. It only locked me in with my pain, leaving it to fester and spoil. I'd locked out all hope, all pleasure, and now, with a force like the ocean, the wall had crumbled, and my protection was gone.

Maude gently withdrew her hand and wrapped her arms around my chest, hugging me, whispering in my ear. I realized Madame had stopped poking me. I opened my eyes.

Madame, Kat, Carrie-Ann, and Maude were sitting around me, smiling, eager to soothe me. The servants were back, watching from their spot against the wall, ready to serve, anxious for my happiness.

"Look," Madame said. I looked at my leg and it took me a minute to identify the design. She'd etched me with a tiny pomegranate fruit, not much bigger than my thumbnail. She covered it up with a bandage and surgical tape.

"You've been to the land of the dead," Madame said. "Now, it's time for you to leave, and live again."

"Thank you," I said.

Madame M. looked at me, a question on her face.

"Surely," she said, "you see now—"

"I still want the book," I said.

Madame's smile slid right off her face. It was replaced by a wry smirk.

"Very well," she said, standing up, now efficient and brisk. I could tell I'd disappointed her. "Breakfast will be ready by now. You must be ravenous. Eat, then leave. I'll make sure you have the buyer's name before you go."

I loved Madame now. But I wanted the book more.

We all left the room together. Madame went upstairs, and Kat, Maude, Carrie-Ann, and I went to the dining room, where another maid was waiting to serve us from a small buffet of scrambled eggs, fresh croissants, cured fish, cheese, cut fruit, and coffee and tea. Everything tasted delicious. We made ordinary conversation about my business, the region, things I ought to see while I was in France.

I'd checked the schedule; the train back to Paris left at 10:15. After we ate, it was time for me to get dressed and go.

Madame and Maude didn't say goodbye at all. Kat and Carrie-Ann met me at the door, and Kat walked me to my taxi when it came. She hugged me tight before I left.

"Remember," she said as we hugged, "no magic is stronger than a true connection with another person."

"And Madame said to give you this—"

From her pocket she took a piece of creamy thick paper.

I took it from her. There was a short note in handwriting so perfect, it was almost calligraphy.

> *The owner of The Book of the Most Precious Substance is Jean-Michel Florian. He's a famously difficult man, and I doubt he's looking to sell, but I wish you luck anyway.*
>
> *I think you'll live to regret this. But I hope, very sincerely, that I'm wrong.*
>
> *M.*

24.

I took the train back to Paris with a clear head and a light heart, tiny tattoo burning. I felt pleasantly high from the sex and the drugs and most of all from the bizarre, intense release of the Precious Substance. I understood now why it was such an important part of magic. I'd read that Crowley said magic was "the Science and Art of causing Change to occur in conformity with Will." That took a clear vision (will) and the means to execute it (power). It seemed obvious to me now that you could get that power from ritual, from herbs and minerals, from charms, you could steal it from others—or you could find it in yourself. Likewise with will—it could come from anywhere, but the best, most genuine will was deep inside you. And releasing the Precious Substance was like breaking a wall around that will. The wired, crabby exhaustion that had been my default mood over the past few years had dissipated. My thoughts were clear and focused.

As I walked onto the train, an old woman, small and bent over, pushed me out of her way to get on board. She had two big bags and a sour expression. I reached out to take one of her bags and begrudgingly she let me. She ranted in French as I followed her to her seat. When we reached it she settled in and I put her bags on the rack above her. As I did I brushed against a man standing next to me, also putting a bag up on the rack. He was in his twenties, and when he lifted his bag he accidentally pulled up his shirt, revealing the breathtaking expanse of his slim rib cage and taut torso. He caught me looking and smiled. I smiled back. We were both happy with the moment and happy to let it end.

Lucas and I texted on the train and made plans to meet at a café near the train station. Lucas was at the café when I arrived. He was smiling and excited. We greeted each other with a kiss and I sat down and ordered more food—all this sex was making me hungry— and a glass of wine. Our reunion was strangely happy for both of us.

"I think I missed you," Lucas said, seemingly surprised.

I was pretty sure I'd missed him too, although I wasn't going to say it. I asked him about his day before I launched into mine. He told me quickly about his book shopping and wandering Paris in between phone calls and emails to librarians, book dealers, and collectors, none of which produced anything fruitful but seemed to have added up to a nice day. I told Lucas everything I'd learned: that I knew who had the book, and that I'd learned that my body could, indeed, produce the Precious Substance, although the question remained if Lucas and I could produce it together.

But it wasn't all good news. On the train, I'd read on the internet about Jean-Michel Florian, the man who had the last complete copy of *The Book of the Most Precious Substance*. He was born into

poverty in a small town near Lourdes. But a Christian he was not. Jean-Michel began, at an early age, to worship money. He delivered newspapers at nine. By twelve he was working in the printing presses; by twenty, editing the local paper; by thirty, running a chain of papers; and now, at fifty, he owned and ran one of the biggest media companies in the world, including four book publishers, countless websites, one giant news service, and most of what was left of the newspaper business. He was, maybe, the most ruthless businessman in the world.

"I know who he is," Lucas said. "He outbid me a few times. I wasn't supposed to know it was him. He keeps his collecting under wraps. All very mysterious."

Money was exciting to Lucas. You could see it in his eyes as he talked. Not for the first time, I wondered how far he'd go to get it.

We were about to find out.

Lucas had a good reputation in the book world, although more as a buyer than a seller, and it wasn't all that hard for him to get in touch with Florian's first assistant, Julien, who handled all his book business. Lucas sent him an email. We walked around Paris while we waited for a reply.

Everywhere you looked in Paris there was something beautiful, something designed to feed your eye and, maybe, through that window, your soul. We stopped to look in a little beauty shop on Rue Bonaparte. I sampled from a beautiful little glass pot of hand cream, tested rose perfume from a tiny vial. Both together cost more than my food budget for a normal month. The saleswoman mistook me for a potential paying customer and gave me a handful of samples in little packets and vials to take home.

Now I told Lucas about the non-book-related parts of the past few days. He seemed to enjoy hearing about it all. By then we'd reached the Seine. Of course Lucas wanted to stop into Shakespeare and Company. I glanced at a few shelves and then waited outside while Lucas picked up a few things. Strangely, I didn't feel like looking at books. I walked over to the river and looked at the view. In a few minutes Lucas came over to join me. He slid up next to me and put his arm around my waist.

"So," he half whispered into my ear, "how exactly did you make the Precious Substance with the witches?"

I turned to Lucas. His eyes were bright in a way I now recognized. I half whispered back some of the details.

But when we got back to the hotel room, it didn't happen. Plenty of other things happened. We spent a highly pleasurable evening together. Lucas looked for the previously unknown spot Maude had known about. He got close. I felt a pressure grow in me and I thought maybe we were there, but it was just normal, if wonderful, sex. No waves, no floods, no ocean.

We were both too satisfied to be disappointed. After, I took a bath. I was washing my hair when I heard Lucas say, "Holy shit."

"What?" I said.

"He wrote back," Lucas said. "Julien. The assistant. *Of course we are able to meet. If acceptable and convenient, please meet at our lawyer's office on Monday at ten in the morning.*"

"Holy shit," I said again.

"Holy shit," Lucas repeated. The meeting was both acceptable and convenient. We accepted.

Room service came. Lucas had ordered us an indulgent, expensive dinner of roast beef with fancy potatoes, red wine, and slices of apple tart for dessert. We ate in bed, sharing everything, and then I fell asleep as we watched bad Hollywood movies dubbed in French. I woke up in the middle of the night. Lucas had turned out the lights and turned off the TV and put our dirty dishes in the hall and straightened the blankets. It was nice to wake up to. I turned and put my arm around him. I'd become used to having him close.

The next day, after coffee and croissants, Lucas set up a video chat with Haber for that afternoon. In the meantime, we bought sandwiches from a café and ate them in our room, fooled around a little after lunch, didn't consummate it, and sorted and straightened ourselves just in time for the incoming call.

"Do you have the book?" Haber said as soon as he saw us.

"No," I said. "But we're close. We need to know exactly what your offer is."

"I told you," Haber barked. "There's no limit. No reasonable request will be denied."

"A million?" I said. Haber nodded.

"Two million?" Lucas ventured.

Haber looked annoyed and nodded again.

"I need that book," Haber said.

"Who's your man in Paris?" Lucas said, which was a very Lucas thing to say. "We're going to need him to put a reasonable amount, as you put it, in an escrow account."

Haber looked annoyed again. He never smiled or looked excited or happy. Just nothing or annoyed or occasionally smirking. Hearing we were close to the book only made him hungrier. All that money and no happiness.

People thought money would make them happy. But money was the consolation prize in life. Money was what you had left to dream for when all the other dreams died. Money was what would keep you going when nothing else could delight you again.

He had his man in Paris put $2.5 million in escrow. We got off the phone. It was time to go get the book.

25.

We met Jean-Michel Florian's assistant, Julien, the next day at Florian's lawyer's office in the business district. The building was a very Parisian combination of whipped cream baroque plaster and stern governmental limestone. The office itself was both luxurious and slightly shabby; the waiting room had two old leather sofas and dusty paintings of hunting scenes on the wall. The secretary who let us in was sixty-ish and didn't smile at us before, during, or after our meeting. We got there at 9:55. At exactly 10:00 the secretary led us into a conference room with a long wooden table and dark green leather chairs and more hunting scenes on the wall. Julien was around forty, blond, with a wide face and a wide smile. He wore a suit worth more than everything I owned. We all introduced ourselves and shook hands and sat down.

"Good afternoon," he said in heavily accented, but flawless, English. "Mr. Markson, Ms. Albrecht, both of you are of course well known to me. I had no idea you were in business together."

"It's limited," I said. "We share a client for this one book."

I felt Lucas look at me, and then back at Julien. Was it limited? Neither of us was sure yet.

"Ah," Julien said, skimming over the potentially awkward moment. "Ms. Albrecht—"

"Lily," I said. "Please."

"Lily," he said. "I hope another book is coming soon?"

"Absolutely," I said. "Next year."

I wondered if it was true. Maybe, finally, it was. That morning, for the first time in years, I'd found myself making notes on the desk pad in the hotel room. I remembered that I used to always carry a notebook with me, and a decent pen. It was just a few words about a book theft in Paris I'd always been intrigued by. But it was something. After years of nothing, it was something.

Julien smiled. "And Mr. Markson? I hear the library collection is absolutely exquisite."

"Just Lucas," Lucas said. "And thank you. It's a labor of love."

"So," Julien said, "what brings us all here today?"

"We've heard," I began, as we'd agreed in a morning of strategizing, "that Monsieur Florian has the only known copy of an extremely rare book. And we have a client who would like to buy it for a very, very generous amount."

"Oh, really?" Julien said, still smiling.

"Yes," I said. *The Book of the Most Precious Substance.*"

Now Julien's smile froze.

"No," he said. "I'm sorry, but I don't believe this book is in our library."

"It is," I said. "And—"

"*Non,*" Julien said. "Monsieur Florian owns no such book. And under no circumstances will Monsieur Florian be discussing such book, not with you or anyone else."

"But we've heard—" I began.

Julien cut me off. "What you've heard is immaterial. Monsieur Florian owns no such book, and does not collect in the area."

"Which area?" I said, getting annoyed.

"Any area you might be interested in," Julien said. "Thank you very much for your time, and goodbye."

Julien stood up and left the room. Lucas and I looked at each other, eyes wide.

"Well," Lucas said, "I think he has the book."

"I think so," I said.

We left the office. Over lunch in a Cameroonian restaurant, sharing peanut stew, greens, and plantains, we talked about what to do next. I'd never had Cameroonian food. Lucas liked to try new things, which reminded me that I did too.

"We could ask again," I said. I knew it was a bad idea, but we had to start somewhere. Lucas shrugged, and I knew that he knew that I knew it was a bad idea. I wondered if that meant we were in a relationship now. Of course, we *were* in a relationship. The question was: what kind?

"You know people," he said. "I mean, people in the book world. The literary world. Want to see what you can find out about Florian?"

"Blackmail?" I said.

Lucas shrugged again, this one a shrug of nonchalance. Lucas, I'd learned, was fairly immune from shame. Getting what he wanted was a priority to him. I wasn't sure if I liked it or not. It was certainly handy now.

"Not necessarily," he said. "Maybe there's something he wants. Maybe something we can do for him. We need leverage," Lucas said. This was his area: the ways of men and money. "Let's see what we can find."

After lunch I bought a cheap plain notebook and a better pen in a little stationery shop and I wrote a few more paragraphs about the book thief. He detested movies. He fed stray cats. Then Lucas and I sat at a café and I made a list of people I knew who might know Jean-Michel Florian. I came up with eight: two editors, two writers, three bookstore owners, and a man who owned five office buildings in Paris and was a bit of a literary groupie, always hanging around literary fairs and taking writers out to expensive meals. He was a decent guy with too much money and was a frustrated writer himself. Yves something-or-other. Yves, I figured, might know Jean-Michel.

I emailed an American novelist I knew from my *Beauty* days, Jim Vivian. We hadn't spoken in a few years. Did he know Yves's last name? Or how to get in touch with him?

Lucas and I walked back to the room, detouring to the Tuileries for a walk on the way. Spring was early, and no flowers were out yet, but the sun was shining and the grass was green. Parents and grandparents walked with children, gardeners trimmed, and a beekeeper tweaked his hives.

Lucas held my hand as we walked. It was a minute before I even realized we were doing it. Somehow, over the past week, it had become a natural, easy habit to take each other's hands as we walked.

"What if this was our life?" Lucas said.

"This *is* our life," I said.

"No," he said. *"Our* life. In the lawyer's office, you said this was temporary. But what if it wasn't?"

"I'm—" I began automatically. I was going to say *I'm married.* But that was ridiculous. I would always take care of Abel. That didn't mean I couldn't be in a relationship with someone else.

"Think about it," Lucas said. "Maybe we never have to go back to the real world. Maybe this never has to end."

Of course I'd been thinking the same. Abel wouldn't miss me. Awe wouldn't mind a generous bump in salary for more responsibility. Lucas and I could get a little place in Paris. Stay for a while, then move on to Milan or London. Buy, sell, and read books. Fuck whoever we wanted.

I said nothing and put all thoughts of the future aside. For now, we had to get the book. By the time we were back in our hotel, Jim Vivian had responded:

> *Lily, it's so good to hear from you. I hope you've gotten*
> *my emails over the years. I would love to hear from*
> *you when you have the time. How's the book business?*
> *How's Abel? Anyway, yes, Yves is Yves Saint Claire*
> *and his contact info is below. Are you ever in the city?*
> *Lunch sometime? Angela is OK and the kids are doing*
> *great—Adrian is 11 and Kitty is 13, if you can believe*
> *it. Angela sends her best and would love to see you as*
> *well. Please call when you can.*

I searched through my emails. I'd last emailed with Jim five years ago. He'd written every year since then, sometimes twice a year, and I hadn't replied.

I wrote back right away. *Thanks so much. I'm sorry I haven't responded to your emails. I'll call you soon.*

I didn't send it. Instead, I called him. We talked for forty-five minutes. I didn't tell him about the book or about Lucas. I just told him about selling books and Abel's ever-declining health. And he told me about his kids, about his new novel, about people we knew in common—friends, or people who used to be friends—and commiserated with me that life, sometimes, was not very fucking fair. He'd lost both his parents since we'd last talked, and his wife, Angela, was struggling with health problems no one seemed able to diagnose. We agreed to have lunch in Brooklyn exactly one month from today.

"Who was that?" Lucas asked.

"An old friend," I told him.

I texted Yves Saint Claire. We'd only met a few times and I thought calling might be awkward. But Yves lived to do favors for writers, and he called me back right away.

"You're in Paris?" Yves said. "It's too late to get reservations at Le Cinq, but I'm sure we can find something good. And hopefully you've got good news about a new book?"

I laughed. I told him I did not have good news about a new book yet, and I would love to have dinner another time, but first, I had a question. I needed to get to Jean-Michel Florian.

"Ahh," Yves said. "Now that I cannot do for you. We're not friends. Jean-Michel Florian has no friends. He has enemies, and people he does business with, and as far as I know, that's the sum total of his human relations. I've always thought he's not really a man at all, but more like a machine that prints money. He controls four publishers, and has one of the best book collections in the world, but I honestly don't think he reads. I mean, not like you and I read. He reads for *information*." Yves spat out the last word like a curse. "For *facts*. And, of course, tips on how to dominate the world and slay his enemies. Believe me, whatever you're selling, or buying, I can find you a better client."

I asked if they'd ever met. Many times, Yves said, through business and through the kind of social events that are actually business affairs. But they'd never exchanged more than a few words.

"You know who really loathes him," Yves said, as an afterthought, "is Lucien."

"Lucien?" I said.

"Lucien Roche," he said. "The writer? Friends with your late husband?"

Lucien Roche was the writer Abel had introduced me to in Paris our first year of dating. Lucien had written five books, and as far as I was concerned he was the best writer alive. But he didn't sell all that well, and I couldn't imagine his connection to Jean-Michel Florian, who published glossy bestsellers. Lucien wrote strange little memoir-novel hybrids that sold maybe two thousand copies each, mostly to other writers. One book ended in the middle of a paragraph. Another was told nearly entirely in footnotes to a strange political screed about dreams.

"Abel isn't quite 'late' yet," I said. "But you're right. They were friends."

Yves was mortified and apologized profusely and unnecessarily. I promised it was okay. And did he know how I could find Lucien?

Yes, he would send me his contact information immediately. And dinner next time I was in Paris? Absolutely, I promised.

"And, Lily," he said, "if there's ever anything I can do…I know the life of a writer is not always so secure, and I've been very fortunate."

"Yves," I said. I was about to make a series of defensive reassurances—*I'm fine, I don't need help, I need nothing and no one, especially not your pity*—but instead I thought, *Why not?*

"Thank you," I finally said. "Maybe I'll take you up on that someday." With many thanks and goodbyes, we hung up.

I'd met Lucien Roche with Abel. He'd been something like a hero to me when I was young and still had heroes. He wrote what he wanted and people could take it or not. Most other writers I knew of when I was writing my first book were already trying to climb over each other to reach the top of the sales charts—and in a few years, social media would inspire them to stomp even harder on each other as they did, rendering sales and cash as the only worthy measure of a book. Lucien seemed, almost on purpose, to write things that had no chance at all of selling wide. When a Hollywood actor tried to option one of his books—how you would have made a movie out of Lucien's biography of his first dog, I have no idea—Lucien burned the book in a Paris art gallery in protest. He knew something everyone else had forgotten. Including me.

Now I texted him, writing and rewriting probably ten times before I sent it.

Hi, this is Lily Albrecht, Abel's wife. We met ten years

ago. I don't know if you remember me. I'm in Paris and could use a favor—may I take you out to lunch tomorrow?

He texted back in ten minutes: *Dinner tonight 8 pm you're buying I'm broke.* I smiled. Underneath was an address. I read it to Lucas.

"This really might work," Lucas said.

"It really might," I agreed.

26.

As we got ready for dinner, I thought about what Lucas said. This didn't have to end. I couldn't see us ever becoming a regular couple, monogamous and married. Maybe, I let myself think, we could just keep going like this—sleeping together, sleeping with other people, doing as we wished. But we could stick together. Maybe.

But first, we had to get the book. And by now, I was sure I was going to get it. Almost sure. My doubts were smaller every day. A much larger force was at work now, pulling me toward the book like gravity. I half believed that I could stand perfectly still and the book would find its way to me, if I let it. But I wasn't confident enough to test it out.

Going home without it was impossible. It just couldn't happen.

Lucien had picked out an excellent restaurant for us to meet at for dinner, which was a good thing, because he was an hour late. Lucas and I had eaten our way through half the menu by the time

Lucien showed up, not just late but also drunk, glowing, and smiling like a child on Christmas. His hair was gray and his face had shifted but he had the same impish look as when I'd met him.

He attacked me with a giant hug and kissed me on both cheeks. I introduced him to Lucas and we caught up. Lucien said we were lucky to find him in Paris—most of his time these days was spent in Morocco or Exarchia, the anarchist community in Athens.

"Paris has become a fucking...what do you call it? Like a corporate cow house," Lucien said after we ordered.

"A factory farm?" I said after a moment.

"Yes," Lucien said with excitement. "Too expensive, too corporate, no real characters left. I mean, except me, but I bought my apartment thirty years ago and I'm almost never here. Bah. Tell me about Abel. Can he talk? Eat? Who's taking care of him?"

I bristled a little, defensive, and then I remembered that Lucien loved Abel and was right to ask about him. I was just so unused to his honesty, it almost felt like an insult. I answered all his questions: no talking, no eating without help, Awe. Lucien put a hand over his face, not hiding his sorrow.

"Shit," he said after a few more questions. "Who deserved this shit less than you? Than Abel?"

"Lots of people, I guess," I said. "I'm not special."

"Of course you are," Lucien said. He shook his head and made a gesture with his hands, knocking over the salt and pepper in the process. "Not special? How could you say that. We're the most special people in the world, people like you and me. We can create"—he tapped his forehead—"with nothing but this. That's magic, Lily. That's power. You're still writing?"

"Yes," I lied. "But—"

"No no no," Lucien said. "No *but*. What *but* could matter compared to doing what you're meant to do? Of course, you're living with a tragedy. But tragedy makes writers, it doesn't end them. I myself lost my wife." He caught the look on my face. "You didn't know that. I was very young. I almost killed myself. Yes, hospitals, restraints, all that. But then, I wrote again. You will too. That's what we do, us writers. It's alchemy. We turn shit into gold."

Suddenly I had tears in my eyes. Lucien reached over and took my hand.

"Lily," he said. "I have faith in you."

No one had said that to me, I realized, since I'd lost Abel. Tears were streaming down my face. Lucas put his hand on my shoulder. I felt so overwhelmed by affection, from both of them, that I couldn't stand it. I shook them both off.

"I *am* writing again," I said to Lucien. "And I'm going to finish another book. Soon."

The waiter brought more appetizers. Lucas had picked out three for us to share: a bright bowl of pickled pink cauliflower, green cucumber, and white asparagus; a small salad of fennel and sweet, fresh baby lettuce; and some tiny hearts of rabbits or chickens that I wasn't inclined to eat but Lucas and Lucien wolfed down and declared excellent.

"So," Lucien said, "we talked about the important topics. Now you said you need a favor. What is it?"

I told him a short version of the situation: I sold books, I had a customer who wanted a book expensive enough that it could change my life, I'd lied and said I could get it, Jean-Michel Florian had it and he didn't want to sell it. Yves had mentioned to me that Lucien hated Jean-Michel, and I wondered why. I was trying to find out everything I could about him, in order to entice, manipulate, or bully him into selling the book to me.

Lucien's face lit up.

"Oh, Lily," he said. "I've been waiting for this day for a long, long time."

As we ate, Lucien told us brief snippets of a story that seemed too wild to be true. And if it was true, it wasn't immediately clear what we could do with it. But after a long series of questions and answers over our main course, dessert, and bottle after bottle of wine, we came up with an idea.

Lucien sent out a long series of texts. After dinner we went to his apartment. He poured wine and an hour later we were joined by one of the most beautiful women I'd ever seen. She said her name was Helene, which I already knew wasn't her real name, because Lucien had told us she wouldn't tell us her real name. She was about thirty, with messy light brown hair, teeth that were slightly too big for her mouth, and lips in a perfect, permanent natural pout. She sat down. Lucien poured more wine. She took a long, thin, elegant joint out of her purse and lit it.

Then she told us how we were going to get the book from Jean-Michel Florian.

"If you were French," she began, "you would know who I am, and I wouldn't be doing this. Not because I'm ashamed. I just don't want the complications in my life. Anyway, as I'm sure Lucien told you, I'm a writer. Coincidence in life is a strange thing. It was my dream in life to be published by Papier Noir, one of Jean-Michel's publishing houses. I don't believe in fate, you know. Not fate, not God, none of it. It's all horseshit as far as I'm concerned.

"I was working as a call girl. I wasn't ashamed of it then and I'm not now. I don't care about sex. It doesn't bother me. I don't particularly like it, but I don't care about it. But I never told my clients I was a writer. They would have found a way to use it against me. They were always looking for some little crumb of your real self to grab on to. They say men don't pay prostitutes for sex, they pay them to leave when the sex is done. But what they really pay for is the game of trying to get more than they agreed to. The game is, the girl leaves, but you have a little something of her to hold on to. Something you stole.

"Jean-Michel was a regular customer. I told him a fake story and he believed it—that I was a girl from a shitty part of Paris, that I had no family, that I wanted to be a hair cutter and was going to school to get a certificate to cut hair. I liked Jean-Michel, relatively speaking— he was smart, generous, and never dull. Not generous—how do you say—he was generous with money. A big spender. I mean, with money. Only money. Not, like, *sympathique*. Not kind. I saw him ten or fifteen times, maybe more, maybe less. Also, he had a beautiful house and a beautiful library. Always good food and excellent wine, usually champagne. I knew he was interested in magic and all that horseshit. I don't believe in any of it, but I find it interesting. Gullibility interests me. So does, how do you call it, the other magic, perception, magic on the stage. So I enjoyed to talk with him about this.

"I should mention here that I'm very good at sex. I don't say this to brag, but it will help you understand why he was fond of me. I don't have a gag reflex and I have a very high threshold for pain.

In fact, the only part that interests me is the extremity of it—but I hate all the theatrics and costumes and all that foolishness, so I don't indulge often. All this, I think, is why he called me to participate in the acts with him. That stupid game with the book.

"He thought I had no limits. In that regard, he's quite stupid. Jean-Michel isn't quite capable of seeing other people as real. To him, they're all either a tool or an obstacle. Use them or destroy them. That's all. He had no idea who I was, even after we'd spent twenty or thirty hours together.

"One night, he called and asked if I could come over in an hour or two. This wasn't so unusual—his schedule was very, how do you say, much variation, so he never planned ahead. He called me when he found himself with some free time, I think. When I got there, the house was dark, which was not unusual, and the room was lit by candles, which was also not unusual. Have you seen his house? It's tremendous, very modern, totally cold. All gray and black. Sometimes we had wine or dinner first, but this night, we got right to it. He sat on the bed and I got on top of him, straddling him. He touched me and he became excited, as expected. He liked to proceed a little on the slow side, as if we were regular people having regular sex, so we kept going like that for a while. I took off my clothes one piece at a time. After a while I'm in my lingerie, and his shirt is undone. Jean-Michel, as you may know, is a famously handsome man. More so, of course, if you don't know him.

"And then he stops me, and tells me to stand up. He has a look on his face as if he's giving me a gift. Why he thought I'd enjoy his filthy little things, I have no idea.

"Let me go back a little: For a few dates previous to this, he always had this dirty old book in the room with us when we had sex. Occasionally he would jump up out of bed, rush to the book, and rub some sweat or come or whatever on it. I didn't know what it was and I didn't care. After five or ten ordinary visits, he became obsessed with making me—" She conferred with Lucien in French for a few minutes.

"Squirt," she continued, having confirmed the lingo. "I don't do that. I never have. After a few times of failing, I peed on his hand and pretended to come. Of course, all my coming was fake. What he thought was wetness was a—she made a gesture of insertion—"I put in before I saw clients. Jean-Michel was very sexually sophisticated in terms of acts, anatomy, techniques, but he didn't understand pleasure. I don't think he was really capable of it.

"So the previous time, he'd smeared some of my piss on the book. Now, before we got going, we stood up off the bed. Jean-Michel had this smile on his face—it made me wary. He didn't ordinarily smile much. He took my hand and led me to another room down the hall. A guest bedroom. And there, tied up on the bed with ropes, was a girl with a cloth over her mouth. A young woman. She was maybe nineteen, long hair, also a prostitute. You can tell, don't ask me how. You just can. She was terrified, and it was clear she was not here by choice. This wasn't a sex game. It was a kidnapping.

"I didn't let on that I was absolutely horrified. Instantly I saw that I was this girl's only chance. I pretended to be intrigued. Turned on. Jean-Michel was thrilled, of course. I stroked the girl's legs, her face. Jean-Michel was going on and on about power and completion and the magical working. As I said, I don't understand, or care about, any of that. On a nightstand was the same dirty old book, and next to that was a knife—an expensive Japanese kitchen knife.

"I pretended this situation turned me on immensely, and I straddled the girl and began to touch myself, my cunt above hers, touching myself with one hand and squeezing her breasts with the other. The knife was in reach, but I waited until Jean-Michel sat down in a chair a few feet away, had his dick out, and was stroking himself. His dick was very red—very big and red. I don't really like any of them, but his was particularly repulsive at that moment. Like a horrible, overstuffed worm. When I could tell he was entirely wrapped up in his dick, and his pants were at an awkward angle, I grabbed the knife and, as quickly as I could, cut the girl free, took her hand, and we ran to the bedroom, where I had my purse. I never went on a date without weapons, without a knife and, how do you say? Buzz-buzz."

She held her hand out and made a buzzing sound.

"A taser," I said.

"Yes," she said. "Jean-Michel was still stumbling around with his pants down and his dick out. I gave the girl the knife, grabbed my taser from my purse, grabbed my purse, which still had *my* knife in it, and we ran toward the door. All this was maybe two minutes, maybe five. We were both terrified. The girl was smart, though, had her head together, didn't scream. We both wanted to live.

"We made it almost to the door when Jean-Michel got his pants up and caught up with us. He was holding another knife, similar to the first. A sharp kitchen knife, very big. It was very, how do you say, a rough little fight—he attacked, he cut me a little, I cut him, he grabbed the other girl by her hair, he got her away from me for a moment. Then I used the taser and he fell down. I used it again, and again. He was—" She made a flat gesture: unconscious.

"So we ran. I was in my underwear, she had no clothes at all. But I had my purse, and so I called a friend. Remember, this was outside of Paris, so it was dark and we saw no one. We ran as fast as we could until we couldn't really run anymore, then we walked, and then finally, after maybe an hour, my friend found us. Both of us—our feet were bleeding, we were freezing, but we were alive.

"I know it doesn't prove much, but I kept the knife. It has his blood on it, and, I think, both of our fingerprints. At least it shows we were in the same place at the same time. I truly believe he would have killed us both if I didn't have my buzz-buzz—my taser."

"Has he ever come after you?" I asked.

"No," Helene said. "Well, yes, but not how you mean. A week or so after this I was called to his lawyer's office. Julien, his little pig of an assistant, was there. He had a stack of money and wanted me to sign a bunch of papers. I took the money and didn't sign any of the papers. Jean-Michel would do anything rather than let the public know about his little hobbies. I'm sure of that. But he can't quite kill me now, because he doesn't know if I've told anyone, and it could be traced back to him. I can't tell anyone, because if I do, he might kill me. Quite a little puzzle."

I explained to her that we wanted that book, and we wanted her to help us get it from him.

"Yes, OK," Helene said immediately. "I'll do it. For twenty thousand euros."

"Done," Lucas said just as quickly. They shook hands, and we had a deal.

27.

Coming up with an exact plan took me and Lucas the better part of the next day. First we had to think about it, which, both of us being fairly good at thinking, was not too hard. We came up with an idea over a three-hour breakfast in a café. Then we had to figure out how to make it work. This was a little harder, and a little out of our respective wheelhouses, neither of us being all that experienced with actually doing things. Lucas and I weren't people who bought audiovisual equipment and arranged busy people's schedules. But we got it done.

Setting up a meeting with Jean-Michel was easy. We lied. The lie took less than ten minutes to come up with. Lucas emailed Jean-Michel's assistant, Julien, again, this time claiming to have a book for sale that Lucas and I were both fairly sure he would be interested in: a handwritten British manual from 1605 that told the story of exactly how the author had raised the devil, and met him in the author's own home one midnight full moon in spring. Asking price: seven thousand dollars. He wrote back within the day. Yes, he was interested. I insisted we would only deal with Jean-Michel directly. After some back-and-forth, this was agreed to as well. We'd put Julien in a bit of a bind: If he refused our offer to sell him this lesser, second book, one that was in the dead center of his collection, it would look like he was avoiding us, and be more evidence that Jean-Michel really did have *The Precious Substance*. Now we knew he had a good reason to make sure no one could prove he owned the book. He intended to use it.

The hard part was arranging to meet. Naturally, Julien expected us to come to him. We tried to talk him into a rented conference room, but it didn't work. Come to him or no sale—which was, after all, the expected way of doing business. We went back to the store and got different, smaller audiovisual equipment.

The whole thing took two days. When I woke up on the day we were to meet, I felt a sick anxiety in my stomach. What I was about to do was outside of anything I'd even dreamed of doing before. I could tell Lucas was just as anxious. We drank our coffee in near silence, talking only to double-check that all was in place. It was.

I took a shower and when I stepped out, I happened to see myself in the mirror, naked and dripping wet.

Maybe it was the dam that broke around the Precious Substance. Maybe it was all the excitement of the last few weeks. Or jet lag. Most likely, it was the book.

But when I saw myself in the mirror, I didn't see the lonely, left-behind, failed woman I'd seen for the past few years. I saw someone who was going to win. Someone beautiful, even with lines etched in her face and hollows in her cheeks. I put on a new dress and red lipstick and I looked like I fit right in in Paris.

But now I know what I was really looking at: a tool, convenient and flexible, used by the book to get what it wanted.

Lucas wore a dark-gray slim-cut suit I'd seen him in before and an expensive dark tie. We drank more coffee and then it was time for our car, which came exactly on time. It stopped to pick up Helene. As we requested, she'd disguised herself well. No one would recognize her on first glance. Red wig, a layer of makeup, lipstick that changed the shape of her perfect lips, and a cheap black suit. She looked like a real estate agent.

We'd told her she didn't have to come in person. A video would suffice. She was insistent. She wanted to be there.

She didn't exactly smile, but she flashed a cynical, pleased look as we checked her out.

"I'm going to enjoy this," she said.

"Me too," I said.

Who am I? I wondered as we drove. I didn't have an answer anymore. I liked the way that felt.

We all checked our technology one more time. All systems go.

After two hours the car pulled up to a huge, modern house on the outskirts of Paris. We went past a set of frosted-glass sliding doors instead of gates. The house was black and glass and looked empty, although I knew Jean-Michel had lived here for twelve years. Surrounding it was acres of perfect bright green grass and nothing else—no trees, no weeds, no flowers, until a sharp line demarcated the woods on three sides and the frosted-glass privacy wall on the fourth.

I gave the driver five hundred euros, as agreed, with strict instructions to wait at a hidden spot down the road. He promised he would. Lucas also had a backup car waiting for us down the road just in case our guy was scared off.

Our concerns were twofold: One, a flaw in the plan and leaving without the book. Two, Jean-Michel killing all of us.

We arrived at the house ten minutes early, which was perfect, as the property was huge and the house was equally oversize. It was nearly nine minutes just to reach the door. A man in a black suit let us in.

"Henri," he introduced himself. "I'm Julien's assistant. May I see the book?" he said.

"Of course," I said. We'd anticipated this. Yesterday, Lucas had bought a little pamphlet from a rare book dealer that could easily pass for the bullshit we were pretending it was. In reality, it was a nothing little grimoire by a third-rate magician, full of useless spells easily found elsewhere, that was not unique and was worth maybe three or four hundred euros.

Henri took a quick look at the book and nodded. Then another surprise: He wanded us for weapons. We had none. Jean-Michel was known to have a small arsenal in the house. Nothing we could bring with us could compete with that. Nothing except Helene.

We were led down a long, cold stone-walled hallway to a big formal room, empty except for a highly modern, expensive-looking white conference table and ten white leather futuristic-looking chairs around it. Without discussing it, we all gravitated toward the perfect seats: Helene and I on one side of the table, Lucas on the other, ready to face any direction depending on where Jean-Michel would sit.

We waited nineteen minutes before Jean-Michel and Julien came in. Jean-Michel had a glittering smile, looking for all the world like a normal, sane, charming businessman. French businessmen tended toward a sexuality and whimsicality that was absent in their American counterparts; they looked like they laughed and fucked, Jean-Michel included. He wore a black suit, precisely cut to his body, and a white shirt, open at the collar. No tie. His hair was thick, dark, and perfectly trimmed, bringing out the best in his dark eyes and tan, perfectly-cared-for skin. I imagined he didn't care much about his appearance—there were no extras, no jewelry, no flourishes that would indicate any real joy in fashion—but paid people to care about it for him.

"You must be Lucas," Jean-Michel said, flashing that smile, "and you must be the great Lily Albrecht. Of course, your work precedes you. I think we published your book here in France a few years back. Such a pleasure."

The gears in my head quickly turned—I'd been published in France by a small publisher that was owned by a bigger publisher that was owned by a media corporation that was, yes, I now saw, owned by Jean-Michel. Funny how things work out.

Jean-Michel turned to Helene.

"And you must be—"

I have never seen a human face change like Jean-Michel's changed as he slowly recognized Helene. Her disguise was good enough to get us through the door and whatever invisible security we'd passed through, but up close, he recognized her as soon as their eyes met. Over the course of thirty or sixty seconds, Jean-Michel's handsome face morphed from charm to confusion to shock to ugly, hateful rage.

Maybe murderous rage. It was now obvious that everything I'd heard about him was true. I had a sense of something like evil—something so dark and so selfish it was beyond redemption. So bad that it now reveled in its own misguided darkness, and worshipped it.

My heart raced. I was scared. But I kept my face calm, forcing my jaw and my forehead to relax. I couldn't tell what the inscrutable Helene was thinking.

Lucas, though, was as cool as rainwater. I could tell he was relishing this moment. He loved power games and money and deals. Why he'd been a librarian all these years, if a renowned one, was beyond me. I suspected that, now, that he wasn't so sure either.

"You should know," Lucas said, offhandedly, as if he said it twice a week, "this is all being live-streamed to our lawyers in Paris. Say hello."

Each of us, somewhere on our body, had a small wireless voice recorder and camera. They were astonishing little implements. The ones on Helene and Lucas just recorded. Mine, hidden in a button on my dress, was wirelessly connected to my phone, which was connected with the cellular network which somehow met with Helene's lawyers, who were sitting in a conference room in Paris with Lucien.

"And," Helene added, "Lucien Roche. He was very interested to follow the proceedings. He isn't a rich man like you, Jean. But he has a lot of friends in publishing. I think it would be a very big problem if any of us was to get hurt."

After Lucas and Helene spoke, Jean-Michel's face reversed, like film rewinding, from rage to anger to confusion back to charm.

"Very well," Jean-Michel said. He walked around the table to stand at the head of it, smiling, as much as possible taking back control of the situation.

He said something in French to Julien and Julien left the room. Lucas and I exchanged a quick, barely visible nod: wordlessly we agreed to give Jean-Michel some power back. Humiliating him wouldn't get us what we wanted, and could be dangerous. We needed the book and we needed to live the rest of our lives in peace, and it probably served us best to let him think he was getting a fair trade, or better, and we were just nudging him into it.

Lucas was doing well so far, so I let him continue talking.

"All we want," Lucas said, "is to make a fair deal. A generous deal. We're interested in buying a book we know you have: *The Book of the Most Precious Substance*. We have half a million dollars in escrow, and as soon as we have the book, we can transfer that money to you immediately."

Jean-Michel looked at us.

"And what if I don't want to sell?"

"Then," Helene said, "I'll have something to say."

Jean-Michel's smile became tense.

"Very well," he said. He tapped on the table. Henri, who had apparently been waiting just outside, practically jumped into the room.

Jean-Michel turned to him and nodded. Henri bowed slightly and turned to Lucas.

"If you'll come with me—" Henri began.

"He will not," I said. "We can complete all of our business right here."

Henri looked at Jean-Michel, who nodded.

Henri went to go get the book. Jean-Michel sat down and put his feet up on the table, drawing on all of his powers of intimidation and authority.

He looked at Helene. She was ice cold.

"How have you been, Helene?" Jean-Michel said.

"Very well, thanks," she said. "Yourself?"

Jean-Michel smiled the cruelest, angriest smile I'd ever seen in my life, and didn't answer.

Henri came back in with the book, housed in a clamshell case. The box was dove gray. Next to the book he set a pair of white cotton gloves. Maybe it was my imagination, but I seemed to feel a hum from the book, something in between a feeling and a sound. The hum pulled me in and kept me close. The book, the book, the book. It was mine, mine, mine.

"Ready for business?" Jean-Michel said.

"Of course," I said. But my stomach fluttered. I'd never spent a half million dollars on anything before. Everyone looked at me.

I stood up, walked to the book, and opened the case. At first, I pretended I wasn't scared out of my mind, and after a moment, I wasn't. Once I saw the book, I remembered that I actually knew what I was doing. I was always at home with a book in my hands, even here.

It looked nearly indistinguishable from the Fool's copy. I picked it up. I didn't wear the gloves. I wanted to feel the paper and the leather. It was part of authenticating it. On closer inspection, the leather was a slightly different shade, and it was definitely more worn. In fact, this copy was more worn all around, probably because Jean-Michel, along with others, had used it more.

I put the book on the table and carefully went through it, page by page. I was checking for authenticity and for completeness. As far as I could tell, it was all there. Each seal was intact, if slightly marred by spunk and sweat. I got to the last seal. This was my first time seeing it. It was, somehow, a triangle and a circle at the same time, with a countless number of stars and crescent moons scattered around. The word seemed to be all vowels, a piece of dry cotton in my mouth I couldn't chew. There was one small, very old streak of brown blood on it. Someone in the past four hundred years had completed the last act, or tried. Not Jean-Michel.

Then I went back to the first page and did it all again. I slid it across the table to Lucas, who did the exact same thing, three times. When he was done he looked at me and nodded. I nodded back. As far as it was possible to tell, this was real. This was the book.

"It's perfect," I said. "Let's proceed."

While I was looking at the book, Henri had brought in a laptop. He and Lucas exchanged bank account numbers and routing numbers, each offering to eat the fees, pretending anyone here was a gentleman.

Together they transferred the money. It was an agonizing three and a half minutes between when the money left the escrow account and showed up in Jean-Michel's private bank. Henri was cool as a cucumber, as if he did this every day, which he probably did.

"Here we go," Henri said, once the money was transferred.

And that was that. The book was ours. Jean-Michel dropped his smile.

"Take the book and get out of my house," Jean-Michel said.

We stood up to leave.

"Remember," Jean-Michel said, "the world is a small place. I'm sure we'll be seeing each other again."

"You're leaving this room with a half million dollars," I said. "I'm leaving this room with a book. If we see each other again, you should thank me."

He looked at me and smiled again.

"Good luck with the book," he said. "I don't like you, but I'll tell you this anyway: Whatever you think it's going to do for you, it won't. It doesn't work."

"What did you want," I asked, "that you didn't get?"

"Get out of my house," Jean-Michel said.

He turned around and left the room, and so did we.

As we left the house Helene smiled for the first time since I'd met her, and she continued to smile as we walked to the waiting taxi, got in, drove back to Paris, and dropped her off on the opposite side of town from her real apartment, just in case we were being followed.

Before she got out of the car she turned to me and shook my hand. I could tell something had been restored to her—a part of herself that Jean-Michel had stolen. Now she had it back.

"Thank you," she said. "I now consider this chapter of my life closed."

She got out of the car, and I watched her walk away.

28.

Having the book was more frightening than not having it. I could drop it, burn it, flood it, ruin it a hundred different ways. Right away Lucas and I made a rule: No food, drink, fire, or water within twenty feet of it.

Lucien called, elated, having heard the whole thing. He didn't care too much about our book but he cared about fucking Jean-Michel and protecting Helene.

"Now go write your book," he said, after we celebrated together. "The next time I see you, you'll sign it for me."

Lucas sent Haber a photo of the book to prove we had it. He didn't know what we'd paid, and he never would. That was how this business worked, and everyone knew it. Neither of us particularly liked Haber, and we both particularly wanted his money. There was no question of cutting him a break.

After some negotiation, Lucas got us to the price we'd hoped for:

two million dollars.

When Lucas got off the phone with Haber, we looked at each other, smiling, nearly dizzy. The money was in an account under both our names.

We were both elated, hyper, buzzing with energy. Surprisingly, neither of us had much to say. It was all still sinking in. We went for a walk, not talking much, finally stopping in a seafood restaurant for shellfish and wine. With some food and drink in us, we relaxed enough to start rehashing it all: Jean-Michel's face, Helene's righteousness, the long, excruciating minutes of transferring the money.

"You were really made for days like this," I told Lucas.

"I know," he said. "I never felt like that before. But I do now. I feel…like someone else. Like a new person."

But something in his face put a thought in my head that I didn't want to see, and quickly pushed out.

After dessert and more wine we walked back to the hotel. On a quiet street, around the corner from the hotel, Lucas suddenly pushed me up against the wall, pinning my arms behind me. He leaned in as if he were going to kiss me. But he didn't. He put his lips close to mine and reached one hand up my dress and pinched the inside of my thigh, hard. I gasped. He pulled me away from the wall and we kept walking.

Inside the door, back in the hotel room, Lucas gently pushed me down on the bed, holding my hands over my head as he kissed me. He let go. We were both excited and exhausted and utterly wired.

"Take off your clothes," he said. "Right now."

I did as he said. When I got to my bra and underwear, he said, "Stop."

I did. I knew I didn't have to—if I'd objected, at any step, Lucas would have stopped. I didn't want him to stop. For five years I had made every fucking decision, every moment, every day, myself. Having someone just take everything over—even only in bed, even only for a few minutes or hours—felt like a glass of cold water after a hike through the desert. I loved it. I knew Lucas was imitating what I'd told him Madame M. and her witches had done—the acts that had produced the Precious Substance. That was fine. Originality does not score points in bed.

"Kneel," he said. I did. He undid his pants and started stroking himself, growing bigger and rock hard, more so than I'd seen him before.

"Turn around," he said. I did, and he kneeled behind me. He put his hands on my ass and explored. Then he drew both hands away and one flew forward to spank me with a loud crack. I gasped. He did it again, and again. I loved it. He could see that I was ready, but we weren't looking for ordinary good sex here. We were looking for magic.

Lucas pushed aside my underwear and began to use his hands and tongue, getting me closer and closer to climax, twisting and biting—but each time, before I got there, he stopped and pulled away and then raised his hand and spanked me again. He repeated this pattern of intense pleasure and light pain until I thought I might die from it. I had no thoughts and no ideas and no capacity to participate in life at any level beyond sex. Everything else had slipped away and this was all there was now: This was everything. Pleasure and pain lost all distinction—everything was silencing, life-obliterating sensation: a blankness of overwhelming feeling. But through my mute wordless storm, I felt it build—the wave reaching, and reaching, and reaching, straining to break the dam. Now that I knew the feeling, I could lean into it and coax it along.

Lucas entered me and just as quickly withdrew, teasing me more. He did this a few more times before he plunged in with full dedication. I could feel the wave coming closer, and closer still. The precipice of it was almost frightening, as if I might fall apart altogether and never set myself right again. The fear was so strong I almost backed off. As strong as the urge was to the breaking wave, there was another, almost equally strong urge to end this, to go back to safety. But Lucas kept fucking me and the wave caught me up and in another minute I fell off the precipice. I shook and fell down, saturated with pleasure as the Precious Substance flooded me.

I felt Lucas shudder, withdraw, and likewise release himself in a series of stuttering shots across my back, his substances mixing with mine. His orgasm set off mine, and just as the Precious Substance was dying down I came in a strange, rough climax that seemed to turn me inside out.

We lay on the bed, breathing, as the strong waves washed away, leaving us ourselves again. I'd forgotten about the book. Lucas hadn't. He ran his fingers over me, collecting and combining both our fluids on his fingertips, and rushed to the book. I righted myself, sat up, and turned around to watch him.

"Get some on your hands," he said. "Come here. Quickly."

I did as he said. The Precious Substance was different than ordinary wetness: thinner, saltier. I collected some on my fingertips, stood up on wobbly legs, and approached the book. Together, we both touched our wet fingers to the symbol and said ██████████

This time felt different than the other times. Stronger. Darker. I'd been in a small earthquake in San Francisco once, and somehow I'd felt it the moment before. This felt like that. My vision went blurry for a moment. Before my eyes I saw a quick series of strange images: a strange, burrowing little animal, a forest of dead trees taken over by insects, and then that same woman's face, peering at me as if I were appearing to her and not the other way around.

I rubbed my eyes and the visions went away, if they were ever there at all. I could barely keep my eyes open. I crawled into bed. Lucas crawled in next to me and put his arms around me. He was as warm as an oven.

"Feel OK?" I said.

"Better than OK," he said. I pulled the blankets up around us and fell into a deep, deathlike sleep.

I woke up at around two, in the middle of the night. Lucas was sitting on his side of the bed, looking out the window.

We had fallen asleep in a post-sex bliss, but now the mood in the room was somber.

"You OK?" I asked again. He glanced at me and then turned back to the window, distracted.

"Of course," Lucas said. "Better than OK. Just thinking. There's a lot to do. You know we have to report this."

"To whom?" I said.

"The IRS," he said. "They track anything over ten grand."

"Well, that's OK," I said.

"Of course," he said, "it's gonna be a hell of a tax hit. I'll talk to my accountant. He might know a way to whittle it down. Splitting it will help, of course."

"Excellent," I said.

It was like we were actors in a play, saying lines we didn't believe. Neither of us was really thinking about taxes, or even money. We were thinking about the last act.

We looked at each other. Lucas had a pleading look on his face. Was it my imagination or did his face look a little different—features sharper, eyes deeper?

"I'm not doing it," I said. "Not a baboon. Not a cat. Nothing."

"There must be another way," Lucas said instantly. "A substitute for the blood. What did you say Imogen had done? An art project? We could do something like that. We could at least try."

"Look at everyone who's done it," I said. "Nothing good happened to them. To any of them. We've gotten further, with better results, than anyone else. Anyone ever, as far as we know. We got the book. The money. Let's just be grateful and leave it at that."

Lucas smiled a fake smile.

"You're right," he said. "Of course."

We looked at each other again.

"I'll book our flights home," he said.

"First class," I said.

"Absolutely," he said. "Let's get out. Enjoy our last night in Paris."

I was still half asleep.

"You go out," I said. "I'm exhausted. I'll meet you later."

"You sure?" Lucas said.

"Go," I said. "I can tell you're restless. It's Paris, I'm sure there's something to do. I'll see you in the morning."

I lay on the bed. Lucas came and sat next to me. I thought he was going to kiss me. Instead, he spoke. I noticed he was already fully dressed.

"Think about what I said," he said. "We could stay in Paris, at least for a while. Travel to Rome. To Tokyo. Once word of this deal gets out, people will be throwing expensive books at us to sell, let alone the money from this sale. A whole new life."

I said something noncommittal. Lucas kissed me goodbye and I heard the door click closed when he left. In minutes I was back asleep, but it was fitful and troubled, twisting up the sheets and blankets, leaving me sweaty and more tired than when I'd started.

I got out of bed at six and took a long, hot shower. But I didn't feel better afterward. Instead I felt a nameless, anxious dread.

After the shower, I checked my phone. Lucas had called, twice.

I felt a sickening feeling in my stomach. Nothing was right. We should be celebrating. But Lucas sounded frantic and scared.

"Call me. Lily, it's urgent. Call me right away."

I called him back, hair still dripping wet, still wrapped in a towel.

"Lily," he said. "Thank God you're OK. You aren't safe there. Come meet me."

He gave me a long address with complicated instructions on how to find it. Left off the river. Right under the bridge. Smells like coffee.

"What about the book?" I said. "I can't leave it here."

"Don't worry," he said. "I've got it."

I felt sicker still.

29.

I got dressed and gathered up my things and took a cab a half-mile from the location Lucas had given me. Then, just in case anyone was watching, I walked in a roundabout route to get to the destination, cutting through a crowded, busy market under a bridge. I was near the Seine in a nearly unfathomably old part of Paris—probably as old as the book. Around the market were some cute shops and pubs, but a few blocks away was a more industrial stretch, and then a few blocks further, a warren of industrial streets. Finally I reached the address. It did indeed smell like coffee.

It was a warehouse. There was a big sliding door above a loading dock and, next to it, a regular door. The loading dock was only a few feet high and I hopped up on it easily. The door was shut tight, but not locked. I pushed a little and it slid open and I let myself in.

Inside was a vast, dark cluttered space. Machinery and stacks of boxes loomed. After a moment I realized it was a coffee roasting operation, abandoned with beans still in the roasting and grinding machines.

It was dark but not black; dim light came from the back. I followed it. After a minute I saw Lucas. He was in a clear area toward the back of the building. Pacing, holding the book. In the wall behind him was a door marked BATHROOM. Nearby was a big metal desk and a matching chair.

"Lucas," I said.

He turned to me.

"Lily," he said. "You won't fucking believe it."

Just then someone knocked on the door.

The bathroom door. From the inside.

I looked at Lucas.

"It was the person who was following us in Los Angeles," he said. "In Paris. I think he's working for Haber. He was going to kill me. He was going to take the book and take the money back. I was on a walk, he was following me…I'm lucky I got him in here. He's been following us for days."

"How?" I said. I didn't know, but I doubted Lucas was telling the truth. Maybe he was. But nothing about this seemed right. If someone wanted to kill us, last night would have been a good time.

Lucas looked different. It seemed like his face was shifting before my eyes. His eyes were sinking into his face, his chin moving forward. I rubbed my eyes.

"Lily," Lucas said, urgent and angry. "He wanted us dead. Both of us. He was going to kill us and take the book."

"Then we should call the police," I said calmly.

"Or," Lucas said. "Or."

He looked at me, big eyes pleading. My knees felt weak. I knew exactly what that *or* was.

"No," I said. "No. I told you no a dozen times. I'm not doing it."

"It wouldn't be wrong," Lucas said. "He was going to kill us. He isn't a good person."

"It would still be wrong," I said. "Why did you bring the book with you?"

He came toward me. He tried to put his arms around me. I stepped away.

"Think of the life we could have," he said, avoiding my question. "Life like the past few weeks have been. But better. Even better. We can spend the rest of our lives like this."

"We already have plenty of money," I said.

"But money isn't everything," Lucas said. "Think of what we could do with unlimited power." When he saw the disgusted look on my face, he rushed to add: "Think of all the good you could do."

"Right," I said. "If we only do the worst thing—take another life for our own selfish goals."

"It isn't selfish!" Lucas rushed to justify. "He was going to kill us!"

And then I saw it. The knife on the table. It was a big all-purpose kitchen knife, sharp and long. This had all been well planned. I had no idea where or when he'd gotten it.

Next to the desk, on the other side, was a big transparent plastic tarp.

"So now we have to kill him," I said. "Right? Like you killed Shyman."

Lucas's face twisted, as if he tasted something ugly, and then for a moment he looked like his old self. His old charming self, but sadder. Older.

"No," he said. "How could you say that? Of course I—"

But then his face twisted again, this time with confusion.

"Shit," he said. "I'm so confused. I feel like maybe I— But I couldn't have. Lily, you know that. I couldn't have."

"Like you killed the General," I said.

"No," he said. "No, no, you have it all wrong. Someone—I mean. Jesus. I don't know what happened. I think I was there. I think— fuck. I don't know. I couldn't have. You know that. I couldn't have."

I hadn't really been sure until right now. Not until I saw the tarp and the knife. I'd suspected, but I hadn't wanted to believe it. Hadn't wanted it to be true. But he'd mentioned the Admiral had wanted to run for president. The Admiral hadn't said that—not while I was there. Until now, I'd gone over and over it in my head, coming up with excuse after excuse—Lucas had heard something I hadn't, he'd remembered something I'd overlooked. Now I had to admit: All my excuses were lies. Shit and lies.

Lucas had gone back that night and killed him to prevent him from getting the book. Or, I like to think, something, someone, made Lucas do those things. That Lucas was, once, someone better than he was in that warehouse. Someone imperfect, but still full of life and joy and pleasure. Not just this monster of desire. Of greed. I like to think that our moments of closeness were real and organic, and that Lucas, a mildly selfish and thoughtless person, was just that—a confused, somewhat selfish man taken over by a power stronger than him.

Maybe. Maybe not. Maybe this ugly man was who Lucas really was and always had been, and the book was just an excuse to let that man out.

Now Lucas's face had that sharp, wild look to it again, eyes bright, cheeks hollow.

"Lily," he said. "Lily, you have to trust me. I have not steered us wrong. This is all coming to its natural conclusion. This is how it has to end."

He didn't even sound like himself anymore. Something about the words, the order he'd put them in—it was all so different.

"I told you," I said. "I'm not doing the last act."

"OK," Lucas said, clearly not OK at all. "Then what do you suggest we do with the man in the bathroom? The man who wanted to kill us and steal our book?"

"Let him go," I said. "I don't think he was going to kill us. We haven't done anything so wrong yet. He's done worse. He won't tell anyone."

Lucas set his mouth and jaw and I knew that wasn't going to happen.

I wish I could say I hadn't thought of it before. I wish I could say in all the weeks since I first learned about the book, it had never crossed my mind.

Of course it was wrong. But Lucas was making it so easy. Maybe I was the sociopath. Maybe I was the one the demons took over.

Or maybe I just had a moment of clear, cold intelligence.

The rest of the world could go to hell. I wanted what I wanted.

I walked to the dusty, creaking chair behind the desk and pulled it out. I gently pushed Lucas into the chair.

He looked at me, face changing so rapidly now I couldn't quite believe what I was seeing: It was as if every facet of him, good and ill, was having a moment of expression.

"OK?" Lucas said. "OK?"

"OK," I said.

I'd been such a good fucking person, for so long. How good could a person be expected to be?

I took a step toward him and over him, so I was straddling him. Now Lucas started to relax again. He breathed a sigh of relief.

"Lily," he said. "I love you."

"I know," I said. "And I think I kind of love you, too."

I sat down on his lap, facing him. I kissed him. Lucas was ready almost instantly. We'd been having so much sex our bodies were attuned to each other, Pavlovian.

I lifted up my dress and pushed my underwear aside. Lucas unzipped his pants. I sat on top of him, touching myself until I was ready too, then gently sliding over him. He leaned his head back, moaning, as I twisted and turned on him. I knew his body by now, and I knew when he was close.

Just before he lost control, I reached behind me, and picked up the knife.

Lucas didn't see. He didn't know. I didn't want him to know. But at the last moment, he opened his eyes.

Now his face looked different yet again. I saw how the book had truly warped him. He smiled a twisted smile, almost more like a grimace. He looked like an animal. Like a devil. No one, it seemed, could handle the power unscathed.

No one except me.

I could call the police and destroy both our lives.

Or I could end this fucked-up mess I'd made, and save another.

Lucas came, shuddering and shaking. Then he saw the knife.

"No," he said. "No no no. You're not going to kill me," he said.

I still felt him throbbing inside me.

"I am," I said, and I stuck the knife into his chest.

At first I wasn't sure if I could do it. I'd thrown a few punches in my life, all one hundred and thirty pounds of me, and never caused anyone greater harm than a few bruises. But I had to move quickly—Lucas had easily fifty pounds of muscle on me. I'd studied Helene's story well, and waited until the right moment.

It was hard. There was muscle and flesh and bone and organs to cut through. I knew it wouldn't be easy, but it was even harder than I'd imagined. But I did it. I wasn't sure if I'd hit his heart, but I'd at least punctured his lung.

Lucas gasped, in what would be the first of his last three breaths. He tried to move his arms, hoping to push me off him, but he was already dying, and all he could do was wave his arms a few inches. He looked astonished and ugly. He took another horrible, wheezing breath, and then another, and I stabbed him again, on the other side of his chest, not wanting him to be in pain. The second time was not easier, but by the third, I felt something rise in me, and I stabbed him as if driven by the pure rage that was starting to trickle out of me, now pour—

And then I stopped myself. I wouldn't become what the book wanted me to be. The book would work for me. I wouldn't work for it.

The blood started to bubble out from Lucas's wounds in big spurts, then stronger, more, and then trickled to a long, slow leak. As he died I pushed away my squeamishness and sadness and disgust and ran my hand through the blood coming up from Lucas's chest. Then I stood up and ran to the book.

I knew what I wanted. What I'd wanted all along.

I smeared the blood on the symbol and said the last word.

I felt the world fall down around me. I lost my balance, and as I fell I saw a series of visions and felt a rush of emotions: a black animal trapped in dirt, no chance to scream; a woman with a horribly distorted face laughing at me with disgust; an overwhelming rush of sickening shame; the birth of something wiggling and evil from a black hole, entering a world where it shouldn't exist...

Then I was in that filthy little workshop with Heironymus Zeel and Princess Isabelle. She gave me a knowing look, but I didn't know what knowledge it was that she imagined we shared.

She turned and looked at me directly. Now I saw she was looking in a scrying mirror. Somehow she knew I was here, hundreds of years on the other side.

"My congratulations," she said. "Now you'll learn."

"Learn what?" I said.

"That remains to be seen," she said.

"What did you want?" I said.

But she didn't answer. And for the rest of my life, I was never sure: Had she wanted me to end the book? To destroy this ugly creature that she'd created? Or had she wanted me to feed it one more fantastic meal—Lucas, and the piece of me that died with him?

Who had won, and what was the prize?

I woke up an hour later.

Lucas was dead. I was alive. I'd completed the fifth act. And there still a man in the bathroom to deal with.

30.

I put the book in my dress. My waistband held it against my belly. It was heavily used, and a little more human oil and sweat wouldn't ruin it. Then I knocked on the bathroom door. I felt strangely calm. The reality of what I'd done wouldn't truly hit me for weeks. For now I was efficient and collected.

The first thing was to deal with the man in the bathroom.

"I'm going to give you a piece of fabric," I said, distorting my voice with a fake accent. "You're going to cover your eyes. You're going to leave here, see nothing, and forget you were ever here. Otherwise you will die. Understand?"

"Yes, ma'am," I heard through the door.

"Close your eyes," I said.

I took off my jacket and tossed it in the room. His eyes were closed. He was a big man, solid, looked vaguely military.

"Who hired you?" I asked, as he wrapped the jacket around his head.

"Haber," he said. "No one was supposed to get hurt. I was supposed to bring back the book before he paid you. I was supposed to follow you, find it, and undercut you. I failed. That was all."

He finished tying the jacket around his head. He hadn't seen me. I took the knife, grabbed his right hand, and stuck the knife right into the center of it. The man grimaced and grunted but didn't scream.

"Remember," I said. "You were never here. If you look for me, it's your throat."

I took him by the arm, roughly, walked him outside the warehouse, made sure no one was around, walked him out to the corner, left him, and walked away. I walked the other direction, going in impulsive circles to guarantee no one would spot me.

In a drug store, searching for translations on my phone, I picked up the bottles of chemicals I needed—nail polish remover, rubbing alcohol, a few more. Back in the hotel room, I carefully opened the book and mixed chemicals in a plastic bowl. With a cotton swab, I dabbed the chemical mix on the last symbol in the book, erasing both Lucas's blood and a good piece of the symbol below it. I made my erasures carefully symmetrical, so the book still looked accurate and untampered with. Then I did the same to the fourth act. No one would ever get past it again.

No one would ever know I had done it. It was impossible to distinguish from ordinary wear and tear. Haber would never know I had ruined the book I was selling him.

And no one could ever use it again. It was dead. Maybe it was my imagination, but I thought I felt it die as I held it, felt the power of the book recede, felt it wither down to just a little scrap of animal bits and ink. I could only hope it had already given me what I'd asked for. I knew it might take a few days, maybe a few months, to become material. But I couldn't risk Haber, or anyone, getting the book intact, even if it meant not getting what I asked for. It was evil, and it never should have existed. Now it didn't.

Then I went to Haber's Paris office and delivered the book.

I told the hotel Lucas had left early, with a dramatic tone. I knew everyone would believe the simple, believable story I had ready if anyone asked: We'd been lovers, we'd had a quarrel, we'd split up. Someone had killed him. No one would suspect me. No one would suspect anyone.

Eventually Lucas's body would be found. I'd made an effort to get rid of any fingerprints from the warehouse, but given the general mess of the place, I wasn't too worried about any forensic evidence. No one had seen me enter. I would never touch his half of the money. He'd mentioned a cousin in Westchester once, and once he was officially pronounced dead, I made sure she got every last penny from the sale of the book, and made sure she got his library properly valued as well.

Six months later, when his body was finally found, it was imagined to be a hook-up turned badger game turned murder. A spontaneous sex encounter that led to extortion that led to death.

But for now, I was alone in Paris, with blood on my hands and a life to go back to.

I was back in my hotel that night, packing, when my phone rang.

It was Awe.

"Lily," he said. "Lily, come home. There's been a miracle."

I flew back to New York that night. I brought Lucas's luggage with my own and threw it away before I got to the airport. Every minute was an hour; every hour was a day. In my first taste of what my new life might be like, I got off the airplane and went right to the limo I'd booked to pick me up; the limo took me right to my door upstate, where Awe was waiting.

"I swear," Awe said. "Lily, I swear, he was watching me."

The story Awe had told me on the phone was that he'd been bringing Abel his dinner when Awe had noticed Abel's eyes tracking him as he walked across the room.

It wasn't much. But it was something. Now Abel seemed as unfocused and absent as he had before I left. But a few days later, I thought I saw the same: I could swear his eyes followed me as I walked toward him. A few days later, it happened again.

In a week, there was a smile. Now we were both sure, Awe and me: Something was different. I tried talking to Dr. Richards, the latest neurologist. She didn't believe me. But over the next few weeks the smiles became regular occurrences.

Then, on the twenty-eighth day after I killed Lucas, Abel spoke. We were sitting in the kitchen in the morning—Awe and I were having coffee, Abel positioned in a nice sunny spot. When a cloud came over the sun, Abel made a sound that was very close to the word *cold*.

Awe and I looked at each other, astonished. A few weeks after that, we took Abel to the doctor. She was discouraging.

"I wouldn't get your hopes up," Dr. Richards said, face firm, lips in a straight line. "Ups and downs are normal. But cures are impossible."

She didn't know what impossible was. She ran some tests. At the end, she admitted he did seem to follow some motion with his eyes, a little, and that some basic reflexes seemed to have returned.

"You can't read too much into it," she said. "He's not going to recover."

I knew better.

Three months after I killed Lucas, Abel said my name. I was taking him out for a spin in the garden. It was a sunny early summer day. I stopped us in a warm spot and crouched down next to him.

"Lily," he said. I hadn't heard his voice in years. It was different now, of course, crooked from atrophy. But it was him.

My knees shook under me. I kneeled down and put my head on Abel's lap and sobbed.

It had worked. The book had worked. I had gotten what I'd asked for.

After that, Abel improved a little more rapidly every day. Within another six weeks he could complete a simple sentence: *Cold here. TV off.* In a few more months he could, on shaky legs, with my and Awe's help, stand up.

No doctors could explain it, of course, and soon they stopped trying. They found their ways to sleep at night. It was the hormone cocktail I'd fed him. It was a virus that died.

Soon Abel could walk a few steps. Another few months and he could articulate a preference: ice cream or cake, indoors or out.

Abel needed speech therapy to use his voice again and physical therapy to control his legs and arms and bladder and bowels again. It was three more months before he understood that he'd lost over five years. It was eight months before he could walk alone and two years before he could write.

But he was here. All of him. Restored.

I told the police and anyone else who asked that I'd left Lucas in Paris, alive and well. The story went down in bookseller lore as one of the racier biblio-mysteries in our dull little world. A lot of people missed Lucas. But no one missed him enough to figure out what happened to him. It was just like when Shyman died: Everyone was sad, and everyone talked about him, and then everyone forgot about it and moved on. Everyone except me.

After two years of recovery and work, we were nearly back to normal. Abel started writing again, and in a few more years he'd finished another book, this one a mix of memoir and research about the various states of consciousness he'd encountered over the past years. He remembered strange little flashes of visions, dreams, cognitive blips. Especially a recurring dream about a strange young woman with an odd pointed hat, staring into his face as if he were appearing in her dream. Sometimes, she laughed at him. The book climbed the bestseller list. He went on TV shows and drive-time radio. Abel became a star, more famous than we'd ever imagined.

I also wrote another book, a new novel. It didn't fare as well as Abel's, or my first book, but it held its own. I was proud of it. And of course I had the money from the *Precious Substance* sale, so sales of my own book didn't matter as much. I kept one hand in the book trade; I'd developed a reputation as maybe the most rarefied book dealer in the world, dealing with only the most exotic of works at the highest prices. It took me on some interesting adventures, and brought in a lucrative side income.

Most importantly, I had my love, my family, my best friend back.

Here was Abel: Here was his ridiculous sense of humor, finding something to laugh at in the bleakest turns. Here was his playfulness, insisting that we drive out to Stockbridge for the day just for pumpkin ice cream and good apple pie. Here was his brilliance, reading medical books and diagnosing himself with a rare form of encephalitis, putting the question of what had actually happened to bed—at least for him. All the old friends came crawling out of the woodwork, and while I resented some of them—all of them, really, every last one—for drifting away while Abel had been sick, I put that aside so Abel could enjoy his reunions. Soon the house was a kind of salon, just like I'd always dreamed of, with writers and artists coming and going, dropping off food and wine and books every weekend.

One day, twenty-four months after I'd killed Lucas, I was washing dishes in the kitchen sink and Abel came up behind me and put his arms around my waist. He kissed the back of my neck. It was such an ordinary, familiar gesture of marital affection. So normal—the kind of thing I would have taken for granted before. But this time, I started to cry—and I cried, and cried, and couldn't stop.

It was like the past seven years had never happened. Like it was all just a horrible nightmare, and I had finally woken up.

I fell to the floor, crying. Abel kissed me, and kissed me, and told me he loved me.

"It's me," he said. "It's me. And I'm never leaving you again. I am so, so sorry, baby. So sorry for what I put you through."

"I just missed you," I said. "I just missed you so much."

Of course, *missed* was a wholly inadequate word, but there was no better. Abel kept kissing me and we made love on the kitchen floor, and when we were done I cried again—this time, tears of happiness. I had it back. All of it. Everything I'd wanted. It had worked. It was all over. And I'd won.

31.

One night, after a few more years had passed, I saw Leo Singleton. It was a party to celebrate the publication of Abel's newest book. The party was, ironically, in an art gallery in Paris, not far from where I'd murdered Lucas. Abel read the first few pages of the book, gave a little talk about how grateful he was to be there, about how strange life was in its ups and downs, and, of course, he thanked his wife. The crowd gave him a standing ovation. People knew our story, or thought they did, and found it moving.

After his talk we mingled in the crowd, separately. People brought me little toasts with caviar on top, and tidbits of salmon and crab. Abel's books now sold well enough for shellfish and champagne.

Abel was across the room, holding court with fans, a smile on his face, enjoying the attention. He was talking to a pretty young woman in a black dress. He put a hand on her arm. Abel had developed new habits in his new life. Before, we'd been monogamous by choice, never by rule. Now, given the undeniably extreme torments he'd been through, taking every last bite out of life, exploring every last corner, only seemed fair. And, often, a more appealing prospect than nights at home with me. We spent less and less time together.

And of course, he was always the smarter one. He found the work I'd done to support us, selling books, distasteful. So did I, I tried to explain. But I had not exactly been rolling in fucking choices. Still, it seemed to be something he was having trouble forgiving me for.

But my lack of intellectual output was my worst sin. He never said so out loud, but I could see that I'd become dull to him. He was not happy to see what our life had become—or, in his words, what I "had done to" him or what what I'd "let happen." He hated the house in upstate New York, and was more than happy to let Awe go.

Awe, who for three years had cleaned Abel, fed him, and cared for him like he was his own child, hated the real, living Abel. We didn't need Awe anymore anyway. In return for his service I gave him a hundred and fifty grand, or tried to, when I let him go. He asked me to give it to his daughters instead, and I did. Awe had done more for me than anyone in my life had, ever. Abel was angry about it. I told him my money was mine, and he was lucky I shared it with him, and we never fought about money again.

Soon enough Abel had his own money coming in, anyway, far more than I had made from selling the book. Book sales, a TED Talk, film options, consultancy fees. We sold the house upstate and bought a co-op in Manhattan. Then, when even more money came, we bought a house on the beach on Long Island, like I'd always wanted. Abel was a star now, in his own stratosphere. For years he'd needed me to care for him and keep him and bring him back to life. Now he didn't need me at all. Sometimes I thought about telling him what I'd done for him—when I saw him with another woman, when he was dismissive of my ideas, when he came home late and wouldn't say where he'd been.

But there was no point. He loved me, and I loved him. If our life wasn't perfect, well, whose was? We had fun together, just like we had before. We talked for hours about books, art, ideas. We spent three weeks in Japan, like we'd always wanted. We went to flea markets and restaurants and saw friends and made love and planned the garden for the big Long Island house together. In the nursery, Abel picked out strange plants and exotic trees. We both started painting, him again, me for the first time, and Abel encouraged me every step of the way, even getting one of my silly little experiments framed and hanging it above his desk.

After we'd gotten back to regular sex, I told him about the Precious Substance—not the magical aspects of it, of course, but just that it was something fun we might want to try. We did try, once or twice, but it never happened, and then it started to seem like a chore, and we forgot about it. Or at least Abel did. That dam never broke with Abel, or with anyone else, again.

Of course, I was free to see others too, just like Abel was, but just as when he was sick, nothing ever seemed right. There were a few people I saw when the scheduling worked out, but I could take them or leave them. There was no one like Abel.

Or Lucas.

In marriage therapy, I tried to explain it to Abel. That all I'd ever wanted was to get him back. That restoring him was my sole focus for all the years he was gone. That I'd given up everything to get us here. That I was sure he'd have done the same for me. But a dark look crossed his face and the therapist and I met eyes and all three of us knew something that none of us would ever say out loud: Abel, at least this new Abel, would not have done the same for me. This Abel would have put me in the public nursing home and moved on with his life.

In the art gallery in Paris, I was talking to one of the bigwigs at Abel's publishing house when I saw him. Singleton.

Leo Singleton was still handsome, still had that same smile. But now that smile was a little older, a little rueful, and I knew. I could just tell. I knew he knew about Lucas. He'd figured it out.

I knew he would never tell, and he hasn't.

In his elegant way, Singleton moved through the crowd to me. He kissed me delicately on the cheek.

"Lily," he said. "It's been too long."

"It has," I said. "How have you been?"

We talked like regular people for a few minutes. He'd read my newest book. I was interested in his big-ticket sales. He told me he'd met Haber a few years back, and he'd ranted and raved about how the book was a fucking con. He did all the steps he could—I didn't know how many—and nothing happened.

Just when our small talk was winding down, Singleton leaned in, close, and whispered:

"Was it worth it?"

I looked around at what I had. Money. Friends. My career. And most of all, my Abel, shining, smiling, alive again, brilliant again, in love with me. I wasn't sure if we would stay together. We were different people now. But at least I was free of that other Abel, that drooling, howling thing that had been such a burden to me.

But sometimes, I would think of the little house in upstate New York, warm nights with Awe and Abel, and wonder if I shouldn't have appreciated those simple, safe nights more. I could have tried harder to make friends in town. Gotten to know the other booksellers more. Called those old friends I'd walled myself off from. People found happiness in worse circumstances.

I spent most of my time alone now, in the house on Long Island, while Abel stayed in the city. At least I had my place on the beach, finally. At least I had that.

"I guess that was a foolish question," Singleton said, feeling my hesitation.

"No," I said. "It was a good one. And I'm not sure. I'm sure I'll pay for it someday."

"Maybe," Singleton said, in his usual gentlemanly way. "Who knows?"

"Who knows?" I agreed. We looked at Abel.

Maybe I'm paying for it now, I thought.

"Well, best of luck," Singleton said. "It was a pleasure to see you."

"You too," I said.

Singleton walked away, and out of the building. Abel came over and wrapped an arm around me.

"Who was that?" he said.

"No one," I said. "No one you know."

Abel looked anxiously at the young woman across the room.

"I'm going back early," I said. "You have fun."

Abel gave me a quick kiss and a bright smile and went back to the girl.

"I love you," he said.

I knew he did.

In his own way.

I left the party and walked out into the cool, glittering night. I wasn't in a hurry. Back in my hotel I would take some sleeping pills or tranquilizers and drink some wine and watch a cop show on my computer until I fell asleep—the same thing I did every night, lately.

And so I took a crooked route to the hotel, snaking around the city, thinking as little as possible.

Sometimes I would wake up in the middle of the night and have to convince myself, all over again, that it was real. I was sure that Lucas was still alive, that we were still in Paris, that we had continued on together, like he'd wanted. Then, once I remembered what had really happened, a strange anxiety would come up on me and I'd be convinced that Lucas was in the house somewhere, lurking in some unearthly form. I'd turn on the lights and creep through the house, heart pounding. But I never found anyone. *None of this is real,* I would think. *I never killed anyone, I couldn't have.*

But as I prowled around the house I would remember, *I have. I did. I had to. I had no choice. He wasn't Lucas anymore and I couldn't fix him. No one could.*

On one of those nights I walked out to the yard to find Abel standing there, doing nothing, looking at nothing, fully dressed, eyes wide open, arms hanging lifelessly at his sides. I walked over to him through the wet grass. It was almost a full moon and there was a silvery light across the yard. When I reached Abel he turned to me with flat eyes and an expressionless face.

"Who are you?" I asked.

"I don't know," he said.

"Where did you come from?" I asked.

He said nothing, and looked back out to the black horizon.

I walked around Paris with no particular plan, until I was in a familiar neighborhood. But I still didn't recognize the building until I was practically on top of it. The building where I'd killed Lucas. I stopped for a moment when I realized where I was. Of course it looked the same. Paris doesn't change much. The building was now some kind of tech operation, and they'd replaced the sliding door with a regular one. Other than that it was the same. I wondered how they'd gotten all the blood out of the floor.

Funny how it had all turned out. I had no idea if any of my choices were right. Or if they'd even been choices at all. Sometimes, at night, as I was falling asleep, I still saw that woman's face, looking at me with a satisfied look. Of course by now I knew: She was Princess Isabelle of Luxembourg, the real author of the book. Had she wanted me to destroy the book all along? Or was this just one chapter in its long, ugly history, with more to come?

Maybe someday I'd find out.

I reached into my pocket for a pill, swallowed it, and walked back to my hotel, to go to bed alone.

THE END

About the Author

SARA GRAN is the founder of Dreamland Books and the author of seven previous novels, including *Come Closer* and the Claire DeWitt series.

CPSIA information can be obtained
at www.ICGtesting.com
Printed in the USA
LVHW021517090222
710690LV00004B/294

9 780578 947099